A Trick of The Light

By K.J. Rabane

Copyright © 2013 K.J.Rabane

All rights reserved.

ISBN: 10: : 1482581442
ISBN-13: 978-1482581447

DEDICATION

To my family and friends

CONTENTS

Chapter 1

Chapter 2

Chapter 3

Chapter 4

Chapter 5

Chapter 6

Chapter 7

Chapter 8

Chapter 9

Chapter 10

Chapter 11

Chapter 12

Chapter 13

Chapter 14

Chapter 15

A Trick of the Light

Chapter 16

Chapter 17

Chapter 18

Chapter 19

Chapter 20

Chapter 21

Chapter 22

Chapter 23

Chapter 24

Chapter 25

Chapter 26

Chapter 27

Chapter 28

Chapter 29

Chapter 30

Chapter 31

Chapter 32

Chapter 33

Chapter 34

Chapter 35

Chapter 36

Chapter 37

Chapter 38

Chapter 39

Chapter 40

Chapter 41

Chapter 42

Chapter 43

Chapter 44

Chapter 45

Chapter 46

Chapter 47

Chapter 48

Chapter 49

Chapter 50

Chapter 51

Chapter 52

Chapter 53

Chapter 54

Chapter 55

A Trick of the Light

Chapter 56

Chapter 57

Chapter 58

Chapter 59

Chapter 60

Chapter 61

Chapter 62

Chapter 63

ACKNOWLEDGMENTS
I wish to thank Nona Evans for proof reading
this Manuscript, Rebecca Sian Photography
for the cover images and Frank for his support and
suggestions.

Now

I never thought I'd return to the house on Ransome's Point. But time alters one's perspective. I'm surprised it's still there. It stands facing the sea, isolated from the other dwellings on the promontory, its empty rooms echoing with voices. On the top floor, where it happened, a window is cracked leaving a jagged spear aimed at the sky. The sight of it drags back a memory that I struggle with then shake my head and let it slide out of reach.

The screeching of herring gulls overhead fills me with dread and I think that perhaps it's a mistake to return after all. I hunch my shoulders, place chilled hands over my ears and with eyes tightly shut, practice breathing slowly and deeply but the feeling of panic refuses to subside. A cold wind sweeps in from the sea, grains of sand mixing with its icy fingers as it touches my cheek.

If a prism of light entices onlookers to search

for that elusive pot of gold, then maybe I have imagined it all. My mind is a mixture of half-remembered images as elusive as the rainbow's end.

I open the garden gate, stumble over the cracked paving stones, and reach a steadying hand towards the gatepost, scraping my finger on its uneven surface. Blood mixes with rust - rust with blood, mingling into a reddish brown smear that tingles on my tongue as I suck at the cut. This time I have no excuse. The house is unmoved by the horror seeping through my body and I feel its dissatisfaction at my intrusion. It seems to be saying 'stay away' but my feet have led me towards it and I have no choice but to enter.

THEN

CHAPTER 1

I suppose you could say I'm a creature of routine, even at the weekends. On Sunday morning, I have breakfast in bed, read the paper, listen to the early morning D.J. and, after having a bath and dressing, I start the ironing. So at half past eleven on the day that would change my life, I was ironing a white blouse ready for work the next day whilst listening to the radio.

"Now for our regular feature - *Finding Forgotten Friends,*" the presenter announced.

Half listening, I slid the iron under the collar and sprayed starch along the body of the garment. The partners of Boysey, Rankin and Hawke insisted on a strict dress code amongst its secretaries, dark suit and starched white blouse in keeping with their professional image. The radio programme continued. There were the usual requests made by people who were looking for someone they'd known in their youth in the hope that they might recapture some of the energy and excitement that was theirs in days gone by. I reached across the ironing board to change channels when the announcer's voice made me hesitate.

"This morning we are looking for Rachel Weston. Are you out there, Rachel? Finbar is searching the airwaves for news of you. You last met fifteen years ago when you both worked in London and used to meet for lunch in the *Bunch of Grapes*. Sounds a bit fruity to me, folks!"

The fatuous remark, hanging in the air like a flag at half-mast, was accompanied by a burst of sycophantic laughter from an assistant. I stood, steam-iron raised in mid air, and stared at the radio, as the presenter continued.

"Well now, Rachel, if you'd like to give us a ring, we'll soon put you in touch with Finbar. Go on, put the man out of his misery and pick up the phone. Now let's see who's next - yes Norman Richards is looking for......"

Remembering the last time I'd seen Finbar Alexander, I closed my eyes. He'd been standing in the rain, his fair hair hanging in damp waves across his forehead. "Thanks for buying the flowers, sorry I have to dash. I'm meeting Kate in the Dorchester at one. Hope she likes the ring, eh?" he'd said, his eyes anxiously straying to his watch, the words thrown together carelessly in a heap. I'd been grateful for the shower of rain that mingled with my tears as I watched him walk away, praying he would turn around. If he did, then it would mean he loved me. I remember picking up the daisy that had fallen from the bouquet, peeling off its petals one by one, he loves me - he loves me not.

That was the last time I saw him. There were no more meetings for morning coffee in the shop on the corner. No more drinks after work, or lunch in the *Bunch of Grapes*. After that it was just a newspaper photograph and a report of their wedding. I'd had to get used to them being a couple, removing my name from the scenario and leaving behind - Kate Alexander, the talented dress designer and her husband.

Standing motionlessly at the ironing board, it was as if the past fifteen years had slipped away. I remembered our conversations and how he used to make me laugh at his stories about people we knew. I told him he was wasted working as a draughtsman and that he should be writing his own stories.

The voice from the radio droned on, easing me back to the present. "Contact us on 0890 66 33 44 to get in touch with your 'Forgotten Friends'."

Without thinking twice I copied the number

down on the yellow 'post it' pad on the worktop whilst wondering - what harm could there be in thinking about it for a while?

The next day, I found it impossible to concentrate on the files that Peter Rankin had stacked in my in-tray. The trials and tribulations of his clients paled into insignificance in view of the previous day's radio programme. The contact telephone number I'd memorised, wouldn't allow me to settle and forget the whole thing. The question that kept resurfacing was 'what did he want, after all these years?'

Later, sitting on a seat on the tube, avoiding the pressure of a fat man's belly to my left and a pregnant woman's to my right, I thought, what's wrong with you? You've nothing to lose by ringing the radio station and getting his contact details. It doesn't mean you have to act on them.

I was still arguing with myself the next morning, over a breakfast of strong coffee and tepid toast, in my second floor flat above a Chinese Takeaway. The smell of stale soy sauce and soggy chips were not conducive to eating a hearty breakfast so I left the toast untouched and concentrated on my coffee. My laptop was open at the Heart and Soul Internet dating site. How sad was that? Looking at it and never acting on it, wondering if there was someone who felt just like me but unlike me had taken that extra step and contacted that 'someone special'. After all Susan, Alan Hawks's secretary, had found her husband on a similar site and they were expecting the birth of their first child in June. He hadn't turned out to be an oddball or a pervert, just a nice shy man who didn't feel comfortable with the modern dating scene. I couldn't blame him; it felt like a cattle market - being on show, waiting to be chosen, like some medieval slave or courtesan.

Afterwards, standing in the shower feeling the cleansing spray washing away the tang of Takeaway from my skin, I came to a decision. During my eleven o'clock coffee break I would ring the number. There could be no harm in that now could there?

Later, when I rang Finbar's contact number, I expected I would at least speak to him and was surprised to be greeted by a woman's voice announcing that Finbar and Kate were not able to take the call at present but if you'd leave a message etc.,. At that point my courage almost failed me but I heard my voice saying that I understood that Finbar Alexander had been trying to contact Rachel Weston and I would leave my number for him to do so.

It was almost two weeks later when I received the call. Two weeks during which I vacillated between believing that Finbar and Kate were relaxing somewhere on the continent enjoying a fortnight's holiday of sun, sea, and sex, to wondering why, if they were still united, did he want to contact me? As it was, my soul-searching conversations were not greatly resolved by the call when it came.

"Is that Ms Rachel Weston?" a woman asked, her voice sounding clipped, her manner professional. "I'm ringing on behalf of Mr Finbar Alexander. He wishes me to arrange a suitable time when you can both meet."

Being unprepared I stammered, "Cccould you tell me what this is all about, please? I'm completely in the dark as to why Mr Alexander should wish to contact me, after such a long time."

"I'm sorry. All Mr Alexander asked me to do is to arrange a meeting. Are you agreeable, or shall I tell him it's not possible?" She sounded impatient, as if this phone call was a nuisance.

Picking up my diary from the side table, I opened it to the following week. "Friday 13th, at two thirty?" I asked.

A rustle of papers from the end of the phone

followed by a clipped confirmation ended the conversation. Still confused, I was aware that the glamorous Kate had dashed any immature thoughts of Finbar and me becoming an item fifteen years ago. Since that day, I'd followed her career via the pages of the glossy magazines. Kate Alexander, dress designer to the glitterati, tripping down the catwalk on impossibly high heels, the anorexic clotheshorses she employed to model her designs applauding her expertise as she smiled and acknowledged the accolades. Then there were pictures of them both in 'The Tatler' sipping champagne at a posh party, Finbar looking even more handsome than he had all those years ago. It didn't help to think about the past. Friday 13th began to assume even greater significance as the week wore on and the day itself approached.

Friday was always a slack working day in the offices of Boysey, Rankin and Hawke. I had no trouble rearranging my schedule in order to meet Finbar. Ironically the meeting place I'd chosen was the Dorchester. It wasn't coincidental; I found it vaguely satisfying to anticipate the meeting place where fifteen years previously he had asked Kate Ripton to become his wife. I doubted that he would realise the significance of it. In my experience men never did. Their brains were unable to function when hindered by emotion and dealing with the consequences of their actions was an unknown concept to them.

Jackie, the junior typist, had been prattling on all morning, much to my annoyance; if only she would get on with her work, stop intruding with her mindless drivel and leave me to concentrate on meeting Finbar.

"I hate Friday the thirteenth. I just know that something bad is going to happen. It took me ten minutes to walk through Maunder's passage this morning, just to avoid walking under the ladder standing outside the house next to my flat," Jackie said, filing her nails and examining the result at arm's length.

"I'd rather take my chances with the ladder than risk being mugged by the louts that hang around on the corner of Maunder's passage," I said, looking over the top of my reading glasses at her.

Jackie shifted uncomfortably in her seat. "They're all right. Actually I made a date with one of them. Kept whistling at me, he did - wouldn't take no for an answer. I'm meeting him in the 'Bunch of Grapes' at six."

Of course, it *would* be there, I thought. I can just see them both; they would have been just the sort to give Finbar inspiration for one of his amusing stories.

"Did I mention that Wayne's got the most wicked tattoo?" Jackie had given up filing her nails and was pouring her third cup of coffee of the morning from the newly installed coffee machine.

So his name was Wayne. I doubted whether he would fit in with the crowd that used to gather in 'The Grapes' but thought, at least he would have made Finbar smile.

"Pity about the date, though. Normally I wouldn't have gone out tonight, tempting fate, I always say; a good film, box of chocs., and feet up in front of the telly, nothing bad can happen to you then. But Wayne was very keen and he's got the most wickedest stud through his nose and well you got to take a chance now and then 'aven't you?" Jackie said.

Absentmindedly agreeing, I shut down my P.C., picked up a carrier bag from the bottom drawer of my desk and made for the rest room. Touching up my make-up, I searched my face for signs of aging. Without the aid of my reading glasses, my skin appeared to be unlined. I was only thirty-four, so what if there were a few crow's-feet, I'd never been considered to be anything other than plain, so what did it matter? But it did. Admitting the fact to my reflection, I realised that the moment I'd been waiting for was about to arrive. For fifteen years I'd existed, going through the motions, waiting for the time when I'd see him again. I'd known it would happen one day and now that day had arrived.

Whilst sitting in the back of the black cab, I felt the first flutter of apprehension. The traffic on the outskirts of Hyde Park was at a standstill. A niggle in the back of my mind began to dampen my euphoria - was I leaving myself open to more heartache by meeting him again? Ignoring the warning voice, I shrugged. This time I'd make sure that things were different.

As the cab drew up outside the Dorchester and the hotel's doorman reached for the door to help me out, Jackie's words kept ringing in my ear, 'you've got to take a chance now and then haven't you?'

CHAPTER 2

In the turret room of a house overlooking the sea, a pile of paperbacks with lurid covers, each depicting a murder, assassination or death by misadventure, lay on a shelf behind a large wooden desk that had been turned to face the window. The author, Alex Finn, had been churning out crime novels with a moderate degree of success for the past ten years; his task made easier by a competent secretary who'd converted his untidy manuscripts into copies suitable for publication. The author, having never mastered the art of typing using all his fingers, was beginning to wonder if he would ever manage to complete another draft without going mad. It was all Alice's fault for leaving him in such a mess. She'd said it was time she retired and no amount of charm or persuasion on his part had made her change her mind.

To make matters worse Kate was in New York, Mrs Goodrich was visiting a sick relative and he had to make his own meals, which was a distraction he could have done without. When he was in the middle of writing a novel, time had no meaning and it was only hunger pains gnawing at his insides like a ravenous beast, which drew him out of his lair and into the kitchen.

To be fair, Alice had given him three months' notice. But time was speeding by and he was at a loss find a replacement. The agency in town had sent a few girls to see him, half of them being incompetent, the other half showing comparable skills to the sainted Alice but unfortunately having attributes that his beautiful, but green-eyed, Kate would consider to be unacceptable. He could hear her now, 'If you think I'm going to sit back and watch you and little *Miss Butter-wouldn't-melt* lock yourselves away in the turret room for hours on end, you're much mistaken'. He smiled. Being an author had its advantages; he could write her script for her before she even opened her mouth.

Two days later, sipping from a cool can of lager and eating cold baked beans out of a tin, he'd turned on the T.V. and started watching a documentary. Gordon Hibbard, roving reporter for the BBC, was presenting a programme about 18th century London pubs and there it was – The Bunch of Grapes. He'd almost forgotten its existence. He sat up straight, watched Gordon talking to the customers and gradually began to remember that odd girl who used to follow him around. What was her name? Rachel something, she'd worked in a solicitor's office. It took him a while to remember clearly but once he did, he recalled another important fact - a fact, which could mean the difference to him finishing his latest novel in time for his deadline.

Rachel was a rare commodity, he'd recognised that all those years ago. She was conscientious, competent and intensely loyal. A friend of his, Malcolm Peters, had introduced her to him and was vociferous in praise of her abilities as his private secretary. Afterwards, she seemed to turn up whenever he was in the pub or coffee shop and occasionally he'd ask her out for dinner when he'd been at a loose end. Although she was nothing to look at, she did laugh at his jokes and having a captive audience had flattered his ego. However, he remembered, she'd become a bit of a drag, always being around. Kate came on the scene at just the right time, otherwise he might have had a problem getting rid of little Miss Rachel Weston.

Now things were different, he needed her. She could fill Alice's shoes without any problem. Of course there was always the possibility that in the meantime she'd found herself a husband and raised a family but there was no harm in trying to find out. He couldn't remember the name of the firm she'd worked for and Malcolm had dropped out of sight after moving to the States years ago. So how was he going to contact her?

It was a pure coincidence he'd been listening to the Sunday morning radio programme the following day and heard the item about contacting people who'd lost touch with each other. It was a long shot but it might work, he thought. Kate would have called him an idiot if she'd been around but as he was more widely know by his nom de plume, he doubted whether anyone would connect Finbar Alexander with the moderately successful novelist Alex Finn.

After he'd asked Alice to fix up an appointment for them to meet, he began wonder if he'd done the right thing; he half expected his spur of the moment action in ringing the radio station to bear no fruit. In fact he'd been extremely surprised to learn that this was not the case and as Friday the thirteenth approached, he anticipated the meeting with a mixture of satisfaction and trepidation.

His concern stemmed from the fact that he'd remembered little Miss Weston definitely had some sort of crush on him and he didn't want to stir anything up between him and Kate - not after the Sylvia Marchant affair. Kate had been ready to leave him, was in the middle of packing her case, but he'd managed to win her around with abject apologies and promises of future fidelity. Even then, for months after, she'd been suspicious - still was as a matter of fact. If he was to continue with his occasional clandestine and frequently short-lived relationships with the opposite sex, he had to be very careful not to make Kate jealous.

A look of frustration settled on his face puckering his brow and tugging at the corners of his mouth. Perhaps he could prevail on Alice once more and ask her to check her over? No, that wouldn't do. He'd have to see her for himself and if he had the slightest doubt then he'd make up some tale about a friend wanting a secretary. He'd soon think of a plausible excuse, after all he did write fiction. He was sure he could soon assess whether she would be a threat to Kate's newly found trust in him. He was desperate not to upset her; an expensive divorce was not on his agenda. Kate's brother, the eminent Guy Ripton Q.C., would soon see to it that his assets were stripped to the bone, especially as there was no love lost between him and his brother-in-law.

On Thursday the twelfth, Finbar Alexander checked into the Dorchester Hotel for an overnight stay. He'd decided not to travel up on the thirteenth for a number of reasons beginning and ending with a superstitious fear instilled in him by a mother with a penchant for Fortune Tellers and Clairvoyants.

Strolling around Hyde Park in the sunshine on a slightly chilly Friday morning, he wondered if he would recognise Rachel. He doubted it, as he could hardly recall what she'd looked like before and was sure her appearance would have changed during the past fifteen years. He couldn't even remember the colour of her hair. Nondescript was the word that sprang to mind. Part of him hoped she'd remained so; it would make things a lot easier and provide him with a secretary he could trust. *Death on a Wet Afternoon* was crying out to be typed into an acceptable form and he was in need of a new bestseller to prop up his dwindling finances. He was hopeless with money but Kate usually came to his rescue and bailed him out.

Hunger gnawed at his belly. He was almost sorry she'd agreed to join him for a late lunch. Finn looked at his watch - two fifteen. He decided, the time had come to find a suitable seat in the foyer, one with a restricted view from the doorway giving him am advantageous position in order to see her before she saw him. It would allow him those few precious moments during which he could decide which expression he should assume. It was always useful to be one step ahead of the game, he'd found.

CHAPTER 3

Moonlight touched the stark branches of the frost-coated trees in Central Park making them sparkle in the darkness. Kate Alexander, drinking chilled Chablis from a long stemmed glass, reflected on the finale of the show. Success was an aphrodisiac that brought an uplifting of the spirits to the point of euphoria. It was a pity she was so far away from Finn, she thought.

She watched a man dressed in a hooded jacket and brightly coloured scarf walking his dog on the periphery of the park. Steve's penthouse apartment had a fantastic view. She'd told him he'd been lucky to find this place but he'd said, "Luck or money darling? In my experience you make your own luck and having a sizable bank balance encourages its formation, I always think."

The sound of a shower being turned on made her smile. Steve was fastidious, neat and ordered in a way she could never be. She liked to work in a state of permanent disarray believing it encouraged her creativity and liked nothing better than to escape to her workroom where she could begin producing the designs that had made her a household name.

She almost wished she were there now, in her haven, away from all the glitz and glamour. She'd been right about buying the house on Ransome's Point. It had been just what she needed, her refuge in a world of synthetic instability. When she'd first shown it to Finn, he'd been horrified at the thought of them being buried away in such an isolated spot. The nearest house was just a blur in the distance, but Kate had insisted it would be in an ideal situation, where he could write in peace. The room on the ground floor with its views of the rocky coastline, she'd found enchanting. It was the perfect place to set up as a workroom having large picture windows on three sides allowing a diffusion of light, which would provide a perfect setting for her drawing board.

"Penny for them?" Steve, fresh from the shower and dressed in a white towelling bathrobe, was holding a freshly opened bottle of champagne and two glasses. He walked towards her wafting Chanel shower gel in his wake.

"Cheer up, you are Queen of the catwalk after all. Still got some room for another celebratory drink?" he asked, not waiting for a reply, whilst filling their glasses to the brim.

The celebrations had started at the after the show party and now it looked as though they were set to continue, just when she'd thought a last minute nightcap with Steve, followed by a cab to her lonely hotel room to sleep it off, was all that was on offer. Her head was beginning to spin but he was insistent that she should relax and let him pour the drinks.

"Good conversation and excellent champagne is always a recipe for a grand night's entertainment," he said, sitting alongside her on the long leather couch and refilling her glass. "How are things with the fabulous Finn these days?"

"So, so." Tears prickled behind her eyelids. "It's the booze, take no notice," she whispered. "I'm getting drunk. Finn is being a good boy, my show is a success and everything in the garden is wonderful."

Steve slid his arm around her shoulder. "Come on, have a good cry, lean on me, There now, that's better."

"Did I ever tell you that you remind me of my father?" Kate asked drying her tears on the sleeve of his bathrobe.

"I'll take it as a compliment, shall I?"

The flood gates opened and to Kate's horror she found her laughter suddenly turning to an outpouring of grief, the cause of which was a combination of sorrow at the loss of her father, even though she'd come to terms with it years ago, and the almost unbearable sadness at the thought of her husband's numerous affairs, which had continued throughout their marriage.

Steve waited until her tears were spent then said, "Well, do you want to tell me what that was all about or shall I open another bottle?"

Kate placed her hand firmly over the top of her champagne glass and shook her head, "I'll pass out if I have another. Anyway I must ring for a taxi. I've imposed on your hospitality long enough."

"Nonsense; and I won't hear of you ringing for a cab. You'll stay the night - sleep it off here." Steve kissed the top of her head.

"What will Frankie say - if I stay?" Kate frowned running her finger along the silver photo frame - Frankie and Steve kissing in the sun.

"You know Frankie, it's the Italian ancestry and all that. Besides Frankie's in Canada at the funeral of an old school chum and what the eye doesn't see, eh?" Steve held out his hand and pulled her to her feet, leading her towards the bedroom.

Frankie Gordino watched the snowflakes falling faster with each flurry, covering the frozen ground in a layer of white, covering the coffin as it was lowered into the shallow grave and floating down on the heads of the friends and relatives gathered to mourn the passing of Nina Ponti.

Nina and Frankie had been the only children with Italian surnames in their class and somehow it had become a bond between them, cementing a friendship which was to last until Nina's sad demise. Glad to have been able to make the journey in time, Frankie stared through tear-filled eyes as a layer of earth was scattered over the coffin but memories of the two school friends as children and as adults threatened to turn a contained measure of grief into a catastrophic outpouring. Entering the church, Frankie sat with head bowed in a pew at the back, alone with thoughts of days long gone.

If only Steve had been able to come, it might have been different. This feeling of isolation and loss would have been made more bearable by the sight of his face, the touch of his hand. Steve was the one person who had awakened feelings of love in Frankie to such an extent that it was impossible to think of anyone ever taking his place. The first time they had made love was a revelation; to feel such joy; no one else had even come close.

After the funeral, Frankie decided to make the

journey home - to Steve. It would be a surprise; he'd believed the journey to Canada was to be a nostalgic trip that would take at least two weeks but Frankie had soon discovered that home no longer existed amongst the snow covered conifers but was in an apartment overlooking Central Park.

She must have cried out in her sleep. It had been a bad dream. Finn had found another love; she could see them together, in their bed. She could hear the waves crashing against the rocks beneath their window and see his fair hair mingling with a stranger's on the pillow. It had been so vivid. She had woken, heart thumping against her ribs and sweat pouring in deep rivulets between her breasts. She looked at the clock; it was six a.m.

"It's OK. Just a dream." Steve stood at the foot of the bed. "C'mon old thing don't look so terrified. Here let me give you a cuddle, it'll soon pass."

Kate leaned her head against Steve's shoulder. As a rosy dawn lit the room, they neither heard the key being turned in the lock of the front door nor Frankie's footsteps making for the bedroom.

CHAPTER 4

The view from the cottage window was restricted by the weather. Rain clouds hanging heavy across the bay had preceded a heavy downfall, which now coated the small window in continuous rivulets obliterating all but the wavy outline of the garden wall.

Alice Phillips sat in her front room reading a book. It wasn't an Alex Finn novel; she didn't really care for them, having had the doubtful pleasure of enforced reading over a ten-year period. No more, thank God, she thought, drinking her tea then turning the page. Retirement was a promise she'd made to herself - at sixty she would finish - no matter how persuasive Mr Alexander might be.

He hadn't liked it of course. He began by making her feel sorry for him; what was he going to do without her, how would she cope, and finished by getting ratty; she was leaving him in a very awkward position - he had a manuscript to complete. In the end she agreed that, should he find a suitable replacement, she would give up three months of her time to show the new person the ropes. Alice thought that was a more than fair compromise, and when he saw she would not be moved on the subject, he'd agreed.

The April shower stopped and the windows cleared allowing the view to return. Alice walked to the window and peered across the bay to Ransome's Point. The house stood defiantly facing the elements; the turret room, where she'd spent so many hours, was shuttered against the weather. In the summer it was a beautiful room with a view from every corner and bathed in bright light until dusk. But when winter arrived, it assumed an altogether different aspect, a haven against the fierce winds blowing in from the sea, a sanctuary of silence only broken by the click of a computer's mouse.

Spending so much time in the turret room, Alice hadn't failed to notice the tension that sometimes existed between the author and his spouse and it had become clear that, on many of those occasions, Finbar Alexander's infidelity lay at the root of the problem. There was that time when he'd insisted on hiring an additional typist to help Alice. The girl he'd employed was neither competent nor even a typist as far as she could make out as she'd used two fingers to type and the time she took was longer than someone using a pen and paper. But she was good-looking in a rather obvious way and before long had become the topic of many a heated discussion between husband and wife.

Then there was the affair with Mrs Alexander's friend. Simone was French, chic and charming and very soon, after spending a holiday at Ransome's Point, fell for the author's calculating charms causing a great deal of distress to his wife. The after effects of which resulted in Alice becoming an unwitting eavesdropper on a number of ensuing arguments. Simone was dispatched with haste and Mrs Alexander had gone to stay with her mother in Yorkshire for a few weeks, until her husband finally came to his senses and followed her in order to beg for her return. Back then, it was Alice who had seen to it that the house had run efficiently. In addition to her duties as secretary, she had arranged with her friend Mrs Goodrich to come in to cook for him, tidy the place, dust and wash his clothes. The only good thing to be said about working with Alex Finn was - life was never dull.

Since her retirement, she'd taken to watching the house. She wasn't really sure why. She found herself checking on the daily comings and goings as a matter of course, and if she didn't, she fretted about what was going on there. For instance, she noticed that Mrs Alexander had been away for a spell and that during the last few days the author too had vacated the house. The winds still buffeted the stone walls of the property, the rain continued to soak the garden and the sun still lit the rooms with light. She noticed the postman regularly called and only this morning saw that the window cleaner was cleaning the circular window on the staircase near the turret room.

Life it seemed was going on in the house across the bay as usual but without her. She couldn't understand why it mattered so much, when she could have returned at anytime during the past month. The frantic phone calls over the first fortnight had dwindled to the odd calls begging her to return but for the past four days she had heard nothing. It began to occur to Alice that maybe her replacement had been found and was surprised to discover that the thought disturbed her. She sighed, as the realisation dawned that part of her already missed the routine of her working life and a large part of her missed her employer. He had what her mother would have called the three C's – charm, charisma, and celebrity, the one almost certainly following on from the other but there was another side to his character which was not so endearing. Finbar Alexander was a liar.

CHAPTER 5

He was the first to see her, as had been his intention. He recognised her walk; shoulders held stiffly, as if expecting a bolt of lightening to strike her somewhere in the middle of her back, taking diffident steps through the doorway and into the foyer. Her eyes searched the carpeted area between them both in nervous anticipation. He watched as her gaze lingered on a businessman in a dark suit drinking a large whisky, a black leather laptop case standing at his feet, but lack of recognition finally made her move on.

He stood up when she reached his chair. "Rachel?" Holding out his hand he felt chilly fingers touching his in a hesitant handshake.

"Hello, Finbar. It's good to see you again."

Finbar, that's right, he'd forgotten that; she never would call him Finn, always Finbar. She was looking up at him through a thick fringe of brown hair. Still nothing much to look at, plain, really, but at push……….Her voice was soft, her eyes refusing to meet his as he suggested they make for the dining room.

"Would you mind if I took the liberty of ordering lunch? The salmon is really rather good and I seem to remember it was one of your favourites." He was guessing but she nodded. He couldn't go wrong, he thought, the old charm was working like a dream. "I expect you're hungry. Sorry I couldn't make it any earlier."

"It's no problem. I usually skip lunch anyway."

The meal was successfully and swiftly concluded, with a strange mixture of small talk on his part and hesitancy on hers. Afterwards, he suggested they discuss business over coffee and brandy in the bar.

"I expect you're wondering what this is all about?" He was watching her reaction; his eyes fixed on hers, knowing the effect it would have.

She didn't speak, just sat and waited.

"Well no doubt you realise that I have made a very profitable career as an author. However, now I find I'm in somewhat of a pickle." He was wearing his 'little boy lost' expression, his dark eyes large and soulful. He found it usually worked.

"Author?" She sat forward in her seat, suddenly animated. "So you took my advice, after all?"

He wasn't sure what she was on about but nodded, slightly miffed she hadn't realised he was

Alex Finn.

"Yes, well, for years I've had a secretary I could trust with my manuscripts but she has up and left me, just when I've a deadline to meet and not a hope in hell of finding someone satisfactory to take her place."

"I had no idea that you were Alex Finn, the crime writer," she said.

"No? Ah well, anonymity has its advantages. You do see, Rachel, that I'm in the most dreadful spot, Alice having left me and a deadline looming?" He picked up his glass and looked into her eyes.

"I understand. But I'm not sure I'd be able to help. I couldn't come to Devon at the moment. There's my flat, my job and well - how long would this job last Finbar? You see I'm settled here." She looked away so missed his carefully contrived melancholic expression.

Hello, he thought, she wasn't going to be a pushover after all. Well so be it. He was always game for a chase.

I was beginning to see the light and it was not a flattering one. He was still as attractive as ever, still able to make my heart flutter like a love-sick schoolgirl but I was no longer nineteen and certainly wasn't going to rush headlong into anything I didn't feel comfortable with, even for him. There was no doubt in my mind that he was using me. It wasn't because of a sudden longing to see me again but on a whim that I could help him out of a spot. Everything had changed. He wanted something from me, not the other way around. He was waiting, so sure of himself, smiling over the rim of his coffee cup.

"I thought of you instantly. I remembered how competent you were and I knew we could get on together. We did, didn't we? Got on like a house on fire if I remember correctly."

I could see he was certain his charm was working, so I stayed silent, listening, like I always did. I'd loved all his stories; I remember I used to laugh a lot. But I wasn't laughing now.

"I'm sorry, Finbar. That's just not possible. It's been nice seeing you again but I'm afraid I have another appointment and, as I'm unable to help you, I think it's best if I leave now. Oh, and thank you for the lunch."

"What if I was to employ you on the same terms as Alice? There's always been plenty of work for her in the past and I see no reason why that shouldn't continue in the future. I've hit on a formula, I can churn out as many of the Inspector Flately novels as my publishers want. There's even been talk of a series for television," he said, refilling her wine glass.

"I'm very pleased for you and flattered you thought of me. But…."

"The house is big enough for you to have your own room, Rach - fabulous views - lovely part of the country. What do you say?"

I stood up. I could see the realisation, I wasn't going to be his saviour after all, gradually beginning to sink in.

"Rachel, don't go, please, can't I persuade you to change your mind?" His hand shot out and caught mine.

The warmth of his touch filled me with a rush of long lost desire and I hesitated. "You don't understand. I have a life here in London, a job I like, a flat and friends. How could I travel back and forth from the West Country? I couldn't afford to for a start."

He kept holding my hand. "Look, think about it tonight. Don't say no just yet. There's plenty of room at the house; you could even have a suite of rooms to yourself, if it would make a difference. Alice, my old secretary, is willing to spend some time showing you the ropes, not that you'll have any problem, I'm sure." He was stroking the back of my hand. "I'll match your current salary with another three thousand a year on top. Think about it. You won't have to pay for food or accommodation either. That's got to be an offer you can't refuse, eh?" He was smiling up at me; so sure of himself.

I'll make him wait, I thought, gently easing my hand from his. "I'll think it over, but I can't promise anything, Finbar."

"Good, that's all I ask. I'll ring you tomorrow afternoon. Please don't let me down." The pleading was implicit in his tone, the expression in his eyes attempting to make doubly sure.

As I left the Dorchester, I wondered what it would be like to see him every day, to feel the heat of his body close to mine as we worked together, to wake up each morning knowing I would see him; to discover what his life was like and to play a part in it, however small. The temptation was there - it would be easy to say, 'Yes'. But although it was a tantalising proposal, I realised, if I did go to Devon, our relationship would be on a different footing than before. There would be no mistake this time. No thoughts that he might one day fall in love with me, that we might one day marry. Fifteen years had taught me one thing; Rachel Weston was in charge of her own destiny. If I wanted him, I'd have him - come hell or high water, whatever happened.

CHAPTER 6

A cool wind blew across the courtyard as Guy Ripton Q.C. left his chambers; it threaded through his dark hair and made him shiver. The day had started badly for him; an open and shut case had turned into a nightmare situation of unreliable witnesses and insubstantial forensic evidence.

He couldn't wait to get to the *Bunch of Grapes* and down a large glass of red wine whilst standing with his back to the flames of an open log fire. The court case was only partly to blame for his bad humour, the other reason being his argument with Stella last night.

The lounge bar was full of the usual crowd - office workers and court staff mainly. He nodded to a few acquaintances, being not in the mood to stop and discuss the problems of their day, he had enough of his own. Carrying his wine glass towards an unoccupied table, he sat down. At first he didn't see the figure sitting in a high backed settle facing the fire. He stared into the flames and was surprised to hear his brother-in-law's voice.

"Guy, you old devil. Thought I might bump

into you here."

"Finn?" Not exactly the person he wanted to see. This day was going downhill rapidly. In Guy's judgement Finbar Alexander was an opinionated show off, always had been, even before he became a minor celebrity. What his sister saw in him was anyone's guess, even taking into account his obvious attributes.

"Is Kate with you?" Guy asked.

"No, New York fashion show or something similar. So I'm footloose and fancy free in London for a few days. Why don't we see if we can paint the town red? What d'you say?"

"Love to, old man," lied Guy. "Too busy I'm afraid, working all hours. Stella's always complaining, you know how it is." He tipped his glass draining the last of his wine, tapped his briefcase with the palm of his hand, and said, "Sorry to dash off, give my love to Kate."

Outside, the cool air was almost welcoming. He'd made his escape, a night with Finn was the last thing he needed, he had to concentrate on his marriage and clubbing with his brother-in-law was not an option.

The house was in darkness. Guy looked at his watch, it was eight-thirty; where was everyone? A feeling that a bad day was about to get a whole lot worse swept over him. The chill of the evening air was incomparable to the icy feeling gnawing at his heart. Certain that last night had been more than just another disagreement, he slid the key into the lock and opened the front door.

The usual beeps of the house alarm were his only greeting, not a sound broke the silence, not even the electronic hum from the cooker signifying that his dinner was keeping warm. The lack of welcoming cooking smells, when he entered the hallway, had already alerted him to the fact that something was up.

He took the stairs two at a time and threw open Ben's door. The cot was empty. Their bedroom told the same sad story. Stella's cupboards had been cleared of her clothes. In the kitchen, propped up against a cookie jar, was an envelope inside which was a letter from his wife telling him what he already knew. She was taking Ben to her parents' house in Herefordshire. If he needed to see his son, he could arrange mutually agreeable visiting times via her solicitor.

Guy sat on the end of his bed looking at a future, depicted in Stella's sloping hand, that he had seen many times before during his working life. The impact was in no way lessened by his experiences; this was his life, and bleak though it might be, he felt an unaccountable lightening of his mood. Maybe things wouldn't be so bad after all. If he was honest he'd seen this coming for some time. Pursuance of a glittering legal career at the expense of his home life had led him to this end and he had nobody to blame but himself. At least he would make sure in future that he had time for his son, losing Ben was not something he was prepared to contemplate.

In his study, Guy poured a large brandy and drank it down in one gulp, then rang Kate's mobile.

The airport lounge catering for first class passengers was relatively quiet. Kate, sipping a gin and tonic, flipped open her novel to Chapter one. It was Finn's latest. She was bored by the bottom of the fifth page, feeling she hadn't the slightest interest in whether Inspector Flately brought the perpetrator of the docklands murder of a young socialite to book or not.

Her thoughts strayed to earlier that morning, when Frankie had burst in on Steve and her. She shook her head to clear the thought as the metallic strains of Bach's Air on a G String floated up from her handbag.

"Hello. Oh, hi, Guy! No. I'm really sorry. Yes sure, anytime you like. You say you saw Finn in

London? No. I didn't know. I'll be back by eight, aircraft schedules permitting. Mrs Goodrich will let you in if I'm not home by then. See you soon."

Kate slid the mobile back into her handbag and sighed. She knew Stella hadn't been happy for some time. Kate loved Guy and was fiercely loyal to her older brother but even she could see it had been his own fault. Now he was in desperate need of tea and sympathy. She wondered why he'd said Finn was in London. He had been like a bear with a sore head ever since Alice Phillips left him. Maybe that was it; he was after a new secretary.

Kate felt her heart miss a beat. If there was to be a repeat of the last fiasco, she would have it out with Finn and make him realise she wasn't going to stand for it. She'd make him see there would be two divorce cases featuring members of the Ripton family in the offing. It was up to him, she had done nothing to warrant repeatedly being treated in such a manner. She'd always taken him back, always believed the deceiving words that dripped like treacle from his tongue.

Her flight was being called. Kate picked up her hand luggage and made her way to the aircraft. This latest show had proved one thing to her; she had the ability to make her own way in this world - to become as big a 'name' as Alex Finn, if not more so. Admittedly the fashion world was notoriously fickle but she had come away with the strong feeling she could cope with all it had to throw at her.

The house at Ransome's Point was ablaze with light. Guy discovered that Mrs Goodrich had received Kate's call and made sure the house had been cleaned and a casserole was waiting in the Aga cooker for their arrival. When she opened the door to him, she said, "Mr Alexander is staying in London, Mr Ripton. He said to say he'd be home some time tomorrow. I've laid the table in the dining room, sir, so I'll get off now."

"Yes, of course. Thank you, Mrs Goodrich."

Guy was waiting in the living room overlooking the windswept coast when his sister arrived. Dishevelled and travel weary, she still looked beautiful even to him, who was used to seeing her without make-up and lounging around in clothes that would never been seen anywhere near a catwalk.

"Hello, darling. I see Mrs Goodrich has shown you where to find the whisky bottle. God I'm starving. Have you eaten yet?" Kate kissed him and as he hugged her he felt her ribs through her cashmere sweater.

"I see you're still fashionably thin, sis. The answer to your question is, no. I was waiting for you before I tackled the source of the mouth-watering aroma coming from the kitchen and by the look of you, I'm glad I did." Guy held her at arms length, taking in the contours of her face, the well-sculpted cheekbones emphasised by the careful use of make-up, the narrow hips and skin-tight jeans.

"You're beginning to sound like mother. You should know better, Guy. I've an appetite like a horse." Dragging him into the kitchen, she said, "Come on, sit down, eat, and tell me what's been going on. Oh by the way, where *is* Finn?"

"On some sort of business trip I gather; he didn't tell me any details. Well to be honest I had other things on my mind at the time so I didn't really give him a chance to explain."

When the meal was over, Kate poured coffee and they sat on the window seat watching the changing shape of the sea as it swept along the coast, waves flying high into the air in a fountain of spray then dragging back along the pebbles like bath water when the plug has been removed.

"What's all this about Stella?" Kate asked.

"I think it's finally over." Guy lit up a cigarette, drew the smoke deep into his lungs then slowly exhaled.

"I thought you'd given up the filthy habit. It will kill you, you know."

"Lay off. Anyway practice what you preach, dear sister. It's this business with Stella, I've started again, can't seem to do without it."

"Do you want to tell me all about it. I suppose that's why you've come?" Kate put her hand on his arm.

"It's part of it but I've also been wanting to see you for some time. Our lives being what they are, we've not managed to get together as often as we should. Stella's antagonism towards us visiting didn't exactly help matters in that direction either." Stubbing out his cigarette in his saucer, in lieu of an ashtray, Guy realised he couldn't explain to his sister that the real reason for his wife's opposition to visiting Ransome's Point was all due to Finn. Their last visit had been accompanied by harassment, both sexual and persistent, from Kate's half-wit of a husband and had been the last straw as far as Stella was concerned.

"It's all my fault. I knew how important the dinner party was to her. It was a chance for her to shine in her own field. She's spent most of our married life in the shadow of my illustrious career. If only I could have handled things differently, delegated my cases in a more reasonable manner. You know me. I got caught up in the Harrison case, worked every spare minute to the exclusion of everything else including my family. I've no one to blame but myself."

Lighting another cigarette he screwed up his eyes, telling himself it was the smoke that was making his eyes smart.

"There's no one else? No little legal secretary with a firm figure and nice legs, temping my celebrated sibling?" Kate said, waving the smoke away with her hand.

"No." Guy's one word answer was enough. He was no Finbar Alexander. He loved Stella and that should have been enough. The career thing, he should have managed more carefully.

"Right," said Kate, "that being the case. I think we should get drunk and to hell with the lot of them."

The next morning the sun split the space between the badly drawn living-room curtains in a shaft of light so bright Kate had to shield her eyes against its intensity. Drawing the drapes to one side she breathed deeply and wrapped her arms around her body. This was one of the reasons she loved the house - a sunny morning, the view across the bay, the sun shimmering on the surface of the sea – it was heavenly. It looked as if spring had finally arrived. It made her thoughts almost poetic. It was a shame Guy had to leave for London so soon; she'd hoped to walk across the sand with him, show him the cliff walk and chatter away like excited children. She'd missed their talks more than she had realised. Last night had been great, almost worth the hangover which had left her with a persistent ache over her right eye.

"Great view. Now I know why you bury yourselves in the back of beyond." Guy was up and dressed, he kissed the top of her head.

"What time's your train?" Kate asked.

"Eleven thirty, plenty of time for a lingering cup of coffee and a last minute look at the landscape."

At ten o'clock, a taxi drew up outside. Kate and Guy watched from the window as Finn helped a young woman out of the car and carried two sets of luggage up the side path towards the front door.

"Hello. I'm back," Finn announced, opening the living-room door. "Guy, old son, we meet again. Hello, darling. I'd like you both to meet my new secretary." He stood aside. "This is Miss Weston - Rachel."

Kate held out her hand, thinking with a sense

of relief that at least this one wasn't an obvious threat. Finn turned to Guy.

"Rachel, this is my brother-in-law, Mr Guy Ripton Q.C."

"Hello, Rachel, good to see you again." Guy shook her hand.

"Good Lord, you two know each other?" Finn turned to Guy, waiting for an explanation.

"Rachel works for Boysey, Rankin and Hawke. We've often use their firm, excellent solicitors," Guy remarked, adding, "look if you don't mind, sis, I'll flag down Finn's taxi, it's turning at the point. I'll catch the half-ten, I've plenty to do and I can see you've a lot to talk about. I'll give you a ring sometime. Thanks for last night." Guy was out of the door before she could stop him.

Turning back at the gate, Guy raised his hand. He could see Rachel Weston standing behind Kate and the hairs on the back of his neck stood up. He remembered the trouble she'd caused Kenneth Boysey, the solicitor, who was now the late Kenneth Boysey and he shivered, even though the sun was shining out of a clear blue sky.

CHAPTER 7

Alice Phillips was in the garden when her phone rang. She put down the binoculars on the garden table and went inside. It was Mr Alexander asking if she would be willing to spend some time showing his new secretary around. At first Alice felt a little peeved, being supplanted in such a short time, even though it was she who had chosen to leave; it smacked at little of *'the king is dead, long live the king'.* Yes, it was exactly what it was like. Knowing she had always worked in an efficient manner had given Alice the false impression that she was indispensable when in actual fact it wasn't the case. It never was; nobody, however well thought of or seemingly irreplaceable, could escape being substituted for a newer model.

Alice caught sight of her reflection in the hall mirror and scowled. Although the age of sixty today was not what it had been in her mother's day, there was no avoiding the fact she was no longer young and in her prime. Deep lines fanned out from either side of her eyes; eyes that she had once been told were the colour of the ocean. She had been proud of her profile too, mother had said she had a roman nose, long and straight, a nose of which to be proud. Unfortunately for Alice it tended to give the impression of austerity rather than becoming a feature that the opposite sex found attractive.

At the age of forty-five Alice had decided, if she was not going to hook a man by her fiftieth birthday she would give up trying. So after years of succumbing to the vagaries of a succession of dating agencies, she decided she would be destined to enter old age alone. The men she met were mostly a shambolic collection of individuals ranging from mother's boys to the type who were interested in only one thing. The latter reminded her of her employer. It was their intention to have as much sex as possible without committing to anything more serious than a visit to the cinema or a MacDonald's meal, preferably eaten without the use of knives and forks, unless of the plastic kind. So it had been a surprise when love had entered her life, had crept up on her as unexpectedly as a shower on a sunny day.

She shook off the memory, a life lived without male encumbrance hadn't turned out too badly after all and a life attached to the church perhaps wouldn't have been a bed of roses after all. But that was in the past; however, Finbar Alexander was a different proposition, a man she found it difficult to forget. He was nearly twenty years younger than her; not her type at all, but there was something about him that made her break into a hot flush whenever he was near, which had nothing to do with the after effects of the menopause.

She knew he was a liar and a cheat but part of her longed for him to cheat with her. When he stood behind her reading the script she was typing, she felt youth creeping back into her body, firming the sagging muscles, revitalising the skin and making her eyes glow. She recognised the stupidity of her reactions and because they showed no sign of abating had decided the only way to attain a healthy equilibrium was to put the distance of a sandy tide-washed beach between them. Now, in the wake of the phone call, it looked as though her plan was to be shelved for a while. Alice wasn't sorry, it meant she could put away the binoculars and forget about trying to catch a glimpse of him at a distance.

At eleven on the dot, she stood outside the house on Ransome's Point. Kate Alexander answered her knock. "Hello, Alice, nice to see you again. Finn is with Rachel in the turret room. He asked that you go right up."

Climbing the last flight of stairs, she stopped to catch her breath. She could hear the bleep of the computer in the room above her, the sound of a woman's laughter and her employer's hearty bellow. A tightening of the muscles in her chest made her hang her head over the stairwell in an attempt to slow her heartbeat. The door to the turret room was suddenly thrust open.

"Alice, good heavens woman; are you all right?" Finn rushed down the stairs and put his arm around her shoulders.

"I'm fine, Mr Alexander, just catching my breath," she said, opening her eyes wide whilst hoping he would notice they were the colour of the ocean.

The woman, sitting at what Alice considered to be her computer, was nothing much to look at, she thought, and was comforted by the notion. She was relatively young but wore reading glasses and her thick brown hair was tied in an unfashionable knot at the back of her head. She acknowledged Alice with a nod and continued typing with what looked, at first glance, to be a competent degree of speed.

The rest of the morning was spent with Mr

Alexander discussing what he required from his notes and deliberating how the collaboration between Alice and Rachel should be accomplished. To her satisfaction, Alice became aware that Rachel, rather than being a threat, could be moulded into someone who could become an ally. It was quite possible she could stretch a 'couple of weeks' into something a lot longer and she found the thought strangely appealing.

Finn was frustrated. Everything in the garden should have been lovely but it wasn't. He'd never had any trouble churning out his novels before but suddenly even the lure of a lucrative advance hadn't been the necessary spur to his inspiration. He thought that it had something to do with having Rachel and Alice facing each other furiously trying to compete in speed and accuracy. It was decidedly unnerving. It didn't help either that he found neither of them even vaguely attractive. At first he'd thought maybe Rachel could be promising but whether it was Alice's influence or something else he wasn't quite sure.

"Finn, your agent is on the line," Kate called up the stairwell. He'd made it a rule not to allow a telephone connection; the room was meant to be a place where he could write without interruption.

"Coming," he called. His mood had already been disrupted by Rachel asking how old Inspector Flately was, as she liked to get a feel of the character; it hadn't helped that he had no idea, not having given it a moment's thought before. In his irritable state he had snapped back, "Never mind all that, just get on with it, please." He'd seen her jawline tighten, heard her fingers clatter even faster across the keyboard and vowed to be more careful, after all she could up and leave and Alice with her, and then where would he be?

CHAPTER 8

A month after I started work at Ransome's Point, I overheard a conversation between Finbar and his wife. The suite of rooms set aside for me was situated on the first floor; above, lay the turret room and below the kitchen. The view from my sitting room was across the kitchen garden and out on to the cliff path leading down to the cove. On the landing outside my room stood a small spiral staircase leading down from the turret room to the garden below.

It was whilst I was reading a magazine sitting near the open window that I heard raised voices floating up from the garden. I looked down. Kate, dressed in overalls and carrying a wicker basket full of herbs, was facing her husband. She was flushed and her voice was high pitched. "You know what I think of Cameron Blackstone. I can't stand the man."

"He's not as bad as you make out, petal. Fair play now, he's hit a bad patch. No job, thrown out of his flat. I didn't have the heart to let him down." Finn was holding her shoulders trying to get her to look into his eyes, presumably so she could see how sorrowful they were, I decided.

But Kate was having none of it, wriggling free of his hands she almost screamed at him, "His situation is his problem. I don't see why I should open my house to all the waifs and strays you come across."

"It wouldn't be for long; just a week or two." I saw Finn thrust his hands into his trouser pockets. "It's not as if we haven't got bags of room is it?"

"You really are impossible, Finn. I've just about had enough; I've a good mind to ring Steve and see if he and Frankie would like to come over for a holiday. After all, as you said, it's not as if we haven't the room." Kate pushed past her husband in exasperation.

"The more the merrier; that's what I say, even if Steve is…" The rest of Finbar's words were lost to me as they walked towards the front of the house.

So, it looked as if everything was not a bed of roses between Kate and Finbar, I thought, picking up my magazine, my mood inexplicably lightened by the prospect.

The next day Finbar's guest arrived, amid much commotion. I was with Alice busy working on the manuscript in the turret room when the taxi drew up. A loud crash followed by a variety of expletives and the banging of the garden gate had us peering through the window in the hope of an explanation.

The man picking himself up from the floor with Finbar's help was obviously drunk. A battered holdall spilling its contents on to the path lay in front of him. The whole spectacle seemed to amuse his host who slapped him on the back whilst shouting to Mrs Goodrich to see to the luggage. Kate was nowhere in evidence.

"Well I never, Cameron Blackstone! I didn't think we'd ever see him again. Not after the last fiasco," Alice said, backing away from the window. " And the cheek of it, expecting Rhona Goodrich to pick up after him."

"There was trouble?" I asked.

"There was indeed. I'll tell you all about it when I get a chance. All I will say now is that he's not what he seems. No, not by a long chalk."

Intrigued, I continued working, promising myself that before the week was out I would know everything there was to know about Mr Cameron Blackstone.

CHAPTER 9

Cameron Blackstone had been staying at the house for over a month and I was still no nearer discovering the root of the problem, which Alice had referred to, on the day he'd arrived. The main reason for this was, ever since, Finbar had written copiously in the morning and spent his afternoons either walking to the village pub with Blackstone or lying on the garden sun beds drinking beer with him. I sensed Kate found neither of these occupations endearing and understood that a friend of hers was expected to visit from New York soon, which would probably even things up a bit.

From the middle of May the sun rose with consistency every morning and shone out of a clear blue sky until sunset. Weather forecasters speculated that the summer was going to be exceptional and a drought was to be expected.

On one such sunny Saturday morning, I took the cliff path leading to the village of Totbury, which led me past Alice Phillips's cottage. Alice was sitting in the garden reading.

"Lovely morning, Rachel," she called from her

deckchair near the garden wall.

"It is. It makes you wonder how long this will last. I for one can take as much of it as is on offer. I love the sun." I stopped, leaned on the stone wall and smiled. "You look nice and relaxed."

"Would you like to join me for a while? I was about to make a jug of iced tea?" Alice asked.

I accepted the invitation and, as she slipped the latch on the garden gate, thought it might be a good opportunity to find out a little more about Cameron Blackstone.

We chatted inconsequentially for a while over the refreshing drink and then I said, "There doesn't appear to be any time limit on Mr Blackstone's visit. I wonder how much longer he'll be around?"

"That depends on Mrs Alexander." Alice put her glass down on the table and removed her sunglasses from their resting place on the top of her head. "I never did get round to telling you all about him now, did I?"

I shook my head and waited.

"Well it all began some years ago. But I first saw him when Mr Alexander brought him to the house around about the time he was writing *Murder on the Main line.* At first I thought he seemed quite pleasant, even though he did drink too much. But he appeared to be able to handle it without too many incidents. I also noticed Mrs Alexander didn't think he was too bad then. He was amusing company and at the time worked as a journalist in Fleet Street so had a wealth of stories to entertain everyone."

Alice took a deep breath and continued. "I remember overhearing a conversation between Mrs Alexander and Mr Blackstone one evening. She was upset; it was after one of Mr Alexander's little affairs. It was all over some fling with a young girl from the village but naturally it had hurt her and, although she appeared to have dealt with it, her conversation with Cameron Blackstone showed it was still a sore point."

I nodded sympathetically.

"I was put in a very difficult position. You see, I could tell their conversation was turning personal in nature and it had gone too far for me to reveal myself without causing embarrassment. So I stayed effectively hidden from view and became an unwitting eavesdropper."

Alice revealed that Kate had told Blackstone of her fears that her husband would be tempted to stray again and she was sure she wouldn't be capable of dealing with it. She also made the big mistake of confiding in him that she was afraid her husband's drinking was getting out of control.

Apparently Kate's uncle had been an alcoholic and she remembered what devastation his drinking had wreaked on his family. Throughout her youth she had seen her aunt trying to cope with his drink-fuelled moods and the fear of not knowing whether he would come home drunk or sober.

Alice said, "Cameron Blackstone, assured Kate, she had nothing to worry about and he'd take her husband in hand and make sure he stayed on the straight and narrow and soon after Mrs Alexander went to bed."

After she'd finished talking, I asked, "And did he?"

"He did no such thing. He never intended to. It took a while for me to fathom it all out, so many things happened at the same time. But as the weeks passed I began to realise that Blackstone, rather than dissuading Mr Alexander to cut his drinking, was actually encouraging him to drink more. I heard him on more than one occasion insisting they have another drink when it was obvious they'd both had more than enough."

"Perhaps he couldn't help it. If he was a big drinker himself, maybe he didn't realise what he was doing?" I suggested tentatively.

"I wish I could say that was true, my dear. However, I watched as he played his game. First it was the drink, then the girls. I saw him bring one girl after another into the house when he thought Mrs Alexander was away or in town for the day. Each girl was no better than she should be. Pretty in a cheap sort of way, sexy, you know the type. Oh I know I'm an old spinster but I do know what I'm talking about. It was all so obvious."

"Do you mean Cameron Blackstone was acting as a procurer for Finbar?" I sat back in the deck chair.

"That's about the size of it. I'm sure he thought by causing trouble between the two of them it might eventually leave the road open for him to have a chance with Mrs Alexander. Have you noticed the way he looks at her?" Alice sat forward in her seat.

"She is very beautiful."

"She is. Anyway, things didn't turn out in in the way he'd planned. One afternoon when he thought the coast was clear, there being a photo shoot or some such thing in London, meaning Mrs Alexander would be away for a couple of days, he arranged for two rather common - looking types to spend the night with her husband."

"Two? Surely not; perhaps one of them was meant for Cameron Blackstone."

"Not on your life. Mrs Alexander returned

home unexpectedly to find her husband sharing their bed with the two of them and Mr Blackstone in the conservatory drinking whisky as if it had gone out of fashion."

Alice shook her head. "There was all hell to pay, I can tell you. Mrs Alexander refused to enter the house again until the girls and Cameron Blackstone left. In fact she went straight back to London to see her brother in order to arrange divorce proceedings. Mr Alexander soon came to his senses, ate humble pie yet again and, as far as I was aware, promised he would never see Cameron Blackstone again. That's why I am so shocked he's been allowed to stay at the house. I don't know how Mrs Alexander was persuaded to put up with it. In my opinion it was against her better judgement."

"Maybe he's changed - grown up a bit, even apologised and ate his own slice of humble pie?" I suggested.

Alice snorted. "A leopard never changes his spots and mark my words that one is only waiting to pounce again."

A while later, I left Alice relaxing in her deckchair and resumed my walk along the cliff path to the village. My mind was full of Finbar. I was beginning to see him in a new light. Was he so unhappy with Kate that he'd resorted to sleeping with call girls and casual acquaintances? Had he, perhaps, married the wrong woman? The latter, it seemed to me, was a distinct possibility and for some reason the idea was not an unpleasant one.

To either side of me on the path, yellow gorse bushes scraped at my legs their coffee-bean blossoms peppering the cliffs in colour. Below, cutting through the bright blue water, a speedboat left a trail of white spume behind as it circled the bay and then turned towards the open sea. I took a deep breath and smelled the salty air, feeling the heat of the sun on my face even though it was still not yet mid-day.

The cliff path narrowed between two garden walls at the end of which lay a flight of stone steps leading down to the harbour, the smell of fish becoming stronger as I approached the quayside. A hive of activity near two fishing boats unloading their catch caught my eye. I saw the fish being crated into ice-packed containers and transferred to three waiting vans, each with the name and logo of local restaurants emblazoned on the sides.

Away from the shore, the village opened out into the main shopping street at the end of which lay a haphazard collection of cottages looking as if they'd been thrown up the hillside, each brightly painted in vermilion, primrose yellow, cobalt blue and the inevitable whitewash, the sun shining on the small-paned windows making them sparkle like Christmas trimmings. Hanging baskets, beginning to show the early promise of riotous splashes of colour, hung from every spare lamppost and shop front.

The walk from Ransome's Point had been tiring. The house was so isolated that to walk to the nearest village took both time and energy, the latter easily depleted by the hot weather. I walked the length of the High Street, found a teashop, which had some unoccupied seats and gratefully sank into a wicker chair in front of a table spread with a pink gingham cloth. Ordering a scone and coffee I began to think over my earlier conversation with Alice. The older woman had been vituperative in her dislike of Cameron Blackstone to such an extent that I began to wonder if there was more to it than met the eye, but was swiftly brought out of my reverie by a shadow falling over the tablecloth and a voice saying, "Is this seat taken?"

As if I had conjured him up out of thin air I looked up into the brooding dark eyes of the man who had sunk so low in Alice's estimation.

CHAPTER 10

In Central Park the buds had burst into a riot of spring colour. White May blossom drifted down and carpeted the grass. Steve Fiori stopped to catch his breath, although fit from a daily jogging programme, he was finding the heat oppressive. Summer seemed to have come early, before May had officially cast off her coat.

Leaving the park and making for his apartment, he mulled over his earlier telephone conversation with Kate. The prospect of spending a few weeks with her in Devon was definitely appealing; to feel the fresh tang of untainted English air caressing his cheek in preference to suffering the heat of a Manhattan summer, which was already promising to be a scorcher.

The only problem as far as he could see was Frankie. His explanation, as to how Kate and he were in the same bedroom when Frankie arrived home from Canada, had been met, at first with anger, followed by floods of tears. It was all so silly but his protestations that Kate was just a colleague and a friend had done nothing to ease things between them. How would this invitation be received, he wondered? Frankie had been included naturally, Kate had stressed there was plenty of room at the house and they would be welcome to stay as long as they liked.

Steve, sensing there was more to her invitation than met the eye, decided there was a distinct possibility that it had something to do with that fool of a husband of hers. The man was an idiot in his opinion, he didn't deserve a gem like Kate and the irony was she was mad about him. Why else had she put up with all his crap over the years and by the look of it was continuing to do so?

He entered the foyer, deep in thought, and by the time the elevator stopped at his floor, he'd made up his mind. If Frankie kicked off on one then he'd go alone.

The sun shone through Kate's studio window with a burning intensity redolent of high summer and yet it was still only the first week of June. There had been no rain since the middle of May and already the lawn was beginning to turn brown at the edges. The use of sprinklers and hosepipes had been discouraged and the local news reports warned of the imminent likelihood of a total ban.

During the last few days she had suggested Mrs Goodrich save the water she used to clean the vegetables by tipping it into the water butt outside the back kitchen door. However, the lawn was a different proposition, it required a lot more moisture than the stored water to keep it in tip-top condition. She loved gardening, which was just as well as it was no good relying on Finn to help; gardening was a chore to him. In her husband's opinion the garden was simply a place to sit in order to get a tan, read a book or fall asleep after a liquid lunch.

Kate shuddered. There had been rather more liquid lunches since the arrival of that man. She could hardly bear to say his name. She realised she'd been a fool to agree to him staying at all. But then she'd always been a fool as far as Finn was concerned and was aware that most of her friends and relatives recognised the fact. Guy was always on at her to leave him. He'd promised time and time again to see she was given the best legal advice. She kept telling him that, although she appreciated his concern, she loved her husband. But she had to admit there were times when her resolve had been sorely weakened. Finn promised her that Cameron Blackstone would never set foot in the house again but look how it had turned out.

Aware she was being used once more, she turned back to the drawing board and concentrated on compiling her spring collection.

Her studio faced the cliffs; a large double-glazed picture window gave her an unrestricted view of the sky, sea and coastline. In winter, she viewed the constantly dramatic scene converting the images into flowing lines as she sculpted the fabrics and designs into the creations the world's most beautiful women would be wearing. In summer the materials she used were colour-washed by blues and greens of every hue and depth ranging from the deep blue-green of the ocean to the pale opalescent shade of the sky. The greens of the hillside, hedges, foliage, and lawns this summer had faded to yellow and dusty browns. Nevertheless, Kate found the inspiration of the parchment shades so intense that she couldn't wait to start work each morning. It was a pity Finn was finding writing so difficult at the moment.

The telephone on the wall rang, disturbing the complete silence, which helped her concentration. No soothing background music for Kate, she found it a distraction. She picked up the telephone; it was Steve.

"Just you? Oh I am sorry about that. Tell

Frankie I would still like it if the two of you came together, you know there's plenty of room. Come for the summer. I would be grateful for your opinion and help with my latest designs. Oh and by the way bring your swimming costume, the weather is great."

Kate's mood was suddenly lightened by the prospect of seeing Steve again. He always made her laugh. It would be the perfect antidote to having to suffer Blackstone every day. However, it was a pity about Frankie. Steve's powers of persuasion seemed to be sadly lacking. Kate was sure he would have sorted it out by now. Jealousy was such a destructive emotion, as she knew only too well.

It was no good; he'd been sitting in front of a blank sheet of paper for an hour and a half. In his mind the plot could have been completed in twenty-nine short chapters; murder, suspicion, conclusion, done and dusted before Inspector Flately had finished his inspection of the crime scene. It was all too obvious, trite, done before, with no more excitement to be had than with a weeping widow on a wet afternoon.

Where was everyone, Finn wondered - Rachel, Cameron, was no one enjoying the sunny weather?

It was Saturday for heaven's sake. The sun beds lay empty on the baked lawn waiting for what? His irritability was compounded by the fact that he'd just passed Kate's studio and found her deep in concentration whilst crouching over her drawing board. It was all right for some, he thought spitefully. Deciding to abandon the problems with his novel and start again tomorrow, he walked towards the waiting sunbed.

"Hello darling, enjoying the sun?" He wasn't sure how long he'd been asleep when he heard Kate sitting down beside him.

"Something like that," Finn grunted. "Anyway, where is everyone?"

"I don't know. I wasn't aware we were alone, but I can't say that I mind too much." Kate leaned across and kissed his cheek.

"Lets make the most of it then, eh?" Finn took her hand and led her inside towards the staircase. She was very beautiful and he sometimes forgot how fortunate he was. The trouble was, no matter how beautiful she was, he was used to her, and he would always need variety - it *was* the spice of life after all.

Later, satiated and on the edge of slumber, Finn watched his wife emerging from the shower.

"Oh by the way, I forgot to tell you. Steve rang

this morning, he's coming to stay. Should be here the day after tomorrow. But Frankie won't be joining him."

"I wouldn't bank on it," laughed Finn, and as he did so, Kate thought it was the meanest sound she had heard for a long time. She asked herself yet again what kept her with this uncharitable, philandering, husband and found that for once she had no excuses ready to hand.

CHAPTER 11

Cameron Blackstone sat in the chair opposite me and ordered a pot of tea. I wondered why he was here. If Alice was to be believed he should be propping up the bar of 'The Drunken Sailor'.

"I saw you from the street and thought, as we haven't had much of a chance to get to know one another, this might be as good a time as any." He smiled and offered to fill my cup.

"I only drink coffee thanks," I explained resting my hand over the rim of the cup.

"There we are then, that's something I didn't know about you before." His laughter was light and appealing. I found him easy to talk to, as we discussed topics as diverse as the approaching tennis season at Wimbledon to the state of the country. An hour passed in a moment and I was almost sorry when it became obvious that the small café was busy making preparations for the lunchtime trade.

Standing outside on the pavement, he asked, "Do you fancy a bite to eat? I thought I might take a stroll down to the harbour. I'm not used to so much fresh air but I'm finding I can't get enough of it."

"Yes, I'd like that," I replied the words spilling out before I could stop them.

It was no surprise that he guided me towards The Drunken Sailor where he assured me the freshest fish, cooked to perfection, featured on its lunchtime menu. The surprise came when we reached the bar; he ordered a white wine for me, and an orange juice for himself. Maybe he would have a drink with his meal, I thought.

The food was as he'd said it would be. I agreed, the fish was like nothing I'd ever tasted, having previously resorted to the supermarket or the fish and chip shop variety. And as the time wore on and he still hadn't drunk any alcohol, I asked, " Why don't you join me? I'm getting slightly tight here and you are stone cold sober."

"I have no problem with that," he said. "I don't drink, if I can help it. It doesn't bother me."

I suddenly felt as if the afternoon had turned chilly. It didn't make any sense. I'd seen him lurching out of the taxi when he'd arrived and heard about his history from Alice. What did it matter to him whether I thought he was a drinker or teetotal? Why would he say such a thing?

"I must get back. I didn't realise it was so late.

Thank you for a lovely lunch. My shout next time," I said, getting to my feet, the lie still floating in the shaft of sunlight separating us.

"Hang on, I'll walk back with you."

"No, really, I have some more shopping to do. See you later. Thanks again."

I couldn't wait to get out into the air. My head was buzzing with unanswered questions. To say that Cameron Blackstone was a paradox would be an understatement. I walked towards the shops and turned at the corner to look back. He was climbing the steps to the cliff path. I watched him brush away a wayward lock of hair with his fingertips, run up the last few steps until the gorse bushes on the cliff path swallowed him up, then I walked towards the High Street, lost in conflicting thoughts and emotions. Realising I was still no nearer to understanding the man, I began to wonder if I would ever learn the truth.

Shielding her eyes against the sun, Kate ran towards the gate to meet Steve. "Hello, darling," he said kissing her cheek. "Bloody awful journey. The train from London was two hours late and the catch on the window was stuck. I would have melted into the tasteless imitation leather seats had it not been for a kindly steward who kept me plied with iced drinks from the buffet car."

"Oh you poor old thing," sympathised Kate. "Bring your cases into the house and I'll remove the tang of train from your lips. I'm so pleased to see you, Steve."

"Me too, Duckie. This place looks divine, even better than your colourful descriptions led me to believe. I can see why you were so attracted to the area."

Kate led him into the conservatory overlooking the cliff path and they sat and ate the lunch Mrs Goodrich had prepared for them. "How is Frankie?" she asked

"You know Frankie." Steve was not in the mood to elucidate and changed the subject. "Everything alright between you and Finn?"

"I think so. Cameron Blackstone is still here and you know what I think about that. But as yet nothing too sinister has occurred. In fact he seems to be on his best behaviour, although I try not to spend any time alone with him, if I can possibly avoid it.

Coincidentally the man in question suddenly appeared striding along the cliff path and entering the garden via the wooden style.

"Oh my Lord, talk of the devil and he appears," said Kate

Steve looked up and raising an eyebrow said, " He's not how I imagined him, in fact quite the opposite." Before he could explain further the door to the conservatory opened.

"Sorry, Kate, I didn't realise you had company. I'll be in the living room if anyone wants me." Blackstone acknowledged Steve and walked through the doors leading into the main part of the house.

"Mmm, a man of few words I see," muttered Steve.

"I wish." Kate frowned.

The house was designed so that the main bedrooms were on the first floor. An additional bedroom existed on the second floor and was situated in a turret room of similar proportions to the room at the opposite end of the house, which Finn used as his study/workroom. Linking both rooms was a long landing with a central staircase leading down to the first floor. When Finn told her Cameron Blackstone would be staying with them, Kate had insisted he was to sleep on the second floor in the turret bedroom. It was a condition of his occupancy of the house, from which she refused to budge. However, she showed Steve into the large bedroom, next to theirs, with the same magnificent view of the coastline.

"This is just too, too much, I love it. You'll have trouble getting me to leave," Steve said, standing near the window.

"Stay as long as you like and as I said before, Frankie is welcome, the bed is big enough for two as you can see." Kate left Steve unpacking and ran lightly down the staircase, happy to have a friend in residence, an accomplished antidote to Finn's feckless companion.

Undressing for bed that night, Finn, watching Kate's naked body reflected in the dressing table mirror as she showered, saw the outline of her pert breasts as she lathered her skin with shower gel. He felt his body reacting as it always did at the sight of her and pushing the shower room door closed with his foot slid in beside her then ran his fingertip down the length of her spine until she turned to face him.

Afterwards, they lay on their backs beneath the cool satin sheets; Kate's heartbeat matching his and slowing in the wake of their lovemaking and the satisfying aftermath when every nerve in their bodies tingled with pleasure.

Finn caught her hand and turned on his side to face her. "About Cameron," he began. He continued to keep hold of her hand, although the expression on her face was as if she'd been drenched with cold water. " I want to ask him to stay for the summer. He's been no trouble, has he? It's just until his new job starts in September then he'll have to go back to London anyway. What do you say?"

What could she say? It was his home and if he wanted Blackstone to stay then that was that. Kate shrugged, but not without commenting, "On the understanding, if there is a repeat of what happened last time, I will tell him to go myself."

"Of course. Don't worry; he'll be a model guest. You mark my words." Finn bent towards her and kissed her lips.

The weekends were always the worst Alice found. Living directly across the water from Ransome's Point she couldn't fail to notice the activity in the house. She felt like an aging Cinderella who had not been invited to the ball. It was an iniquitous feeling in the light of Cameron Blackstone's acceptance. Slightly mollified by the fact that she was, at least, wanted in the short term, she opened her bedroom window wide and gazed across the bay.

In the distance, from the direction of the

village, a church bell sounded welcoming worshipers to the Sunday morning service. Once, Alice would have put on her best clothes and strode purposefully along the cliff path to join the congregation in the small church on the hill overlooking the harbour. Not any more-not after Robert- as far as she was concerned, she was done with praying to a God who refused to listen. Anyway she had other fish to fry, she thought, picking up a pair of powerful binoculars from the table.

Although early, the day promised to be a hot one. Around Ransome's Point a heat haze lingered waiting for the sun's rays to burn it off. She angled the binoculars until they focused on the house, scanning the front windows for any signs of life, starting at the turret room. Increasing the magnification by a twist of a dial, she thought she could just see Mr Alexander pacing back and forth at the front window. He liked to start work early, especially if he had an idea in his head, it was another reason why she had decided to retire - early mornings were not her speciality. But the odd thing was, that when she had no need to rise early, she found herself unable to sleep and often got up before seven.

Sliding the magnified view to the opposing

turret, she saw Cameron Blackstone was also standing at the window. She focused on his face and saw he was watching someone intently. Following his gaze she saw Rachel taking an early morning stroll along the cliff path out towards the point. When she tried to focus on him again, she found he was no longer standing in the window and by the time she had managed to pick out Rachel's figure once more she could see that she was no longer alone.

CHAPTER 12

Inhaling the early morning air and the fresh smell of salt rising up the cliffs from the sea, I was concentrating hard on how I was going to tell Finbar I wasn't really cut out for working for him and that I was missing the bustle of the city, when I heard someone calling my name.

"I thought it was you." Cameron Blackstone, breathing heavily after his run along the cliff path, caught up with me and fell into step at my side.

"Do you run every morning?" I asked, noting his shorts and vest top and wondering why, if that was the case, was he so out of breath.

"Not at all but I thought I might start, especially as the weather is so good. I need to get fit as you can see." His smile lit up his face changing his rather stern features into an altogether more pleasing aspect. "I've had some good news this morning. Finn has asked if I would like to stay for the summer and I've accepted. In fact it couldn't come at a better time for me - being between jobs so to speak."

They had reached the Point, so named by the

formation of the cliff, which ended in a sharp spur of rock. In front of them stood a wooden bench facing out to sea.

"Join me? I need to sit for a while. I'm more out of condition than I thought." He held out his hand to help me over a raised hump of earth.

"Just for a moment then." I was astounded at the beauty of the ocean spreading like a sheet of shimmering glass for as far as the eye could see and ending on the horizon. "It's beautiful here," I said.

"It certainly is," he commented and to my surprise saw he was looking at me and not at the view.

I felt my cheeks burning and was annoyed at myself. There was only one man I'd ever loved and if I was honest it was why I wanted to go back to London. It was a lie that I missed the bustle of the city; what could compare with a view such as I was facing? Not high rise buildings and the acrid smell of drains. The problem was what it had always been; Finbar was married to Kate and seeing them together every day had unsettled me more than I'd thought possible.

"I must go. I heard Finbar at work early this morning, I'm sure he'll be calling for me soon." I stood up and he caught my arm

"Let Finn wait. It's Sunday - a day of rest. The old goat shouldn't be making you work on a Sunday, anyway."

His hand was hot on my arm, I stuttered, " It's not that kind of work. It's very flexible and I - I might only be working for an hour or two today. It all depends on him."

"It always did," he said taking his hand away from my arm. "I'll see you later then?"

I nodded and hurried back down the path. I was beginning to think I might have been a bit hasty in deciding to go back to London. Perhaps I would stay for the rest of the summer. It was promising to be a hot one and stuck in a sweltering city was not the best place to be during a heat wave.

The night of the storm, Steve Fiori tossed and turned until he woke at half past three. The green LED numerals on his bedside clock glowed in the darkness as a thunder clap resounded overhead. The heat had been unbearable the previous day. The hottest June day for over forty years the weather-forecasters had announced.

Steve slipped out of bed and stood at the bedroom window. The sash windowpanes were open to the half but not a breath of air disturbed the stillness. In the distance the sky erupted, as sheet lightning followed by jagged forks of light sped across the heavens. But still there was no rain and the air was as thick and heavy as it had been before the storm began. Thunder rumbled overhead and, as a lightning bolt suddenly lit the sky, Steve thought he saw a shadowy figure in the garden. Someone was out there, creeping stealthily along near the garden wall. He rubbed his eyes with the back of his hand trying to focus more clearly but the night was dark once more and the figure had merged into the darkness.

He remained at the window for some time waiting for the next shaft of light to appear but the storm had moved on and everything was still once more. Finally, deciding that he'd been mistaken, a trick of the light perhaps, Steve went back to bed. This time he slept soundly until daylight shone through the window. Opening his eyes, he became aware of raised voices then footsteps on the stairs followed by his door being thrust open.

"Frankie!" he exclaimed, "How lovely to see you. Come here and give me a kiss; I've really missed you."

"I couldn't stay away a moment longer. The thought of you being here with that woman; I know you said there's nothing in it but, even so,

I've been eaten up by jealously. Her husband's a bore too. He almost stopped me coming in to see you." Frankie slipped into Steve's arms saying, "I'm such a fool."

"You are. You know you're the only one for me," Steve said, as the sound of raised voices drifted up from below the window.

"You know how I feel about them. You didn't tell me the other one was staying. And *you* have the cheek to be affronted by Cameron!"

"You're such a bigot, Finbar Alexander. It's a wonder any of your books sell with the narrow views you hold. It's always been the same, one rule for your friends and one for mine. As far as I'm concerned Frankie and Steve are welcome to stay as long as they like and if that's the whole of the summer, like your buddy Cameron, then so be it."

The turret room was silent; not even the clicking of a computer mouse disturbed the peace. All the windows were thrown open as in the rest in the house. Finn constantly complained that if they'd moved into a more modern house they could be luxuriating in a comfortable air-conditioned environment and at times like this, in the sweltering heat of early summer, he thought she might waver, but Kate was adamant. She kept saying where else would she find such a suitable place to work and lately he'd been inclined to agree. The heat was bearable, when taking into account the view and the lack of noise, in addition to which the only house visible for miles was Alice's cottage across the bay, and after working in cities for most of his early life, he could see the benefit of living in such a location.

Finn sat in an easy chair in the circular bay window and looked towards the point where the sea was beginning to spray upwards as it hit the rocks. He loved to watch it fan out in fine droplets and then fall back on itself. There was something in its cyclical motion that he found both relaxing and inspirational. He picked up his pen and notepad and as he did so, he noticed Rachel walking swiftly back along the cliff path. Extending his field of vision by turning to the right he saw Cameron Blackstone standing in front of the bench at the point, watching her. Finn stroked his chin and muttered, 'I wonder what he's up to now?' then picked up his recorder in an attempt to break his word block of the previous day.

The evening meal was set in the garden. The temperature had dropped a couple of degrees as night approached and Kate had given instructions to Mrs Goodrich, that during the heat wave, the houseguests would eat in the pavilion at the bottom of the garden. It was the only place where the cross winds, blowing in from the sea, met. Most times of the year it was a place to avoid but in the summer it was a haven from the heavy over-heated air of the day.

"Where's Rachel?" Cameron asked, after they were all seated.

"She usually eats her meals in her room," Finn replied, a frown settling between his eyes. It was as he'd suspected then, he had his eye on little Miss Weston. He would never have suspected that she would attract Blackstone - never in a million years. It occurred to him that perhaps he'd have to look more closely at her. What was he missing? Maybe the time had come to find out.

I was reading; my forehead felt damp with beads of perspiration. I put the book down on the table at my side and stood at the window. A slight breeze filtered in through the slats. Unlike the rooms at the front of the house, the windows at the back were smaller, the view less spectacular. Looking out, I was unable to see the pavilion or its occupants, just the kitchen garden and the hedge bordering the steep rocky drop down to the cove.

Then I heard a knock at my door followed by Finbar's voice.

"Rachel, I've brought you a cool drink. Why don't you come and join us all downstairs?"

Opening the door to him, I said, "That's very kind of you. The drink is certainly welcome but I'll stay here if you don't mind."

"No, of course not. Why don't I sit with you for a bit? I've brought enough for us both. We haven't had much chance to talk since you've been here. All work and no play eh?"

In spite of myself I felt a knot tighten in my stomach. He'd not waited for a reply but sat down in the chair I'd recently vacated and begun to pour out two iced cocktails from a large glass jug. He'd intended to stay whatever my reply had been, I realised, and the thought made me even more uncomfortable.

After the jug was empty and the conversation, which had started innocently enough, began to become more intimate, he stood up on hearing Kate's call from downstairs, and left me with a wink that held a promise, but of what exactly? Later, in bed, I stretched out on the cool sheets and wondered what it had all been about. Had I imagined Finbar had just made a pass at me? It must have been the drinks - the heat - it wasn't his fault, it was so hot, the drinks were cool - he was relaxed and no doubt would forget what he'd said by the morning. Excuses piled up. Nevertheless, I lay on top of the bedclothes and caressed my naked body with my fingertips, imagining it was Finbar and that we were about to make love. I told myself it was always meant to be so from the very start. Perhaps it wasn't just the alcohol, perhaps he'd realised his mistake in marrying Kate at last and now had come to his senses. The thought of it brought me to a lingering climax, reawakening my infatuation as if it had be waiting like a sleeping serpent for just such a moment to occur.

CHAPTER 13

In the darkness Finn saw the outline of his wife's sleeping body glowing as moonlight silvered her soft skin. His desire, though satiated, still lingered, he longed to touch her again, ease her into wakefulness, to feel her body stirring against his once more. There was no place in his mind for anyone but his lovely Kate. He wondered why he had so often thought otherwise. It was a madness that swept over him from time to time, a devil that would not be stilled. At times like this he knew he was a fool but folly took over when faced with each new challenge, each new adventure.

He couldn't understand what had made him make a pass at Rachel earlier. He'd hinted he'd drunk too much but he knew it was not the case. It had started with Cameron showing an interest in her. It had driven him to find out if he could get there first. It was his competitive nature driving him on, he decided, remembering school days when he would go all out to win, regardless of whether it was by fair means or foul. It was a trait that no matter how his life panned out, how successful or wealthy he became - the thrill of competition still held him in its thrall.

Kate stirred in her sleep and he began to stroke her back, willing her to wake up all thoughts of Rachel and of future conquests placed firmly in a folder at the back of his mind. A folder he knew he would open again, when the time was right or the urge to win uppermost.

Starting work at ten o'clock in the morning was infinitely more pleasurable than the early starts Alice had endured pre-Rachel days; she closed the side door and climbed the staircase leading to the turret room, pausing to catch her breath where the staircase curved sharply back on itself. Through the circular stained-glass window she saw the coast and her cottage and smiled ruefully. Robert had suggested she buy the place. She believed he'd come and live there after they were married. But Robert had been like all the rest. He'd fallen for a younger woman, a widow five years younger than Alice, a woman with a large house and plenty of money. He'd been the verger in the small village church. But after his marriage he'd transferred his allegiance to another church and worshipped with his new wife in the town of Sowbridge six miles away. It might have been six hundred for all Alice would see of him in the future.

"That you, Alice?"

"It is, Mr Alexander."

"Good. Hurry up then. Rachel is making me a cuppa. Let's get started on Chapter twelve."

When Alice pushed the door open, he was pacing the floor. She recognised the signs. He was impatient to get on. She lost no time in sitting at the old computer. Rachel could keep the new one with its fancy programmes. There was nothing wrong with the old one as far as she was concerned. She'd told him, she was too old to learn new tricks, she didn't want to appear too computer literate, it wouldn't do, he'd expect more of her and she was content to work at a slower pace even though she knew the new programmes like the back of her hand.

It was lunchtime by the time he took a break. Beads of sweat prickled in her armpits. It was bad enough having to cope with this swelteringly hot summer without having hot flushes; she thought she'd seen the end of those years ago but the odd one still crept up on her when she least expected it making her face look like an overripe tomato.

"Right, that should be enough to keep my two favourite girls hard at it for the rest of the afternoon." Finn dropped two small cassettes on to Alice's desk and added, "Do the necessary, Alice love. Rachel knows what to do with the rest."

Alice blushed or flushed she wasn't certain which, only that Mr Alexander was bound to think it was the latter. Then she plugged in one of the recording machines, inserted the tapes and adjusted the headphones, making a meal of it.

Rachel slipped in an earpiece and accessed the voice transmission app,. Watching her, Alice sighed, she had nothing against Rachel personally, just that she was younger and had replaced her. She knew it was her own fault. She should never have retired. But now it was too late. At least she was able to work here for a while, which was some consolation. What would she do when he no longer needed her, she wondered?

At midday, Alice opened her sandwich box and went to sit on the window seat where Rachel was eating her lunch whilst reading a paperback, an Alex Finn novel.

"I never thought I'd be praying for a change in the weather," Alice said.

"Wonderful for lying on the beach and cooling off in the waves but not exactly great up here. I'm sure this room must be the hottest in the house. You could grow orchids on this window sill," Rachel replied then crunched an apple between her teeth.

"There's Cameron Blackstone in the garden. He's talking to that Frankie. I hope he's not about to cause more trouble." Alice stretched her neck and looked down.

"Why would you say that?"

"Take it from me, dear. He's no good. Never has been and never will be." A sandwich crumb lodged itself into a deep crease running from her nose to her mouth of which she was blissfully unaware "If that Steve's not careful he'll be another fly in the ointment too."

Alice saw Frankie and Cameron Blackstone engaged in what appeared to be deep conversation in the garden then saw them walk out of the garden gate towards the cliff path.

"Look, there he is again. It's Frankie this time."

"Surely not."

"I wouldn't trust that man with next door's cat," muttered Alice watching the effect her words had as the crumb dislodged and floated down to her lap.

She began to think about Mr Alexander. She wasn't sure when she'd first recognised her feelings had changed. It was a long time after Robert. After all, it wasn't as if the women, he'd had relationships with, meant anything to him. They were the necessary distractions required by a genius. And Alice was sure he was a genius. She'd been a fool to leave him; lots of famous men liked the company of older women. Dreaming of what might have been, she closed her sandwich box, brushed the crumbs from her skirt and went down to the bathroom to wash her hands.

Later in the afternoon, she collected the manuscripts from her desk and put them on top of the pile Rachel had left. She could hear the young woman's laughter floating up from the garden. She looked out and saw her employer standing with his arm loosely draped around Rachel's shoulder and shuddered when she saw him bend towards her and whisper something in her ear.

Turning back to the completed pages piling up on the desk, Alice picked up a few that Rachel had been working on, switched on the computer and retyped the pages making as many typing errors as she could manage without being too obvious. Her computing skills were excellent, ever since she'd enrolled on the computer course at Sowbridge Technical College. Congratulating herself on keeping the extent of her proficiency a secret, she smiled. Shredding Rachel's neatly typed pages and replacing them with the amended copies, she left the room.

"So you're telling me I have nothing to worry about?" Frankie looked up at Cameron Blackstone.

"Steve loves you, what more could you want?"

"Yes, but does he? I can't compete with Kate. She's ravishing."

"I wouldn't have thought there would be any competition. It doesn't make sense."

Opening the gate leading to the cliff path Cameron followed Frankie in the direction of the harbour.

"Before Steve and I fell in love he was with Dora Metford."

"Good lord! *The* Dora Metford?" Cameron looked shocked.

"The movie star, yes that's the one." There was a catch in Frankie's voice.

"But she's not his type, surely?"

"You know how some men are. Never sure of themselves." Frankie lit a cigarette and inhaled the smoke.

"He is now though. I'm sure of it. You're barking up the wrong tree. Besides Kate Alexander has eyes for no one but Finn."

"I found them together in New York. He said he was comforting her but he was sharing a bed with her at the time."

Cameron stopped and placed his hand on

Frankie's arm. "I don't believe you."

"Well, OK, I exaggerated. But he was lying across the bed and she was resting her head on his shoulders. How d'you think I felt walking in on that?"

Cameron kicked a stone into the air. It came to rest on the cliff edge then clattered and bounced towards the cove beneath them. He didn't answer Frankie's question. There was nothing he could say. He'd been there before, only then Kate had been wrapped in Finn's arms and they were sleeping in the bed he'd shared with her for six months before Finn decided to spoil things. He remembered the choking sensation that had gripped him. The icy fingers plucking at his heart as if removing it piecemeal. He'd closed the bedroom door quietly, neither of them had been aware of his presence, then he'd left the flat and rung Kate the next day to say he wouldn't be coming back. He said he'd met someone else and he'd let her know when he'd be around to pick up his belongings. She'd acted as if it was his fault ever since. Perhaps he should have stayed away this time but Finn had insisted.

Still complaining and jealously commenting on Kate's faults, which it seemed only Frankie could perceive as Steve and the rest of the male population appeared to be blinded by her beauty, Frankie said, "I've tried telling him, she's only out for herself. She doesn't really value him. He's useful to her career. That's all there is to it."

"You think she's as shallow as that?"

"Certain of it. Anyway don't let Kate Alexander spoil our day. The pub suit you for lunch?"

"Yes, fine." Cameron followed Frankie across the harbour and in through the door of the pub. They sat in the same seat he'd shared with Rachel a few days ago.

"You and Finn, been friends long?" Frankie asked.

"Yes. He helped me out of a hole once and we sort of gelled. He's good company even if he's a bit over the top at times. But then geniuses often are."

"You consider him a genius?" Frankie looked disbelieving.

"I suppose I do - in a way. His books certainly sell well and anyone who can plot novels with the speed and competence of Alex Finn deserves to be in the top ten best selling lists."

Frankie frowned. "Never read any of them, so I couldn't say."

"You want to have a word with his secretary she'll tell you."

Rachel?"

"Rachel, yes but I was really thinking about Alice. She's been with him for years; faithful as a puppy. She retired a while ago, I gather, but she doesn't seem able to stay away. As far as she's concerned there's no one quite like Finn. I reckon she'd die for him," Cameron said.

"You're not serious?"

"Well, no, although I think she'd walk on hot coals for him, if he asked her."

"It's exactly how I feel about Steve. I'd do the same if he asked me," Frankie said picking up a large glass of red wine from the table.

Cameron realised the conversation had now taken a turn for the worse and that the rest of the afternoon was likely to be taken up with Steve and Kate. He looked longingly at the wine glass and then raised his hand towards the waiter.

The afternoon heat made the turret room unbearable. Finn left Rachel and Alice with what he considered to be enough work to keep them out of his hair and persuaded his wife to join him in the Jacuzzi, a prelude to what he hoped would be an afternoon spent in the bedroom.

Alice could see Rachel typing furiously, her brow

beaded with sweat. Finishing at break-neck speed, she said, "I'm done here, Alice can I give you a hand?"

The muscles in her neck tightened but she gave no other outward appearance of annoyance. "I'm fine thank you, dear, nearly finished. You go off and enjoy yourself." Yesterday she had managed to alter Rachel's work and had been pleased with the result. Mr Alexander had been quite annoyed. Anyone could see that. How had she managed to finish it all so quickly? Maybe it was time to adjust some of the settings on her computer? It would be sure to delay her tomorrow. Watching her go down the stairs towards her rooms, Alice switched on Rachel's computer.

CHAPTER 14

Looking out of my window, I watched the waves crashing over the rocks in the cove. They looked so cool and enticing. Picking up my swimming costume and a towel, I put them in my canvas backpack together with *The murder of Sleeping Beauty,* an Alex Finn novel, which had been written some years ago and, taking the back staircase, I walked through the garden and out on to the cliffs. There was no one around but I thought I heard Steve talking to Mrs Goodrich somewhere at the front of the house.

The breeze threaded though my hair but gave me no relief. There was a warm wind blowing in from the South. The T.V. weather bulletins had predicted a drought similar in nature to the one experienced back in nineteen-seventy-six. Thunderstorms swept around the coast during May and June, spectacular events with high winds, crashing thunder and sheet lightning but without bringing the rain the ground so badly needed.

I felt damp rivulets of sweat sliding down my back as I climbed down the narrow steps leading from the cliff to the cove, which became more uneven the nearer I came to the pebbles. I could see they had disintegrated into rubble leaving me with a walk of perhaps twenty feet over uneven ground until I could reach the sand.

Panting with relief, I jumped over the remaining two feet of scree to reach the safety of a patch of firm sand. The small cove was deserted. The only sound was the crashing of the waves on the foreshore. Breathing in the salt tainted air, I closed my eyes. I could hardly wait to slip out of my cotton sundress under which I'd worn my swimming costume. Finding a patch of soft sand in front of a flat rock, I unrolled my towel, spread it out and placed my backpack on the rock. Then dipping my toes into the cool water, I took a deep breath, plunged into the shallows and swam towards the deeper water closing my eyes and floating on my back. Cool at last, I made for the shore, ran up the beach and removing my book from my bag stretched out on my towel. The pages began to blur, my eyelids drooped and I fell asleep.

When I awoke, the sun had moved and I was in the shade. Seagulls soared towards the cliffs where someone was feeding them scraps. I thought I saw a flash of green and white and wondered if it might be Alice.

The sea was creeping closer; white-topped waves were caressing the shore enticingly. I raced towards them once more, running to meet the waves and diving beneath them to emerge in the calmer sea beyond the rocky coastline. Lying on my back I kicked my feet and watched the vapour trail of a jet crossing the cloudless sky, spreading its plume like a peacock's tail across the blue. I could see my towel on the sand and above, on the cliffs, a lone figure walking along the path but I couldn't quite make out who it might be.

With eyes closed the sounds became clearer. The screeching of the seagulls as they fed on scraps mingled with the sound of voices from the cliff top. Someone was shouting. I opened my eyes and, blinded by the sun, saw the outline of a figure trying to catch my attention. The person was waving whilst rushing towards the steps leading to the shore. I tilted my head to one side and looked away from the sun. When my eyes re-focused I could see I had drifted dangerously far from the coast and could feel the current tugging at my legs as the tide turned. Feeling panic rising up inside, I steadied myself, bracing my body against the flow of the current. But it was no use; the undertow was dragging me out to sea and the toes on my left foot were beginning to cramp up. I desperately tried to wriggle my foot but nothing happened. Pain seeped into my calf muscles as my movements became restricted still further. I could feel the current winning in my battle to stay afloat.

Hopelessly struggling, I felt the water close over my head as I sank beneath the surface. I fought to raise my head using my arms to keep my body afloat. Spluttering and coughing I re-surfaced but only for a moment, the strength in my arms wasn't enough and I sank once more.

Finbar's face came to meet me as I sank. He was smiling, holding out his arms to me. I would be with him soon. It was me he wanted. I could feel his arms around my waist, lifting me up above the waves, carrying me to the shore. I closed my eyes and drifted away sure that I was safe at last.

"Will she be all right?" Alice Phillips looked down at Rachel's prone body.

Frankie, who had been bending over Rachel, stood up. "What d'you think?"

Cameron didn't reply. He was too busy applying C.P.R. Rachel's skin had whitened under her tan but suddenly she gasped, vomited seawater into his face and opened her eyes. "Quick, give me that towel and your cotton jacket. We've got to keep her warm," he said.

Frankie hesitated. The jacket was a Sam Laurence. It had cost a fortune. "Here, it's not very warm though."

"It'll do," replied Cameron bundling Rachel into it and wrapping the towel around her waist. "Give me a hand up the steps, Frankie."

Alice, carrying Rachel's canvas bag, followed the trio unable to suppress the thought that if Cameron Blackstone hadn't arrived in time then Finbar Alexander would be minus a permanent secretary.

CHAPTER 15

There was no one in the garden. The house was quiet. I found out later that Steve had decided to follow Frankie into the village and had stopped in a shop selling artworks, effectively delaying him so he'd missed Frankie returning to Ransome's Point altogether. Finn and Kate were in bed.

"Put her down on the couch. I'll fetch some brandy," Cameron instructed.

"I'm all right, please. I'll just lie here for a moment longer to get my breath back." I struggled to sit up.

"Sit still and do as you're told. Cameron will kill me if I let you move a muscle." Frankie sat alongside me and took my hand. "You've had a very lucky escape you know."

"I saw you and alerted Mr Blackstone," simpered Alice. Frankie raised an eyebrow. I soon realised it was Cameron who had seen me. Although why Alice, who was looking out to sea whilst feeding the seagulls, had not raised the alarm earlier was a mystery.

"Here, drink this, slowly, now." Cameron handed me a glass and sat down on the couch at my side.

I spluttered, as the brandy hit the back of my throat. "Will I ever be able to thank you? It would seem you've saved my life."

"Just get well enough to have lunch with me in the Drunken Sailor tomorrow and that will be thanks enough," replied Cameron patting my arm.

"Good Lord, what's going on?" Finn, wearing a towel draped loosely around his waist and little else sauntered down the staircase. He was in search of ice, no doubt for the after-lovemaking drinks he and Kate were now enjoying upstairs.

"It's Rachel. She nearly drowned." Alice, suddenly solicitous, bent over me with a concerned look and proceeded to report the afternoon's events to Finn, with herself playing a major role in the unfolding drama.

"Well, well, not a dull moment. No lasting ill effects I trust?" He walked towards me, one hand securing the towel at his waist. "Glad old Cameron here was able to help, otherwise I'd be minus a secretary."

Alice Phillips was a lone voice joining Finn's laughter at his tasteless joke.

"If the drama's over then, I'll carry on," Finn

said making for the kitchen.

I stood up. "I think I'll go and have a lie down in my room for a bit."

"You are sure you don't need a doctor?" Cameron asked.

"Yes, quite sure. And thanks again."

Cameron turned to Frankie. "Your jacket."

"Thanks." Frankie took the damp creased garment, and sighed.

At the beginning of July, Finn was to attend a book signing in Regent Street and had made arrangements to stay in Guy's London flat.

"It makes sense not to shell out bucks to stay in the Dorchester when Guy's pad's a stone's throw away," he told Kate. "Anyway he said it's no problem he won't even be there. He's in Geneva next week for three weeks."

"Did he mention Stella?" Kate asked.

"No, not a word. I think he's putting space between them. They'll work it out, you'll see."

"I don't think so. Not this time. She seems adamant to end the marriage, according to Guy." Kate frowned. "He'll miss Ben. Not seeing him every day will devastate him."

"I wouldn't jump the gun, old thing. You know how these things go. One minute it's the end of a relationship the next it's full steam ahead." Finn threw a few things into a small case that was lying on the bed. "You don't mind if I stay over for a few days? Seems a shame to go to London and not enjoy city life while I'm there."

"No, I don't mind. It will give Steve and me a chance to work on a few ideas." Kate repacked the case and closed the lid.

"That's if Steve's other half will let you." Finn picked up the case and walked to the door. "You do know Frankie is jealous of you."

Kate burst out laughing. "It's the most ridiculous thing I've heard you say in months, Finbar Alexander. Now off you go and leave me in peace."

The book signing was a success. A stand had been erected in the store around which stood a selection of Alex Finn novels. In front of a full-length photo of the author holding up his latest novel *The Slayer of Souls,* stood a table and chair where Finn sat, hoping it was going to be worth his while. The thrill of book-signing events had long since passed for him. He looked upon them as a necessary evil, even the plaudits handed out by his loyal fans had become routine. As it turned out the queue of customers waiting for a chance to speak to the author led through the store and out into the street, each customer clutching a copy of *The Slayer* in eager anticipation. By closing time the store was beginning to run out of copies and the Manager, Rex Bickersley, breathed a sigh of relief as the last customer left.

"A great success, Mr Finn," Rex said shaking Finn's hand. "I wonder if you would care to join me in a drink at *The Keys.* The store would like to show its appreciation."

"If you're in the chair, Rex, I'm right behind you," replied Finn.

The pub was full of the usual mix of office workers desperate for a drink before commuting through the rush hour traffic, and out of work actors hoping to be *seen* by a casting director. Finn followed Rex Bickersley to a table overlooking the street.

"Staying in London long, Mr Finn?" The store Manager handed Finn a bottle of red wine and a glass.

"It's Alexander."

"Pardon me?"

" I said, oh never mind, Finn will do just fine. To answer your question; I'm not sure. Maybe I'll stay over for a week or two - I'll see."

Finn's eyes had rested on a tall brunette

wearing a figure hugging black dress and red high-heeled shoes. She raised her head from her glass and her eyes met his. Rex was rabbiting on about the profits of his store and its admirable location. From time to time Finn noticed that he glanced nervously at his watch. Smiling in the general direction of the bar, Finn said, "Look old man, I don't want to keep you away from your family. I've enjoyed chatting but I think I can see an old friend at the bar." He stood up and raised his hand to the brunette.

A relieved Rex Bickersley picking up his brief case from the floor said, " Right, nice to have met you, Mr Finn."

The brunette raised her eyebrows. "Hope you don't mind; had to get rid of a bore in a hurry." Finn gestured to the barman. " Same again, and for the lady." Turning to face her, he smiled. "Please make, a lonely old man in a big city, happy, by joining him in a drink?" They couldn't resist the smile, Finn thought, and true to type the ice maiden melted. Her smile matched his, her red lips parting to show a row of gleaming white veneered teeth.

"Love to." She held out her hand, "Laura Crighton, struggling actress, waiting for her big break."

"Finbar Alexander. And believe me with a face and figure like yours you'll not be struggling for long."

Sitting at a table near the window were a group of women in their forties. One of them stood up and made her way to the bar. She was short and plump and carried a copy of *The Slayer of Souls*. She approached Finn and said, in a high-pitched voice, "Mr Finn, I wonder if I could bother you for a moment. I don't want to interrupt but I'd be ever so grateful if you would sign this copy of your book for me. My friends all managed to get to the store in time but I was too late." She rambled on, " I bought my copy as soon as it was out last month. I've read every one of your novels. It's such a privilege to meet you."

Finn gritted his teeth and forced a smile, though admittedly not as dazzling as the one he'd displayed for Laura Crighton. "It would be my pleasure. You have a pen ready, I see?"

The plump lady simpered and purred as Finn asked her name and personalised her signed copy. Blushing an unflattering crimson she returned to her seat amid lively chatter from her companions.

"So, Alex Finn, nice to meet you." Laura smirked. "Now all I need is someone to film one of your books with me in the lead role and I'm in business."

"You never know your luck. Look I'm famished. I don't suppose you'd like to join me in a meal. The Ritz is fairly near."

She hesitated but only for a moment. "Why not? It's not as though you're a stranger. "You've been sitting on my beside table for weeks, apparently."

Finn took her arm and guided her past the giggling group seated near the window and out into the street.

At the Ritz, the Maitre d' recognised Finn and realising he was not dining with his wife guided him towards a secluded table in a corner of the dining room. Heavily gilded cherubs danced on the ceiling and Laura's face reflected back at her from the Multi-facetted mirrors lining the walls.

A young man with red hair was playing a selection of ballads on a highly polished grand piano at the entrance to the dining room. Laura sighed, "Oh this is great. It certainly beats grabbing a bite at a fast-food outlet in Covent Garden."

"Quite. Just relax and enjoy the evening. I believe in enjoying life while you have it; and thanks to *The Slayer,* which is jumping off the shelves like a kangaroo on speed - I have it. May I suggest the oysters as a starter?"

Finn was enjoying himself. Kate had become blasé about their elevated status in life and it felt good to play Professor Higgins, a role he'd always admired. It was true Laura was no Eliza but she would do.

By the time the sweet trolley arrived, Finn was staggered at how much food she had managed to consume. Watching her making short work of a white chocolate concoction, he said, "Where do you put it all?"

"High metabolic rate, " Laura mumbled between mouthfuls. "My mother and sister are the same."

"No diets for you then?"

Kate was always on one diet or another, watching every bite. Her ultra slim body never varied in size but it was not without its sacrifices. Laura was a breath of fresh air and he wanted her. He was surprised at how much he wanted her.

Throughout the meal, the wine flowed. Finn found Laura an eager listener and was soon discussing his favourite topic – himself. Whenever her wineglass was empty, he dutifully filled it and by the time the coffee and brandy came Laura was hanging on his every word.

"Excuse me for a moment." She stood up and

walked unsteadily towards the ladies room.

Finn sat back in his chair. The evening had flown by and he'd enjoyed every minute of it. He'd temporarily forgotten how good it felt to flirt with a woman, a complete stranger, who appreciated his anecdotes and laughed in all the right places. He toyed with the stem of his brandy balloon, swirling the amber liquid around in the glass. Should he take her straight back to Guy's flat, or go on to a club? While he was contemplating his next course of action the Maitre d' put a hand on his arm and bent forward.

"I'm afraid your companion is unwell, Mr Alexander. She has fainted in the ladies room. I fear a little too much wine perhaps?" He tapped the side of his nose conspiratorially.

Finn raised his glass to his lips and tipped his head back. "I see. Better get her home then. He handed a passing waiter his credit card, punched in a number then headed towards the ladies room.

Laura was sitting on a chaise longue clutching a small white towel to her mouth.

"Time to get you home, my dear," said Finn. "A taxi is waiting. How d'you feel about walking? If you lean on me, I'll see you're OK."

Laura raised her mascara - streaked eyes to his and nodded. Finn realised that he was no longer facing a dilemma as to how to spend the rest of the evening. Reaching the taxi, he helped her into the seat, her head resting on his shoulder. Then directed the driver to Guy's flat.

During the short drive, Laura fell asleep. Finn looked down at her shining hair resting on his chest and felt a renewed urge stirring inside him. After paying the taxi driver, with Laura draped across him like a marionette, he managed to open the lobby door, reach the lift and finally the seclusion of Guy's second floor apartment.

Half asleep, Laura didn't protest as he removed her dress, lay her down on Guy's overly large bed, and covered her with the satin throw, he'd draped over the chair earlier in the day. Then with a resigned air he removed spare bedding from the linen cupboard and made up a bed on the couch in the living area.

Throughout the night Finn was plagued by dreams; swirling fantasies that drifted out of reach as the first rays of sunlight split through the gap in the blinds to come to rest on his eyelids. It took a while before he remembered the reason why he was lying on Guy's couch and not in the bed. He yawned loudly, stretched his arms above his head and padded across the wooden floor to the kitchen area. Carrying a tray with a mug of hot black coffee and a plate of buttered toast towards Guy's bedroom, Finn knocked on the door and waited. No reply.

"Laura, wake up sleepy head. This should make you feel better."

Still no reply; Finn balanced the tray on his arm and opened the door. The bed was empty. The satin cover replaced as if it had never been disturbed. On the bedside table lay a scrap of paper. Putting the tray on the bed he picked up the note and read;-

Thanks for the best evening I've had in ages. Sorry I had to make such an idiot of myself. I look forward to reading your future novels with the memory of a lovely evening spent with a very special man.

Laura Crighton.

He stared at the sloping handwriting unable to believe he wouldn't see her again. His mouth turned down. He wasn't used to being thwarted when it came to women. And he wasn't going to let it happen now. He picked up the telephone at the side of the bed and rang his home number.

CHAPTER 16

Lance Rodway sat at his desk and sifted through the morning mail. He hadn't had a story he could get his teeth into for ages. Routine, mundane pieces featuring starlets, celebs and wanabees had been his bread and butter for months. He was fed up of interviewing surgically enhanced Californian women with ferociously whitened teeth. It was prostituting his talent; he was an investigative journalist with a talent for getting to the truth. There was a time, during the Falklands war and its aftermath, that he'd felt his talent was being put to good use. He sighed and picked up a brown A5 envelope with a typewritten address sticker bearing his name under which in a handwritten scrawl had been written, PRIVATE AND CONFIDENTIAL, rather as an afterthought.

The contents of the letter made him sit up and take notice. Perhaps this was the one he'd been waiting for. The rest of the morning passed as he continued to feed drivel into his computer and send it off to the magazine, which had been foolish enough to pay for such rubbish. At lunchtime he picked up the phone, rang the number and made an appointment for the following day. For the first time in months he began to feel optimistic about a story.

When he arrived home, later that evening, Emma was waiting in the lobby.

"Forgot my key again," she explained. "I was going to have a meal all ready for you."

"You don't have to worry about feeding me, Em." Lance kissed her cheek then opened the door. " Seeing you is enough."

She laughed and pushed his shoulder. " You won't be saying that when we're an old married couple." She bit her bottom lip. "Did I just say that? Erase it, quick."

Lance smiled, she was great, just what he needed but her joke had set him thinking. Would it be so bad to marry Emma? Kate Ripton, his ideal woman, had been married to that fool Alexander for years. It was time he moved on.

The television was on in the kitchen, the smell of steak cooking reaching his nostrils, when he'd washed the stink of the New York subway from his skin and joined Emma. "Something smells good," he said opening the wine.

"Hope it tastes as good as it looks. You can never tell with steak. Bit like men really." She grinned and looked over her shoulder at the television." Hey isn't that Kate what's her name, the fashion designer, the one you knew way back?"

Lance sat down at the kitchen table and watched the screen. Kate looked the same, she hadn't aged a bit; stick thin, clouds of wavy hair framing her face and touching her shoulders and a smile which still made his insides turn to jelly.

"She's making quite a name for herself. I must admit I do love her clothes but you have to be a size six to wear them properly. I'm really envious, how does she keep so thin?" Emma said turning the steak on the grill.

"You are perfect just as you are, my sweet," Lance replied, realising he meant every word. "Perhaps Kate Ripton/Alexander could at last be put in the past where she belonged.

However, the past has a way of surfacing when you least expect it. He awoke at a quarter to three, Emma still sleeping soundly at his side, and couldn't get the contents of the letter and his appointment the following day out of his mind.

CHAPTER 17

Kate put the phone down and walked to the window. A light breeze had sprung up rustling the leaves on the silver birch. She could hear them, swishing like bails of satin rubbing together, through the open window.

"Everything OK? " Steve asked, looking up from the drawing board.

"Yes. No, not really. That was Finn. He's staying in London until Guy gets back at the end of the month."

"And, that's not good?" Steve's eyes locked onto hers.

"It's just me being silly. Forget it; let's see what you make of my drawings. You haven't said a word yet." Kate walked towards him but Steve was waiting until she stood at his side then put his arm around her waist.

"You don't have to pretend with me," he said.

She sighed and rested against him for a moment. "I know. It's only for a couple of weeks. It may be perfectly innocent. Perhaps Finn has been missing city life. It's so quiet down here; not a bit like he was used to in London."

"But you have your doubts?"

"Yes. Past experience and all that; anyway there's nothing I can do about it. I have to believe him otherwise there's not much point in our being together is there?"

Steve's grip on her waist tightened. "You know what I think about it."

Kate bent to kiss the top of his head. "I know," she said. " Now move up a bit and I can show you the finer points of my spring collection."

The French doors leading to the garden opened, the sound of the latch echoing around the studio. "Oh, so here you are. I was beginning to think I was alone in the house. Where is everyone?" Frankie walked towards them. "This looks cosy. What are you two up to?" A coating of heavy sarcasm lingered on each syllable.

"We've almost finished here. That's right, Kate?" Steve's eyes were imploring her to answer.

"Yes, of course; nothing that won't keep. You scoot off and keep Frankie company. We can look at this again another time."

Watching the pair walk into the garden, Steve's arm around Frankie's shoulders, Kate felt Finn's absence as acutely as ever, although from past experience she usually knew instinctively when he was up to something. But however hard she tried to put it to the back of her mind, it wouldn't stay put. She was sure Finn's excuse for prolonging his stay was just that - an excuse.

Out on the point the breeze had died. A heat haze hung over the sea obscuring the coastline so Alice Phillips's cottage lay shrouded in mist. Frankie flopped down on to the seat as the struts creaked.

"Careful," Steve said.

"You'll be telling me next I should lose a few pounds. Perhaps you prefer your conquests to be stick thin *a la* Kate Alexander."

"Oh, so that's it. I wondered why I'd been getting the cold shoulder on the way here." Steve sat down and took Frankie's hand in his. "Don't be so ridiculous. You know that's nonsense."

"Do I?" Frankie looked out to sea.

"I don't understand where this obsession with Kate has come from. I've never given you any reason to doubt my feelings for you. Kate is a friend who happens to be a work colleague. You know I owe much of my success to her expertise. Not everyone would have been as generous with their time or ideas."

Frankie remained silent looking over the water

then stood up. "Look, out there. Isn't that Rachel Weston and Cameron Blackstone?"

Steve peered into the mist. A small boat with an outside motor attached was slowly drifting out to sea on the current. "Yes, I think you're right. Why don't they use the motor to pull them back to shore? They're drifting towards the *Cobblestones,* quick, try to attract their attention."

Steve and Frankie began to shout in the direction of the boat, their voices carrying on the still air. They raised their arms. "Turn back," Steve shouted but his words drifted back to him, like a slap, on the breeze.

From the cliff top they could see the couple in the boat had acknowledged them but seemed powerless to do anything about the situation they now found themselves in. Cameron mimed the motor was useless and they had no oars. Steve took his mobile from his pocket and dialled the emergency services then taking Frankie's hand ran towards the steps leading to the cove.

"What's the panic? And what for Pete's sake are the *Cobblestones?"* gasped Frankie as they ran.

"They're a treacherous stretch of water lying midway between the point, where the cliffs oppose each other." Steve replied, his breath catching in his throat.

"In simple terms?" Frankie replied, running down the steps.

"They are drifting out to sea but before they reach open water they have to cross the *Cobblestones*. Not a good idea if you're in an open boat without a motor or sail power to see you safely across."

"You mean they could drown?" Frankie stopped, the true horror of the situation suddenly dawning."

"Exactly," said Steve searching the coast for sight of a rescue boat.

CHAPTER 18

"What is it?" I sat up. I'd been lying back with my eyes shut enjoying the sun on my face and the sounds of the sea, the gentle lapping of the water against the wooden sides of the small boat, the screeching of the seagulls as they dived towards the shore in search of food and Cameron's soothing voice as he told me stories of his youth spent in the Scottish borders.

"The motor's dead and that half-soaked idiot who leased us the boat for the day forgot to mention there were no oars on board." The tone of his voice had changed. He sounded worried. "I shouldn't have listened to Finn. I should have gone somewhere else not hired this sieve from one of his doggy mates."

"Never mind. It's a nice day. The water's calm. We'll drift in on the tide, won't we?" I suggested, although I wasn't sure of my facts. However, I couldn't see any problem; it wasn't as if there was a raging storm brewing and we were miles out to sea. But there was a deep furrow between Cameron's eyes and his voice was harsh.

"I think we'll shoot off a flare just to be on the safe side, nothing to worry about just lie back, close your eyes and enjoy the day." He was searching in the emergency supply box situated in the middle of the deck and emerged holding a flare rocket and applicator.

"What's all the shouting about? Look up on the cliff. I think it's Steve and Frankie, though I couldn't be sure from here. They're trying to attract our attention." I sat up and screwed up my eyes against the glare of the sun. "Whatever is it? They're rushing down the steps as if their lives depended on it." I looked to Cameron for reassurance but he fired off the rocket flare and then turned back to the motor in desperation. Each time he tried the engine it groaned and refused to turn over. " Oh God, that's it," I said. "It's not their lives they're concerned about - it's ours. I'm right aren't I?"

Cameron left the engine and came towards me. He sat alongside and took my hand in his. "We'll be OK. I'm sure of it. The coastguard will see the flares."

"But what's the problem? The weather is good..."

"The tide is going out, not coming in. We are

drifting out beyond the point, towards the *Cobblestones,"* he said.

"I don't understand."

"It's the name the locals give to the mix of currents that exist between the two headlands. You can see how rough the sea is, as we are getting closer. It's no problem in a larger boat, or even in one this size with a decent motor or a strong pair of oars. But we are at the mercy of the underlying currents and could be tossed about in that cauldron and capsized by the undertow." Still holding my hand he said, "I hope you are you a strong swimmer, Rachel."

"Do you think it will come to that?" I pulled my hand away from his and cupped my cheeks with my palms. "I can swim, but I'm not used to swimming in a strong current. You saw what happened the other day. I'm used to swimming in a pool, not the sea."

"Don't worry, you'll have me to cling on to. Now for the good news and the bad news," he said trying to sound light-hearted but failing. "The good news is there's a life jacket. The bad news is it's punctured - absolutely useless."

"So there's no good news then?

"No. I'm afraid not."

I sighed, "I think I've changed my mind about

you."

"Really? How?" Cameron's eyes swept around the coastline then reverted to the stretch of water which was ominously near.

"I was under the impression you were some sort of drunken, lecherous, individual whom Finbar had taken a liking to years ago and who was now trading on his generosity for a free holiday."

His laughter had no humour in it. The sound he made was harsh and bitter. "That's so far from the truth, you'll never know. Why the change of mind?" He tried the motor again.

"Oh, I suppose it's been spending time with you, getting to know the real you. Making up my own mind." I eased around to the back of the boat, aware that the sea was getting rougher by the minute.

"So you think you know the real me, eh?" He was trying to keep my attention away from the rocking of the boat. "I wonder if you do?"

"Perhaps I'll never have the chance to find out."

The boat suddenly began rocking, water slurped over the side into the well between the seats. The surface of the sea had changed from being flat to an agitated mass of water; angry, spume-topped waves rose up to either side of us.

"Cam," I was beginning to panic. I clamped my arm through his aware my grip was like a vice.

"Hey, not so tight, I'm not going anywhere. Where on earth is the emergency lifeboat?" He tried to steady the boat by jamming his feet against the side but the current was too strong.

"Perhaps there isn't one." I tried not to sound as terrified as I felt. Swimming in a strong current was my worst nightmare. I knew I was not a good swimmer and hated even putting my head under water in the safety of a swimming pool patrolled by lifeguards.

"There is. Don't fret, they'll be here any minute." The tone of his voice robbed the reassuring words of their impact as the rocking increased. The level of water in the well of the boat was rising and Cameron's attempts to bail out were futile. Adding to my unease, with every movement, water rushed over the side so that my feet were now covered and it was creeping up to my calf and to make matters worse a strong wind had begun blowing in from the sea. It tossed the small boat about threatening to capsize it.

Taking me by the shoulders Cameron said, "When we hit the water, don't struggle; go with the flow of the current. Move your legs to keep afloat and hold on to me. I won't let you go.

You've no need to worry; I'm a strong swimmer. They'll reach us soon. Steve and Frankie will have raised the alarm by now."

It was a shock when I slid overboard. The water was colder than I'd thought possible. My breath left my lungs like the sighing of the wind as my mouth filled with water. Coughing and spluttering I gasped, "Don't let me go"

"No chance," Cameron replied but I had no way of knowing whether it was the truth or not.

CHAPTER 19

Finn felt a slight pang of guilt at the sound of her voice.

"Darling, how are things in London? Have you heard from Guy yet?" Kate was breathless.

"Where've you been?" he asked.

"I've just come in. The house is empty. I don't know where they've all gone. I heard the phone and had to run."

Finn could picture the scene and for a moment wished he were there. But the moment was fleeting. "I see. To answer your question, London's fine and no I haven't heard anything from your brother. You're sure you don't mind me staying on?" He crossed his fingers.

"I'll miss you," she said. "But no, I have so much work on at the moment. Oh Lord I'll have to go, Finn. Frankie and Steve are making the most awful racket. I wonder what's wrong now?"

Putting down the phone Finn shrugged. It was good to get away from those two for a bit at least. Histrionics were their speciality. It was no good

Kate insisting it was a side effect of having an artistic nature. It didn't wash.

Laura's scent lingered in the bedroom; it hung in the air like a memory. The need to find her returned; but where to begin? It had to be the wine bar. The clock in the hall struck mid-day as Finn left the flat. He'd forgotten the difference between spending the summer months in the city and living by the sea. Traffic fumes coated his nostrils with a layer of black carbon and from somewhere nearby he inhaled the acrid smell of cement, tar, and dust from a building site. The heat was more oppressive than on the coast. His shirt began to stick to his body long before he found the wine bar.

He opened the door with a sinking feeling. He'd already searched the bar for sight of her and hungrily gazed at the few tables, which were occupied. The barman was the same person who had served him with drinks the night before.

"Glass of red, please. Oh and by the way, I don't suppose you know the lady I met in here last night, Laura Crighton?"

The barman filled Finn's glass and put it on the counter. "Three-ninety-five. I know the bird you mean, seen her in here before. Laura Crighton you say? Didn't know her name." He handed Finn his change.

"Does she come in here regularly?"

"Not sure, mate. All I know is, I've seen her before. Well, you're not likely to forget a face like that now are you?" He walked to the end of the bar. " Yes, mate, what can I get you?"

By half past three Finn was drunk and sure she wasn't going to turn up. He hailed a taxi and went back to the flat to sleep it off.

She was waiting outside the security doors.

"Laura?"

"Hello, Finn. I'm afraid I've lost an earring. I expect it's fallen off somewhere in the bed. Sorry to be such a nuisance."

"No problem." He had difficulty in punching in the correct security numbers on the pad. His finger felt thick and awkward. His head was swimming. "Look, I need to sober up. Come in, I'll make us some coffee. That's if I can. He laughed and fell against her.

"I'll make the coffee. It's the least I can do. What were you celebrating?" she asked, helping him into the lift.

"The loss of a good woman," he mumbled.

Outside the flat, he gave Laura the key. "Over to you. I can see two of them."

"Men!" Laura smiled. "OK. That's it. Come on

let's get the coffee on."

He must have fallen asleep. When he opened his eyes it was dark outside. He was stretched out on the couch, his head on a pillow. Again the bird had flown leaving a note. This time it read;- *Hope you enjoyed your sleep. No luck in finding my earring. Let me know if it turns up. Phone me; perhaps we could meet up again, this time without one or both of us getting drunk. Laura. Tel no. 0803001556*

"Bingo!"

Finn rubbed his eyes and was making for the shower when the telephone rang. It was Guy. After exchanging pleasantries, he said, "I thought you should know. I've finished up here sooner than I'd anticipated. My flight is due into Heathrow tomorrow at six pm."

Making a face into the phone Finn silently cursed fate. "You'll be wanting the flat then?"

"I will. I trust you've completed your book signing jobby?"

"Ye.....s"

"But?"

"Oh nothing really. I thought I might stay on a bit. Have a drink with you. Catch up on old times." Finn was thinking on his feet.

"No can do, old man, much as I'd like to; busy

time of it at the Old Bailey. Sorry and all that. Give my love to Kate by the way. Say I'll try and come down to Ransome's Point some time in late July-early August. Maybe then you and I can catch up."

"Right," said Finn realising with a sinking feeling that his time in London was up. "I'll leave the key with the janitor."

He thought about ringing Laura but realised it would be futile. There was nothing for it now but to return to Kate. If he tried to book into a hotel, Guy would spring him for sure and Kate would quickly smell a rat.

'C'est la vie' thought Finn, throwing his clothes into his bag. It was a shame. She was a corker, just what he needed.

Picking up the phone he rang his home number and waited. No answer. Where were they all?

CHAPTER 20

The water was unbelievable cold. Cameron held on to me. I couldn't feel my legs but tried to move them to stop myself from sinking. We seemed to have been in the water for ages. Where was the rescue boat? There were people on the cliff top at Ransome's Point watching us; to me they looked like ants. Surely they would have rung for help? Minutes seemed like hours. All the while the strong current tugged at our legs threatening to drag us beneath the surface. It might be good, to just give up, to be taken with the waves. I was so tired, exhausted by the struggle to keep afloat. My limbs ached and my head hurt as the afternoon sun beat down on top of me.

"Hold your chin up, Rachel. You have to keep your head above water," Cameron urged.

"My legs ache. I'm so cold. Why am I so cold on such a hot day?"

"I know. It won't be long now. They'll soon come for us."

"You're sure?"

"Certain." He groaned then and explained that he was struck by an attack of cramp in his calf muscles. His face contorted and he winced. My terror increased as I felt him loosen his grasp on me as the spasm took hold of him. There was nothing more I could do to stop my head dipping beneath the waves.

Kate joined Steve and Frankie on the beach. They were watching helplessly, as the small boat capsized spilling its occupants into the rough water of the *Cobblestone* currents. They'd alerted the emergency services and waited helplessly for sight of the rescue boat. Frustrated at the hopelessness of the situation, Steve paced the beach standing on a rock in an attempt to assess the situation more clearly.

"I can't believe the strength of the current out there. It seems impossible on such a mild summer's day," he shouted to Kate.

"It's a notorious stretch of water. I can't understand why they would be in that vicinity, in such a small boat. Can you see anything yet?" Kate asked.

"No. These binoculars are quite powerful but I can't see a lifeboat. What if we use the yacht? Try to reach them ourselves?" Steve suggested, jumping off the rock.

"It would be madness. Besides, I'm not even sure it's seaworthy. You know Finn, he's not exactly interested in sailing." It was sold with the house. Kate remembered them using it once, not long after they'd moved in. But it had been moored in the small boathouse ever since and to her knowledge Finn had never kept it in order; in fact she doubted if he even remembered its existence.

"It might be better than nothing." Steve was walking towards the boathouse. He thrust the binoculars into Frankie's hand. "Keep a look out."

"I don't like the idea of Steve using the yacht, it's too dangerous. Try and persuade him against it, Frankie," Kate implored.

"He won't listen to me." Frankie raised the binoculars and searched the horizon. "Wait. Look - there. There's something. Yes it's the rescue boat. I can see the spray from its motors." Frankie ran to the boathouse.

"Thank heavens." Kate breathed a sigh of relief.

Returning to where Kate was standing, Steve held the binoculars once more. "Something's happened. One of them has disappeared. "I think it's Rachel. I can see Cameron diving under the water. It looks like he's trying to find her."

In the distance they could hear the sound of the rescue vessel's motor as it cut a path towards them.

"I think he's in trouble now. He's struggling, I don't like the look of it at all." Steve kept the binoculars glued to his eyes. "What the hell are they doing, can't they go any faster? I thought you said it was a new state of the art lifeboat, for goodness sake."

Kate put her hand on his arm. "It is. It looks like they've reached the boat but I can't see Rachel or Cameron. What's happening Steve?"

"I'm not sure. Wait. I think they've found someone."

"Both of them?" Frankie asked.

"Not sure."

Kate ran to the steps. "I'll drive over to the harbour. Perhaps you two would stay near the phone?"

By the time Kate reached the harbour, an ambulance was waiting on the quayside. She saw Blackstone helping Rachel into the back of the vehicle assisted by two Paramedics. He looked unscathed by his ordeal but from what she could see Rachel looked in poor shape. Getting back into her car, she followed the ambulance along the winding coast road to Witcombe Cottage Hospital situated on the outskirts of the town.

Waiting interminably at reception in the small Accident and Emergency department, Kate eventually saw Cameron emerge from a corridor. Seeing her, he raised his hand. She felt her stomach clench. If only she could get rid of the unpleasant sensation she felt every time she saw him.

"Kate."

"How is Rachel?"

"Not good. She's being admitted to a ward for overnight observation. She's suffering from exhaustion and a degree of hypothermia. You wouldn't think it would be possible on a day like today, would you? But the water was extremely cold." He shivered.

"Can I see her?"

"I wouldn't advise it. She was sleeping a moment ago that's why I'm going back to Ransome's Point. I'll come in later."

Kate felt uncomfortable. She couldn't avoid it "I'll give you a lift," she said, over her shoulder as she made for the door.

Driving along the cliff-top road towards the house, Kate said, "I don't understand. What happened exactly?"

"The motor died and the idiot who hired the boat to us forgot to mention the lack of oars." Cameron was looking out of the window.

"Didn't you know about the *Cobblestones*?"

"I'd heard something. But if the motor had been OK there wouldn't have been a problem. We intended to cut through them, head out into the bay and skirt around the coast until we reached Bramble Bay. I'd done it before, I seem to remember."

Kate shivered, was he referring to their relationship and their time together? She couldn't remember if she'd ever been there with him. In fact she'd effectively blocked out memories of anything to do with the part of her life, which had included Cameron Blackstone.

Steve was waiting at the gate. He was looking out to sea through a pair of binoculars, which he lowered as Kate's car appeared. "Finn's on his way home," he called. "He said Guy had returned to the flat unexpectedly early so he decided to cut his stay short."

"Thank God," muttered Kate. At least he could take charge of the obnoxious man who was at present thanking her for driving him back from the hospital. "Excuse me, I'm off for a shower," she said leaving Cameron to explain events. She was impatient to wash herself clean of his presence.

Wrapping a towel around her, Kate sat at her dressing room table combing her wet hair. She looked at her reflection and sighed. Had it been all that bad? Cameron Blackstone, by merely inhabiting her home, had stirred up memories she'd thought were forgotten. She opened the bottom drawer of the dressing table and removed a tin box.

Reaching across for her handbag she slid her fingers in between the lining of the front pocket and the leather and removed a small silver key, which she used to open the tin box. Inside were a stack of diaries; ones which she had never shown to Finn. The reason for her reticence had been simple. Finn was like a dog with a bone if he thought she didn't want to discuss something. He was also extremely jealous where she was concerned. He probed and prodded until she said things almost against her wishes. It was a knack he had. There was no way she wanted him to pry open from her mind the memories of her relationship with the man he thought of as a good friend. It was better if he knew nothing about it.

She opened one of the diaries. The one she had written the year before she had married Finn. It began with the New Year's Eve party. The one

Finn had invited her to, after they'd met by chance at a friend's house. Finn had made straight for her but, although she had initially found him extremely attractive, she thought he was brash and full of himself. She'd made some excuse about having to leave early and left him with a hangdog expression that in latter years she came to know well. She'd noticed the man with the dark eyes and brooding expression who kept looking at her but that had been all.

She turned the pages to the middle of March.

I met him again, she read, *the man at the party. He was looking at me whilst pretending to admire The Van Gogh. I wondered if he remembered me. He followed me around the art gallery but didn't approach me, never said a word, just looked.*

Later, in the park, he came up to me. " I'm not following you, if that's what you think." he said. "Well actually it's not strictly true. You dropped this." He opened his fist and my gold bracelet with the broken safety chain lay in his palm.

That was the beginning of it - of Cameron and me.

Kate closed the diary and put it back in the tin. She didn't want to read the rest. She had locked the memory away with the diary years ago and it would be foolish to dip her toe into that muddy pond. Best left to stagnate, she thought, as the telephone rang.

CHAPTER 21

The ward smelt of disinfectant and alcohol wipes. I wrinkled my nose and opened my eyes. Alice Phillips was sitting on the side of the bed. "Awake at last. I didn't expect to see you sitting in a chair. I heard you were at death's door." She sounded disappointed.

"I'm OK, Alice. I can't stay in bed all day."

She thrust a bag of grapes at me along with a copy of last month's Ladies' Times and I muttered my thanks.

"Getting to be a habit," she said, popping a grape into her mouth.

"Pardon?"

"Being rescued from the sea by Cameron Blackstone." She sniffed loudly. "If you ask me he should have taken more care in the first place. Fancy taking you out near those currents. I told you before he's a man to stay well clear of. He's trouble that one."

"If it wasn't for him, I'd..." I began my defence of him.

"Oh I know all that. Well he couldn't let you

drown without trying to save you, could he? Not with an audience watching his every move through binoculars."

I sighed; I didn't have the energy to counter Alice's cynical remarks. The woman had made up her mind about Cameron and there was no shifting her opinion of him. I closed my eyes and heard her voice drifting towards me, as if through a fog.

"Mr Alexander's coming home today; cutting short his stay in London. I know I for one will be glad to see him. Don't you worry though, I'll keep the work ticking over, until you are fit enough."

I tried to smile; Finbar was coming home. It was strange, I thought, I hadn't the energy to get excited. I couldn't feel the old familiar thrill as my heart lifted with elation at the prospect of seeing him again. Perhaps it was because he'd only been gone a short time and so much had happened since, or perhaps I was finally getting over him.

"I'm off. Here he comes. As if a bunch of flowers is going to make up for nearly getting you killed." Alice picked up her handbag and strode off.

I looked down the ward. Cameron was searching for me. The staff had moved my bed to the end of the ward earlier. He was carrying a large bunch of white daisies. I must have mentioned they were my favourite. I was touched he'd remembered. I raised my hand.

"Feeling better?" he asked taking my hand and kissing my fingers.

I nodded. "How can I thank the man who saved my life twice?"

"Mmm. Let me think. I suggest we talk about it when you are up and about." He grinned and I felt content. It was as if a weight had been lifted from my shoulders. "What do the doctors say?"

"They just want to make sure my chest is clear so I have to go for an X-Ray, later this morning." I thought he looked tired. "How are you?" I asked

"Don't worry about me, I'm fine."

"And how are things at the house? Alice tells me Finbar is coming home."

"He is, the old rascal. I wonder what he's been up to now?"

"What d'you mean?"

"Nothing. Forget it. To answer your question, Kate still treats me like I'm a large dose of poison. Frankie isn't leaving Steve alone, especially if he is in the vicinity of Kate. So no change there."

"I don't understand why Frankie is so jealous of Kate. It doesn't make any sense, considering."

"Jealousy never does." Cameron's brow lowered and his face clouded over.

"You sound as if you've experienced it at first

hand."

"Let's say it's been the ruination of many good relationships and leave it at that, shall we? Anyway, when can I take you home?"

Was Ransome's Point my home, I wondered? I wasn't sure how long my job would last. I was at the mercy of Finbar's whims. Maybe he and Kate would move to the States. His books were selling well there and Kate's fashion empire had its tentacles firmly fastened on Paris, Rome, London and New York.

"I'll see if they have any idea when you can be discharged." He turned away and I watched him as he moved away to talk to the ward Sister.

The grapes Alice had brought me were on top of the side locker. Why was she so vehement in her opinion of Cameron? I prided myself on being a relatively good judge of character and there had been nothing in his manner or behaviour to suggest he was anything other than a decent individual. The fact that Alice held an altogether different viewpoint and had reason to believe him to be a drunken liar and cheat left an unpleasant taste in my mouth.

I watched him talking to the nurse and saw him smile as he returned to my bedside. "Later this afternoon, if the X-Ray results are good." Cameron said.

"I can go home?"

"Yes. So how do you feel?"

"Fine. As long as I can have a rest, I'll be OK." I was trying to sound positive but wasn't as certain as I sounded. The whole experience had left me feeling weak and shaky. But I didn't think there was any point in taking up a hospital bed when I could just as easily rest at Ransome's Point.

"Good. I'll ring for a taxi, grab a bite to eat in the canteen and pick you up later," Cameron said.

"You don't have to wait, really. You've done enough." I stood up and feeling my knees buckle sat back in the chair."

"Rubbish. I'll help you put those few things in this bag, shall I?"

Later, lying on my bed in the house at Ransome's Point, I noticed the flowers Kate had left on my bedside table. They reminded me of the ones Finbar had asked me to buy and which I had dutifully taken to the Dorchester for him to give to Kate, a lifetime ago. I shivered. My obsession with him had coloured my opinion of Kate to such an extent that I found it difficult to converse with her at any length. We merely exchanged pleasantries when forced to do so. I was aware that she kept her distance too and, although polite and solicitous as to my welfare, hadn't taken the trouble to visit me since I'd returned from the hospital.

The sun was sinking lower in the sky, the shadows lengthening. They cast elongated shapes across my bedspread touching my arms with their insubstantial fingers. The windows were open and I could smell the sea. I could almost taste the salt and shuddered at the sensation, reliving my nightmare experience, feeling the chill of the water creeping up my legs, the suffocating sensation of my mouth filling with seawater. I started to take deep breaths in an attempt to still the rising panic but must have fallen asleep for a short while because when I awoke the room was dark, lit only by the faint glow drifting up from the garden lights. The sound that had awakened me was the door opening.

"What's all this - asleep at nine-thirty? Shake a leg, old thing, anyone would think you were recovering from a good drowning or some such nonsense." He flicked on the light with one hand and thrust a large box of chocolates at me with the other.

"Finbar! I didn't know you were back already." I sat up.

"Can't leave you two alone for a minute.

Never know what you'll get up to. Cameron wants a good slap, taking you out in a heap of old junk. He should know better. I'll have a few words to say to him." He was smiling as he lifted the lid on the chocolate box and thrust a dark chocolate concoction in his mouth.

"How did the book signing go?" I asked.

He sat down and told me all about it then said, "It was a shame I had to cut my visit short. But who knows I might manage a few days away in a week or two, depending how we get on with the work."

"I'll be up and about tomorrow, I'm sure of it." I could see he was hoping I wouldn't let him down.

"Good, girl. Glad to hear it. Bright and early I hope." He thrust his hand into the box of chocolates, picked out two, placed one in his mouth and stood up. "Sweet dreams," he said and left without a backward glance.

I climbed out of bed and switched out the light. I doubted if sleep would come so lay back on the pillows and tried to recall a treasured fantasy about Finbar but nothing came. I'd spent a lifetime of daydreams and night-time fancies focussing on him and never had any trouble in conjuring up a suitable scenario. It must be delayed shock, I thought. It would pass.

A breeze blew away the remaining clouds that had littered the night sky revealing a silver crescent moon, which shone over the sea and filtered its beams in through my open windows. Watching the view of the sea from my bed, I thought how odd it was that something so beautiful could be so deadly.

The sound of angry raised voices drifted up from the garden.

"If you hadn't been so careless it wouldn't have happened."

"Careless. I couldn't have taken more care. It's not my fault Tom Clancy's boats are fit for the scrap heap. No one told me. Now it seems everyone knew."

"So you say."

"You're only mad because you're afraid your precious book will be behind schedule. How you could suggest to Rachel she'd be OK to work for you tomorrow is beyond me."

"I don't know why you're getting your knickers in a twist. Anyone would think you care." Finn sniggered.

"I do care. She's a good kid. Pity she has eyes for no one but you. But there we are. They say love is blind."

The voices became fainter and I was unable to

make sense of the rest of the conversation, which, it seemed, was taking place at the bottom of the garden, near the cliff path. I crept out of bed and saw Finbar and Cameron limed by moonlight as they stood side by side.

After a restless night, I awoke to the sun beating down on my face. It was eleven o'clock. I had slept through, without any thought of getting up early to help Finbar. Sliding out of bed I caught sight of my reflection in the wall mirror at the foot of the bed. I hadn't been referred to as a kid for years. My eyes were bright and my hair fanned out in a thick curtain around my shoulders. I wouldn't rush, I told myself. Let him wait. This time it would be on my terms.

CHAPTER 22

The mountain of work in her in-tray was not diminishing. Alice was beginning to feel her age. She hadn't realised how much Rachel had been getting through prior to her accident. Had it been anyone else she would have told him she'd had enough. She would have stuck to her immediate, although somewhat regrettable, decision to retire. But she'd missed him, even though she was fully aware of his bad points and leaving Mr Alexander to the mercy of little Miss Weston was not an option she was willing to contemplate.

She'd dealt with her feelings about his wife some time ago. At least, she believed she had. But the green-eyed monster sometimes had a nasty habit of lying in wait to breathe its destructive breath over the unsuspecting. She hadn't meant it to happen in the way it did, of course she hadn't. She just wanted to wipe the grin off Cameron Blackstone's face, to give him a scare. Ever since he'd 'rescued' Rachel when she'd been swimming in the cove, he'd been basking in a hero's glory, which was completely unjustified in her opinion.

He was using Rachel and no one but she could see it. She'd paid the old fool thirty pounds to remove the oars before he handed over the boat. He didn't want to know why, just slipped the money into the pocket of his dirty jeans and made for the pub. She'd had a shock when she'd seen Blackstone sitting on the harbour wall, but he couldn't have overheard her conversation with the boatman or he'd have done something about it. Nevertheless, she'd only meant to give him a scare, make him look useless in Rachel's eyes. Anyone could see she was just being philanthropic.

Alice bit into a crisp green apple and felt the bitter juice running down her chin. The turret room had become unbearably hot. It was nearly mid-day and although she'd been told that Rachel would probably put in an appearance later, as yet there was no sign of her, and she didn't have time to find out where she was.

In spite of the sash windows being opened halfway, the air that filtered through them was hot and dry. It wafted towards her and she felt her forehead and armpits growing damp. Mopping her brow with a handkerchief, she stood up. In the small sink near the window, she ran the cold-water tap and wrung out her handkerchief, then opened her blouse and dabbed at her armpits. It was then she heard voices drifting upwards and sliding in through the open window. If there was one good thing to be said about this weather, it was the opportunity it gave one to eavesdrop, she thought.

"I don't want Finn to know what happened between us. I can't understand why you are here." Kate was angry.

"Finn was insistent."

"Couldn't you say you were busy; make an excuse?"

"I tried."

"Not hard enough, it would seem."

"You don't have to worry, you know." Looking down, Alice saw Cameron Blackstone put his hand on Kate Alexander's shoulder.

"Don't touch me. I never want you to touch me again. Do I make myself clear?"

"Crystal," he replied, making for the house.

"Well, fancy that now," murmured Alice as the door opened. Walking away from the window, she said, "Ah, Rachel, at last, some help. You look very pale, dear. How are you feeling?" she asked sitting down and accessing the next chapter on her computer.

"I'm OK, thanks. Where would you like me to begin?"

Alice hesitated, unsure for a moment then

seeing Rachel switch on the computer, said, "Before you start, let me tell you what I've just heard."

When she'd finished repeating her overheard conversation, Alice sat back in her chair waiting for a reaction. But Rachel just muttered, "Oh, right," and turned back to her computer screen.

Disappointed that her words hadn't provoked more of a reaction, Alice picked up a tape from her desk and thrust it to the side of Rachel's computer.

"You can start with these chapters," she said.

Soon the room was filled with the sound of Alice's noisy typing accompanied by frustrated sighs and the soft pad of keys from Rachel's computer keyboard. As she typed, Alice wondered if anything she could say would provoke a satisfactory response from her colleague. Maybe she should start to tell her a few home truths about her employer, perhaps they would hit the mark. The trouble was how much of it all should she tell? Whatever else, she was loyal to Mr Alexander; too loyal one might say. There was nothing she wouldn't do for him. She had proved that already. He knew she could keep her mouth shut. And he had repaid her; which was why she'd been able to keep the cottage.

CHAPTER 23

On the Friday morning after Finn's return from London, the weather changed. The clear cornflower blue sky darkened and although the air was humid, grey clouds hung like clumps of dust over the coast obscuring the view of Alice Phillips's cottage in a thin veil of mist.

Leaving Rachel and Alice with sufficient work for the day, Finn paced around the house like a caged lion. In his pocket was the slip of paper bearing Laura's telephone number. He knew he would phone her, he recognised the signs. He couldn't settle, Kate was irritating him and the whole house seemed full of people he didn't want around him, with the possible exception of Cameron. He could hear Steve and Kate talking in her studio, they would be at it for hours. Cameron hadn't surfaced and Frankie was out walking. He scribbled a note telling Kate he was taking the car into the village and not to bother with lunch for him, then left it on the hall table and closed the front door behind him with a determined flourish.

He had made his mind up. He fingered the slip of paper in his pocket reassuringly then backed the car out of the drive and into the lane.

It was early. The village was quiet. In the harbour, mist formed a barrier between it and the open sea. Fishing boats bringing in their catch appeared like ghostly apparitions out of the swirling haze. Finn walked to the sea wall and looked over the side. Oil, salt, fish and seaweed smells rose into his nostrils and he gagged. He'd never been able to understand the fascination with boats; better watched from a distance in his opinion. The smells seemed worse hanging on the still air; they lingered, following him like a faithful hound, as he made his way towards the café. Once inside, his hands wrapped around a mug of coffee and the smell of baking replacing the odour of the sea, he looked out across the limited view of the bay and sighed. What would it be like next winter? It was all very well living here through the spring and summer months. He could even tolerate autumn but the thought of again spending winter days isolated at Ransome's Point filled him with claustrophobic dread. He needed a diversion.

As the proprietor of the café was concentrating on completing the morning's baking in the back room, he had the place much to himself. Taking Laura's note from his pocket, he flipped open his mobile and rang her number.

Her voice sounded thick and full of sleep. Was she alone?

"It's Finn," he said, trying to guess what she felt by the tone of her reply.

"Finn? What a surprise." She sounded non-committal.

"It's complicated. I had to leave London. I'm at Ransome's Point."

"Your seaside home? Lucky you. The heat in London is intolerable." She yawned.

"You're still in bed? Did I wake you?" he hesitated. "Are you alone?"

"Yes to all three."

"I can't stop thinking about you. Can we meet?"

He could see a family approaching the café. Any intimacies would be difficult. "What d'you think?"

"Where?"

"'That's the problem. You could always come here."

"What? Is your wife away then?"

"Not exactly. But she is working very hard at the moment. Hardly ever leaves the house and I thought, if I rented a cottage for you on the coast, then we could meet. Of course I might be taking you away from your work..." He tried to sound dejected, a role he had perfected. It never failed. Women, he'd found, were always keen to make him feel better. It had something to do with the maternal instinct and Finn knew exactly how to play the vulnerable male to perfection.

She was quick to reply, "No, nothing much doing here. I've had a few bit parts but nothing to keep me in the city, especially in this heat.

She sounded eager. Good, thought Finn. "In that case I'll arrange it right away. I'll be in touch with the details, when it's all fixed.

Leaving the café he felt renewed, excited, the thrill of the chase uppermost in his mind; it was as if his mood had lifted much like the haze over the bay, which had now dispersed. A weak ray of sunlight shot through clouds, which were rapidly diminishing; another lovely day, thought Finn, walking toward the estate agents' office.

The uncertain weather that morning had driven another fugitive from Ransome's Point towards the village. Cameron Blackstone walked along the cliff path marvelling at the cloud formations hanging over the harbour. He watched the patterns change as the sun burned through the clouds and dispersed into vapour trails clinging to the coast. He was thinking about the accident.

Seagulls screeched and dived towards the boats as the fishermen unloaded their catches. He scanned the horizon for his prey but he was nowhere to be seen. He would wait; he was bound to show up sooner or later. In the meantime he would look around the bookshop in the village. As he passed the estate agents' office, he saw Finn. The agent had walked him to the door of his office, which was open and Cameron heard him say. "Thank you, Mr Alexander. I'm certain your friend will like Willow Cottage, it's a delightful property in splendid isolation. We'll see you on Monday to finalise the agreement. You're sure you don't want me to drop off the details for you?"

"No. I'll call in." Finn replied abruptly.

Cameron stopped in front of the bookshop and waited for Finn. He could almost see him formulating a story to explain what he'd just overheard. Fabrications came easier than most to an author, he supposed.

"Can we talk? Fancy a pint?" Finn steered Cameron towards the Drunken Sailor.

"Actually I'd prefer a black coffee."

"Nonsense! You don't have to pretend with me. I need a drink and quickly."

It was too early for the locals to have invaded the pub. A young barmaid was polishing glasses at the end of the bar and looked up as Finn stood in front of her. He couldn't resist raising his eyebrows; she was easy on the eye.

"Two pints and two whiskey chasers, my lovely," he said turning on the charm. "My friend and I have important business to discuss. I wonder if you'd be kind enough to bring our drinks over." He handed her the money and a tip and waited for her reply.

"No waitress service here, sir. So you can keep your tip."

Finn did a double take. She was becoming more interesting by the minute. There were not many women who were impervious to his charms and a bit of extra cash. He could hear Cameron's chuckle as he walked back to the table balancing the drinks on a round metal tray.

"Suits you, sir," laughed Cameron. "I hope you don't think I'm going to drink whiskey at this time in the morning. I'm sorry, old chum, I don't feel like a pint either. I'll get a coffee from the machine and join you in a sec."

When Cameron returned and was sitting opposite Finn, he said, "Right spill the beans. What are you up to now?"

Finn hesitated. Should he come clean or make something up? When the reply did come it was more or less the truth. Finn explained about his meeting with Laura in London and how he had been unable to stop thinking about her. The tale ended with an explanation of how he had come to be renting a cottage.

"I thought you were done with all that," Cameron sighed. "You're not thinking straight. What about Kate? What will happen if she finds out? You know you've had your last warning."

Finn fidgeted in his seat. "It will be safe enough. We'll meet in the cottage. No one need know."

"Totbury is a village, Finn. It's not London. People notice things in a village."

"Yeah well. If rumours start I'll use Alice."

"What do you mean?"

Finn downed the whiskey and coughed. "Alice Phillips will do anything I ask."

"Anything?"

"Yeah, anything. Now tell me about your latest project. I hear you're getting quite a reputation in the glossies."

As Finn talked, Cameron began to wonder how long his love-nest would remain a secret. What would be the repercussions of Kate discovering his little secret? Then there was Rachel, what was it about her that made him uneasy? He wasn't sure but thought he would enjoy finding out. Either way he was certain it was going to be an eventful summer.

CHAPTER 24

"With the addition of silk fabric around the neck and armholes I think we can bring this look right up to date," Kate said looking to Steve for agreement.

"You could be right, although I have slight reservations about the colour. I think it's a little dark for the fabric. Try using a cream or maybe pale blue."

Kate hesitated, stood back and tilted her head to one side. "Mmm, as usual I think you're spot on; it is too dark. Look, this swatch of cream silk makes all the difference. Where would I be without your expert eye and invaluable opinion?"

"Still making a fortune," laughed Steve.

Their laughter could be heard in the garden, where Frankie was reading. The sun had at last burned through the clouds and was shining down on Frankie's already sunburnt, body. What was so special about Kate Alexander anyway? Uncharitable thoughts regarding Steve's colleague were never far from the surface. Jealousy was embedded deeply where Kate was concerned and it would take more than a few words of reassurance from Steve to excavate it.

The studio windows were open and Frankie could hear snippets of conversation drifting out and hanging in the humid air. Although work orientated, the tone of their words sounded intimate. Standing on the pile of stones forming a small rockery under the studio window, it was just possible to see them. Steve had his hand on Kate's shoulder and was bending over her as he inspected something pasted on the drawing board. A shiver of pure hatred ran through Frankie as Steve suddenly hugged Kate and said, "This is going to be just great. No one will be able to compete with this collection; it's outstanding."

"You really think so?"

"I do. And I believe that working at Ransome's Point has been the inspiration. I can sense the sun, sand and sea in the fabric, the design and the composition. It will be just right for next year's late spring/early summer collection."

"Mm, I hope, this time, there will be no possibility of copies flooding the high street before I have time to deliver the goods," Kate replied.

"Always a risk but I doubt if there are any spies hanging about Ransome's Point. I shouldn't think any of your competitors have even heard of it." Steve picked up a bolt of fabric. "What d'you think about this colour?"

Frankie's eyes screwed up into slits. Perhaps there were more ways than one to skin a cat, or Kate, to coin a phrase.

"You know what they say about eavesdroppers," Cameron said, closing the garden gate.

"I'm not. Or, well, I suppose I am. I didn't want to disturb the workers. But I wondered how long it would be before I could drag Steve away for an hour or two." Frankie jumped off the rockery.

"Feeling a bit left out?"

"I suppose I shouldn't have come. They were bound to be hard at it. I should have gone to France with my sister," Frankie pouted.

"Look. I'm at a bit of a loose end too. Why don't we use what remains of the day to walk over the cliffs towards Bramble Bay. The surf is high and if nothing else we can watch the more energetic of the species as they ride the waves."

"Sounds good to me."

The cliff walk began with a wide well trodden ash path and at first they walked two abreast. Then as they rounded a bend they felt their calves begin to ache as it steadily climbed upwards. The cliffs to one side of them fell away in a sheer drop.

"Hope you've got a head for heights," Cameron said.

"Well. We'll soon find out, that's for sure." Frankie walked ahead of him and after a while stopped. "I need to catch my breath, hang on for a second."

The heat of the afternoon sun beat down on their heads but a cooling breeze was blowing in off the sea. On the horizon, a container ship loomed large as if painted by a child with no thoughts of perspective. "Do you think Kate and Finn are happy?" Frankie asked.

"Why do you ask?"

"Oh I don't know. Everyone thinks they are the perfect couple but I have my doubts."

Unwilling to enter into a conversation which Cameron knew was bound to lead to him having to lie on Finn's behalf, he attempted to change the subject. "What's that out there?" he asked his eyes focusing on a spurt of white water rising from the sea.

"I'm not sure. No hang on a minute, I think it's a jet ski. From here, it looks like a fountain rising from the surface but I'm sure there's someone riding it." Frankie sighed and continued the ascent.

Effectively having diverted the topic of conversation, Cameron followed until the path narrowed while at the same time levelling out.

"God, I must be out of condition," muttered Frankie. "I'm amazed you're so fit. You are not even the teensy bit out of breath."

"Photographers are used to the outdoor life. It's not all studio work."

Frankie turned towards him and a sudden fall of scree left the path with barely enough room to walk in single file. Clinging to a branch of bracken in an attempt to get a better footing, Frankie said, "For a moment, I thought I was about to meet my maker."

Being careful to place one tentative foot in front of the other they managed to reach a more stable area. Breathing a sign of relief Cameron said, "So far, I have found this place to be a death trap. Was it Finn who suggested I come to the seaside for a rest? I have rescued Rachel from drowning on two separate occasions and was afraid that I was going to have to hang on to you for dear life a moment ago. In my opinion it's far safer to stay indoors. You never know what's going to happen next. "

Frankie smiled. "You could be right there. Oh look, Bramble Bay, what a sight."

"Almost worth the climb," agreed Cameron, feeling the path descending towards a row of stone steps leading to the beach.

But before they reached the steps, Frankie stopped. "I've had enough exercise for one day. I'm going back to the house. You know what they say about mad dogs."

Cameron called out, "Take care on the path. Watch out for the earth slip."

Frankie raised a hand in the air and disappeared behind a gorse hedge.

The steps were steep and uneven. He knew the climb up wouldn't be easy but was determined to make the best of the day. In no time he reached the sand, removed his canvas shoes and felt the heat rising from the soft yellow carpet. Hopping from one foot to another until he became acclimatised to the heat, he made for the compacted sand nearer the shore. His meeting with Finn earlier in the day had unnerved him. He'd thought he was done with all that. He'd given him the impression Kate was all he wanted and that he was going to make up for all the times he'd let her down in the past. But it was all promises written in the sand and washed away on the tide.

If Finn was up to his old tricks and was planning to bring his mess to his own doorstep, he wondered what he could do about it. He wasn't about to cover for him again. No matter what had gone on before, he had to think hard about this one. What was wrong with the man? He seemed to have a self-destruct mechanism which reared its head whenever things were peaceful. It was a dangerous game.

Cameron lay back on the sand, lulled by the waves crashing on the shore and the screams of delight from the young surfers wading out of the shallows. In the distance, the hum of a motorboat buzzed like a swarm of bees looking for a place to land. He could feel the sun burning his face, thought about Frankie's remark and laughed out loud. Wrong on at least one count, he decided, before drifting into a doze.

He dreamed about Alice Phillips and Finn. They were having an affair. Incongruous though it seemed upon waking, in sleep it had appeared perfectly normal. Kate had caught them, in bed together in Alice's cottage. Her furious scream of anguish shrilled into the air. Cameron awoke to hear a group of seagulls screaming over a bag of half-eaten chips, discarded by the surfers. His dream had brought Finn's words concerning Alice to the forefront of his mind. What on earth could he be holding over her head in order for her to lie for him? And how useful was she going to be?

CHAPTER 25

The light was fading fast.

"Let's call it a day?" Kate suggested.

Steve yawned. "Suits me, I could do with one of Frankie's special cocktails. How about you?"

"I'd love one, but later. I'm going to take a walk to the village. Catch the last of the late afternoon sun. I feel like stretching my legs. It's been a long day," Kate replied walking into the hall and out into the garden.

On the cliff path she saw Alice walking home, her back, ramrod straight, her stride strong and sure. Not for the first time she wondered why Alice had decided to retire in the first place and why she had now become what seemed like a permanent fixture once again. Although Alice's stride was brisk, Kate soon caught up with her.

"I expect you're glad it's Friday, Alice. No work for two days," Kate said.

"On the contrary, Mrs Alexander. I consider my occupation with Mr Alexander to be a privilege. I enjoy every day. I can't think why I ever thought otherwise."

Leaving Alice at her cottage gate, Kate thought it odd she had echoed her thoughts so precisely. Finn had the ability to collect his lapdogs at will, it seemed. Not only did he have the faithful Alice at his mercy but also Rachel, who was willing to work at the drop of a hat. How many others did he have waiting in the wings? It was a question of which she dreaded to hear the answer.

She looked back over her shoulder at the house. If anyone had bothered to ask, she knew Finn would have said it was he who had found the house at Ransome's Point. As usual he would have taken the credit and conveniently forgotten that it was she who had first told him about it.

Her father had owned a boat for as long as Kate could remember. They'd lived on the Isle of Wight and summer holidays had always involved visiting the South Coast resorts, the Channel Islands or northern France. Whiskey cove had intrigued Kate's father. He had pinpointed it on the map in his study, told Guy and Kate that they were going on an adventure and for a while they had indulged their father while he read passages to them from Treasure Island. It was the last family holiday they'd had. The next year, Guy went to Oxford, and three years later, while Kate was studying for her A levels, her father died after suffering from a stroke. Their mother seemed to grow smaller in stature afterwards and gradually she too faded away. Guy was the only relative Kate had left and, although they spent long periods away from each other, there was an invisible bond tying them together.

The trip to Whiskey cove had been memorable in more ways than one. It was the first time she had stayed up all night watching the stars fade as a purple dawn crept over the sea. The first time she had lied to her father and the first time she had fallen in love. He was a surfer with bronze rippling muscles and long sun-bleached hair. They swam, laughed and made love in a fumbling naïve breath-taking way and Kate had believed that she would be linked to him forever. His name was Ryan and it was he who'd found the house. They'd walked along the cliff path enjoying the solitary landscape. They met no one. They were alone in the world. Turning the corner at the point, Ryan had dragged her towards it.

"It's empty," he'd said. "C'mon the gate is broken."

Kate followed in a daze, a sleepwalker blinded by first love. If he'd asked her to jump off the cliff she would have asked how high should she jump; it was the first and last time she could remember ever having been totally reckless.

Ryan had picked up a brick that was lying near a wall and had broken a pane of glass in the back door to let them in. He'd kissed her in every room. They ran up the stairs leading to the turret room their breath rasping in their chests as they fell headlong on to the bare boards. Kate remembered how they'd marvelled at the view from the window and later had stopped to kiss on the spiral staircase near the circular window.

"I'm going to live here one day," she'd said.

"After we've been to Bondi? That's where I'm aiming for." Ryan had looked dreamily out at the sea beneath them and it was then, she knew, although they were looking at the same view, they were seeing different things. The holiday had ended, each promising the other undying love. But the letters had dwindled into the odd Christmas card and Ryan and Kate had followed their dreams alone.

A freshening breeze blew up and she took a deep breath. The air in the studio had been stuffy and warm for most of the day and Kate was looking forward to a brisk walk before dinner. Elongated shadows, heralding the onset of dusk, crept across her path and she could see a row of fairy lights twinkling in the distance outside the pub in the harbour. Then she heard Finn. He was talking on his mobile and she could tell by the tone of his voice that he was drunk.

"S'all fixed. As soon as you can. Yes, perfectly safe. I know. I can't wait either."

As she turned the corner Kate saw her husband sitting on a wooden bench, his mobile glued to his ear. "Finn?" She approached him and saw him half rise. He looked like a naughty boy, caught out in a misdemeanour.

"Er, Kate? Whar's up?"

"You tell me. Your conversation sounded interesting."

"What? No, nothing much. Just talking to Jeff."

"Your agent?" Kate asked in disbelief.

"Yes, Jeff Hillgate." Finn repeated.

"He's coming down then? I thought he was in the States?"

"What? Yes, I mean, no. He said he'd pop over soon." Finn was floundering. "Where are you off to?" he asked, effectively changing the subject.

"I fancied a walk to the harbour before dinner."

"Look, do me a favour, old thing. I left the car in the car park of the Drunken Sailor. Cameron and

I sank a few at lunchtime and you know how it is. Couldn't risk driving back."

She noticed he'd slipped his mobile back into his pocket. Kate sighed. Her walk was suddenly reduced to a one-way stroll. She nodded and felt Finn's arms around her. "You're a woman in a million. Have I ever told you that you are the most beautiful creature I've ever laid eyes upon?"

His lips found her mouth as she remembered why he was like a drug to her. She could never break free. She was addicted. She stood for a while and watched him weaving drunkenly along the path towards Alice Phillips's cottage and felt anger at Cameron spurt up inside like a jet of burning oil. He was a bad influence on Finn; he brought out the worst in him. She began to wonder if it was his way of hurting her, for what had happened between them.

When she was satisfied Finn had reached the relative safety of the cottage and had not fallen over the cliff edge, Kate made for the steps leading down into the harbour, silently cursing Cameron Blackstone for being the cause of her truncated walk. She wouldn't hurry home, she decided. Let them worry about her for a change. She walked towards the boats and sat on the harbour wall. A grey dusk settled over the sea and drifted inwards cloaking the masts of the boats moored beyond the harbour wall in a veil of gossamer mist. Green and red navigation lights twinkled on the black sea. Fishermen hurried up the cobbles, desperate to quench their thirsts at the bar of the Drunken Sailor. Kate wondered if she might follow them; drink with them, forget who she was and whom she'd married. She wished she *was* made differently, with the ability to throw caution to the winds. But recklessness was not in her nature, not since that day at Ransome's Point with Ryan.

The car was exactly where Finn said he'd left it. She walked past the car park and up into the village. The grocer was carrying a display of fruit and vegetables inside for the night, office workers spilled out of the bank, building society and estate agents. Two middle-aged ladies in cotton dresses were locking the door of the charity shop.

"Hello. It's Mrs Alexander isn't it?" A young man in a lightweight pinstriped suit was closing the door of the estate agents' office.

"I'm glad I've caught you. I've been trying to ring your husband. He said he'd call in for the details of the cottage, he's renting. Perhaps you could save me the trouble. He seemed quite eager it should all be finalised quickly and this might save some time." He stepped back inside and, returning, handed her an envelope.

Kate accepted the large brown paper envelope with a sinking feeling in the pit of her stomach. It was happening again. Why now? But the answer flew back at her like a fist in the face - Cameron Blackstone.

CHAPTER 26

The letter from Stella's solicitors left him in no doubt as to her intentions. Guy Ripton paced the bedroom, so recently vacated by his brother-in-law. When had it all started to disintegrate? It was no good blaming it on Stella. He'd been too busy furthering his career to spend time with his wife and son. Useless to make an excuse by saying it was for them, the flat in town, the villa in the South of France and the house in the country. What use were they now? They'd become possessions to divide between them. He no longer had strength to argue. She'd made up her mind. She could have what she wanted; there was no point in arguing. However, he would not let her stop him from seeing Ben. He was determined to fight her every inch of the way over it.

His bare foot came down on something sharp and he winced. Bending down, he ran his hand over the thick pile of the carpet. His fingers met the offending object and he picked it up. It was a small silver earring, shaped like a crescent moon.

He had caught the ball of his foot on the backing stud. His eyebrows knitted together. 'The bastard. He was at it again,' he fumed throwing the earring at the dressing table mirror. He wasn't going to let him get away with it this time, if he could help it. Kate had been hurt on too many occasions. There would be no turning a blind eye to his brother-in-law's infidelities, as he had done on other occasions.

He frowned at his reflection, he could do with a break and he knew of a way to kill two birds with one stone. Picking up the telephone, he rang her number. "It's me," he said, relieved it was she and not Finn who'd answered the phone. He wasn't in the right frame of mind to speak to Finbar Alexander."

"Guy! How lovely to hear from you. I've been worried, you know."

"I know, well don't worry about me anymore. Everything's OK, apart from what I'd expected from Stella. Look I won't bore you with the details now. I'm ringing to see if I can pop down for a bit of a holiday. I've just checked my diary and the end of next week would be right for me. What d'you think?"

"You never have to wait for an invitation, you know that. Besides I could do with an ally. I'll look forward to seeing you a week on Friday then. Luv you." Kate blew a kiss down the phone.

Reading between the lines Guy suspected that Kate was concerned about something. When she'd answered the phone, he noticed the usual cheery tone in her voice was missing. He was glad he'd made up his mind to visit. He remembered being there to pick up the pieces after the last time and he'd vowed then, never again.

At the same time as Guy's foot and the earring made contact, Laura Crighton received an envelope from an estate agent in Totbury. Inside were the details of a property on the cliffs at Leaping Lane. It was called Willow Cottage and, it appeared, was isolated from its neighbours. Finn had thought of everything. He must be keen, she decided, tugging a hairbrush through her thick curls. Good, she was beginning to think that acting was not turning out to be quite as lucrative a proposition as she'd once thought. She'd imagined herself in a starring role in a blockbuster movie or leading lady in a West End play but to date her C.V was not exactly promising; a couple of walk on parts in BBC low budget productions, a one liner in a commercial and a part in a soft porn movie, which had required her to strip in a lap dancing club. Not exactly worthwhile roles but meeting Alex Finn the novelist, she was sure, would change all that. He was *in* the business and if nothing else his contacts could be useful to her.

She studied her reflection in her dressing table mirror. There were the beginnings of fine lines forming at the corners of her eyes. Finn wasn't the type of man to let the grass grow either. She could imagine plenty of women eager to take her place in his bed. After all he wasn't bad looking and most men in that position were far less attractive. Ringing his mobile number, she said, "It's me. "Can you speak?"

"Hang on a minute, Simon. I'll take you outside, the signal is fading."

Laura heard the sound of footsteps hurrying down a staircase, accompanied by rapid breathing and a door closing.

"Simon?" she enquired.

"Sorry. I was in my study and two pairs of ears were flapping. My secretaries are both more than capable of typing and listening at the same time." Finn took a deep breath. "What d'you think of the cottage?"

"Great, just the thing. When can I come down?"

"Well, I should think middle of next week

should do it. I've got a few papers to sign. I think it's more or less habitable. Anyway no doubt you'll want to buy a couple things to make it more cosy."

It sounded to Laura as though he was planning this cottage thing to be more than just the odd weekend. "You want me to live there?" she asked.

"It's the general idea. You said you were a bit short of work at the moment and I can guarantee that once you set eyes on the coast, you'll want to stay, at least to see the summer out."

Laura thought on her feet. "Mmm. Let's agree that I'll try it for a week or two to start with."

She didn't want him to get the impression, he only had to lift his finger and she would come running. Putting the telephone down, she opened her laptop, accessed her bank account, which was looking a trifle depleted and logging off felt her mouth stretch into a wide grin. Speculate to accumulate she thought, picking up her handbag and heading for the clothes shops.

Finn was over the moon. Things were turning out well. He was beginning to feel boredom dragging at his heels like mud, threatening to pull him down into domesticity. Plenty of time for that, he thought. Accessing the number of the estate agent in his phone's memory, he rang to see out how long it would be before he could have the key. He'd paid a bond and the first month's rent and knew under normal circumstances there would be a wait until the cheque was cleared but the manager's voice rang in his ear.

"No problem, Mr Alexander. You can pick up the key whenever you are passing. I gather you received the details from Mrs Alexander."

He felt icy fingers run down his spine as he grunted a reply and replaced the phone. Had Tom Darcy made a mistake or was Kate involved? Deciding it was a mistake, he smiled, nothing could spoil today.

That afternoon Finn couldn't contain his excitement. This was the feeling that made it all worthwhile. "Right now, girls I want to discuss the finer points of the next chapter with you. I've decided, Lorimer Hunt is going to arrive at Badger's Drift the same time as Henry Tattersall. Should put the cat amongst the pigeons don't you think?"

Alice nodded and simpered, "That's a brilliant move. Both Lucy Arbiter and Melissa Hughes will have to look to their laurels now."

He could see Rachel didn't agree, "I'm not so sure. I thought Henry's arrival should be delayed," she said. He pretended to listen to her but all he could think about was Laura and the way her hair curled over her forehead. He smiled at Rachel and nodded at Alice, pretence was an attribute he had perfected; oh yes, he *was* the great pretender; he almost laughed at the analogy, the refrain of the song echoing inside his head.

He walked to the window, sat down and stretched his legs out on the window seat. He'd dictated most of the next chapter and was gazing out towards the coast in search of further inspiration. In the distance, he could just see the roof of the cottage where Laura would be living for the rest of the summer, or at least, until he tired of her. He was a pragmatist and knew this was bound to happen at some time. He was a man who liked women, was thrilled by the chase but he knew, more often than not, it was more exciting than the eventual capture of the beast.

The weather showed no signs of change. Through the open window at his side Finn could feel the hot air stroking his skin and began to imagine what it would be like to stroke Laura's naked body in the heat of a summer afternoon. It was all the inspiration he needed. Picking up his small recording machine he walked out of the door leading to the walkway, which linked the turret room to Cameron's bedroom. Looking down into the garden he saw Kate coming up the garden path. She was carrying a large brown envelope. He saw her look up at him, her face as dark as a wet Wimbledon afternoon. The first prickles of unease tugged at the back of his neck and he remembered his conversation with the estate agent; how would he handle it? He shrugged. He'd think of something. Nothing was going to go wrong, he was sure he'd covered every base.

CHAPTER 27

My shoulders ached and what had started as a twinge between my eyes had developed into a thumping headache. I watched Alice typing away, a smug look of self-satisfaction on her face. The woman was a strange mixture of emotions most of them focusing on one person. It was obvious she adored Finbar but then didn't everyone, myself included.

"I'm calling it a day, Alice. My tapes are finished and I've a headache. I don't think I've recovered properly from the other day," I said, closing down my computer.

"No doubt. If I were you, young lady, I'd keep well away from Cameron Blackstone. He's bad news." Alice, churning out the usual warning, didn't look up.

In my bedroom, after taking two painkillers, I lay down on the bed and thought over Alice's earlier remarks. Cameron had given me the impression he was a nice uncomplicated character who enjoyed my company but Alice seemed bent on trying to prove he was anything but. In the past, I'd always relied upon my own judgement and for the most part had been justified with one notable exception. But I'd no intention of repeating the mistakes of my youth. I preferred not to think about the past. Shivering, I pulled the coverlet over my legs and waited for the painkillers to work.

I suppose I must have drifted into a stupor because although I could hear voices, I felt unable to concentrate. Words floated around me in a haze. I tried to lift my arm to brush away a lock of hair that had fallen into my eyes but it felt like lead and unresponsive to simple commands. I tried to cry out, to alert someone, but my tongue felt thick and coated with fur. Somehow I managed to slide my body towards the side of the bed in an attempt to reach my mobile phone on the dressing table but was unable to move any further. Panic set in, what was happening to me? Rational thought began to drift away as my eyes closed.

Rachel wasn't the only person in the house to feel the effects of a rise in temperature and, like her, Kate was searching for some relief. She looked for her paracetamol tablets in order to stave off what she recognised was the beginning of a migraine, then remembere she had given Rachel hers earlier, when she'd seen her making for her bedroom to lie down.

Unable to find any painkillers in the cloakroom cupboard she climbed the stairs to the first floor bathroom. The medical chest was where it always was, in the cupboard under the sink, but there was nothing to be found inside, which would ease her migraine. Kate put her hand to the side of her head in an attempt to ease the pain, which was radiating down the right side of her face. She'd have to disturb Rachel in order to retrieve the bottle of painkillers. She knocked gently on the bedroom door but there was no answer. Realising that Rachel was probably asleep, she opened the door as quietly as she could and went in.

At first it seemed as though she *was* asleep. She was slumped on her side with her back to her. The bottle containing the pills rested on the bedside table and in order to fetch them Kate had to walk around the bed to where Rachel lay facing the window. It was then she realised that something was wrong. Rachel's breathing was laboured and a trickle of white foam was dribbling from her mouth on to the coverlet.

She rushed to the window. "Finn, Steve, anyone, Rachel's ill, please hurry", she shouted.

Cameron was the first to arrive. "Help me to wake her up," he said, placing his hand under Rachel's head and lifting her into a sitting position. As he did so she opened her eyes, heaved and vomited over his shoulder. "Good, that's a good girl," he murmured lifting her until her feet touched the floor. "Kate, take her arm we'll get her to the bathroom and wash her down. She should begin to feel better now she's been sick."

In the bathroom, which was on the small landing outside the bedroom door, Cameron suggested Kate begin to remove Rachel's clothes. "I noticed a towelling dressing gown hanging behind the bedroom door. I won't be a moment. Can you manage?" Cameron said.

Kate nodded.

When he returned, Rachel was wrapped in a towel, her face a pale shade of green, as she hung her head over the sink.

"She's retching, but only bringing up bile as far as I can see." Kate pressed her hand to the side of her eyes. The migraine was now of monumental proportion.

"Where on earth has Finn got to?" she asked.

"I think he's out walking. The air is so still, everyone's suffering."

Cameron held Rachel's forehead as she tried

unsuccessfully to vomit. Her colour was beginning to return; he sighed and patted her shoulder. "You'll soon feel better now."

"I'm sorry to leave you. But I have to take some pills my head is splitting. I'll be back soon, I promise." Kate rushed into Rachel's bedroom looking for the bottle, which she'd seen on her bedside table what seemed like hours ago. They weren't there. She searched under the bed and lifted up the rug in case they'd fallen when Cameron had tried to lift Rachel up from the bed.

If the pain in her head hadn't been so intense she would have been more perceptive but as it was she put the missing bottle to the back of her mind and went in search of relief. Reaching her bedroom, she saw Finn climbing the stairs.

"There you are. You've missed the drama. I don't suppose you know where the headache pills are?" Kate asked.

"Funny you should say that. I couldn't find any earlier. I'm sure there's thunder in the air. The atmosphere is so heavy. I popped into the village. Here….." He tossed a white paper back at her. "Relief is at hand. Now what's this drama I've missed?"

Finn followed her into their bedroom and watched her take two pills in quick succession.

Then listened as she told him about Rachel.

"Is that girl accident prone, or what?" he asked, moving to the window and opening the casement, even wider.

"Just what I've been asking myself," muttered Kate, lying down on the bed. "I don't suppose you'd look in on her would you, darling. I left her in the bathroom on the second floor with Cameron. I did promise to go back there. But I really need to lie down."

"Of course, my little petal. Leave everything to me. You lie back and rest."

The bathroom was empty but Finn could hear voices coming from Rachel's room. He knocked lightly on the closed door, and without waiting for a reply opened it. Rachel was sitting in the chair near the window, Cameron on the window seat.

"Well now what's all this? I can't believe my little secretary is in the wars yet again. Are you feeling better now?" Finn walked towards Rachel, concern clouding his features.

"She's been very sick. It's the weather I expect," said Cameron letting go of Rachel's hand.

"Poor old thing. It must be delayed shock. You mustn't worry, don't even think of coming back to work for the next week. Alice will manage. We're well ahead of schedule, besides I want to think over the next few chapters. So you see, there's no hurry. Just enjoy this weather, it's not fit for working in anyway."

Finn sat alongside Cameron and glanced down into the garden. "I can't take to that Frankie, you know, it's no good. I've tried for Kate's sake but, well it's not happening," he remarked watching Steve and Frankie coming back from their walk.

"Live and let live, Finn." Cameron stood up and I saw him walking towards the door. "I'll bring you up a glass of lemonade, now Finn's here to keep an eye on you. Won't be a minute."

Cameron's footsteps sounded on the stairs to the kitchen. Finn chatted about taking a break to think about the plot of a new novel. Then he too stood up as if something had occurred to him and left the room aiming a kiss in Rachel's direction.

A short while later, Cameron appeared in the doorway. "Where's Finn?" he asked handing Rachel a glass of lemonade.

"He thought I looked tired. He said it was best to leave me alone for a while."

Cameron bit his lip. "Did he now?" he said sitting down at her side. "Well I won't be leaving you alone that's for sure."

"Cameron, what is it?"

He hesitated but changed his mind. "Nothing.

Don't you worry about a thing. I think Finn's right. You do look tired. Come on, let's get you settled into bed. You need to rest."

"It seems funny to be going to bed at four in the afternoon."

Cameron waited until he was sure she was asleep. Then taking the bottle of pills from his pocket, left the room, crossed the landing to the spiral staircase leading to his bedroom and ran up the stairs two at a time. He needed to think things out. He couldn't rush things; he had plans to make.

CHAPTER 28

During the next few days, Kate had no time to concentrate on Finn and his possible infidelities. She and Steve had finalised the drawings for the following spring collection and made arrangements to see the director of their New York fashion house in London the following Monday morning. Kate was sure the episode with Rachel had been due to a migraine and was nothing more. She'd suffered similar attacks herself over the years and, although Rachel had said that she'd never had a migraine before, Kate told her there was always a first time and the heat was enough to bring on such an attack. After all, it had been an unusually hot summer and it seemed there was more to come.

Steve and Kate travelled to London on Sunday evening and booked into a hotel for an overnight stay. Frankie hadn't seemed pleased at the prospect but Steve promised it would only be for one night. The meeting was due to take place in the offices of their subsidiary company in Knightsbridge. Harley Winchester was waiting for them when they arrived. Kate noticed the absence of his usual lop-sided grin as he greeted them.

"What will you have?" Harley asked, crossing the room to the drinks' cabinet.

"It's a bit early, surely?" Kate said, as Steve lifted the design folder on to the large boardroom table in the centre of the room.

"I suggest you're going to need a stiff drink after you've heard what I have to say." Harley was frowning.

Steve stopped sliding the drawings out of the black leather folder. "This sounds serious. A gin and tonic and easy on the tonic," he said.

Kate shook her head. "Not for me. You're beginning to spook me, Harley. Tell me it's not what I think it is."

"I wish I could, Kate. I hope I'm wrong."

He crossed the floor to where a large brown envelope lay propped up against the table leg then lifted it up on to the table alongside Kate's folder and tipped the contents out so that the drawings fell in an untidy heap. Harley waited.

Kate clutched her neck, her fingers feeling the pulse throbbing rhythmically against her palm. In front of her lay her designs. She could see the collection she and Steve had so recently sweated over spilling out of the envelope in front of her.

"I don't understand," she said looking at

Harley.

"This came from the Chambrelle Fashion House. It was waiting for me here this morning. It was too late to contact you, to warn you. I guessed it was authentic. I couldn't mistake your expertise, I'd recognise it anywhere. Look your butterfly signature is plain for all to see on the hem of this garment."

He pointed to the design that they'd had difficulty over deciding which material to use, until Steve had come up with the gossamer fine silk that just happened to have a butterfly effect on the hem.

"Oh no, How? I don't understand." Kate's hands flew to her face.

"It's impossible. We've been nowhere. The designs have been locked up in the safe every night. Ransome's Point is not the middle of London; no one's been near us from the fashion world. How could they have been copied?" Steve was pacing the floor.

"Digital photography, my dear Steve. Look closer, these are photographic prints. Nowadays you don't have to be an artist to copy designs. Anyone with access to the originals can do it." Harley banged his fist down on the desktop. "What a waste."

"I'm going to get to the bottom of this, if it's the last thing I do," said Kate. "Don't worry, Harley. There *will* be a new spring collection for next year, if I have to work twenty-four hours of every day. We have time, not as much as I would have liked but still, I won't rest until it's completed. What do you say, Steve, will you stay on?"

"You better believe it." Steve was beginning to feel uncomfortable. Holiday photographs were rare in their house. Frankie couldn't abide taking photos, but for some reason had arrived at Ransome's Point with a state of the art digital camera and insisted that photography had suddenly become a passion.

CHAPTER 29

Eighteen hours after Cameron left me alone to sleep, I awoke feeling as though my body had been through a mangle and my head was filled with wadding. The following day, I ate little and drank water as though I'd been stranded in the Sahara and had reached an oasis.

I saw Finbar who breezed in and out of the conservatory, briefly asked if I was OK then, once satisfied that I was, seemed to lose interest. I tried to read but failed. Kate was sure I'd had a migraine, but I wasn't so sure. True it had begun with a headache but I hadn't really started to feel peculiar until I'd taken Kate's paracetamol tablets, the ones which had so mysteriously disappeared.

Closing my eyes I let all sorts of possibilities run through my mind. Nothing made sense. The likelihood that someone was trying to poison me flitted in and out of my thoughts but was discarded as a by-product of reading, and being involved with, too many Alex Finn novels. Perhaps it was a one off reaction to the painkillers, perhaps it was delayed shock, as Finn had initially suggested.

In the garden, Frankie was taking photographs of the view over the cliffs. I drifted into sleep in the chair only to be awakened by the sound of Finbar's car backing out of the drive. Evening was approaching and I realised that the person I'd been hoping to see all day hadn't made an appearance. Where was Cameron Blackstone?

At eight, Mrs Goodrich carried in a tray containing my evening meal and placed it on the table at my side. "Thank you, Mrs Goodrich. It's good of you to bring my meal in here. Where is everyone?" I asked.

"Mr Steve's friend is in the dining room and I believe Mr Alexander is meeting an old friend in Witcombe," Mrs Goodrich replied handing me a napkin and generally fussing over me as if having someone to look after was her role in life.

"And Mr Blackstone?"

"I'm not sure, Miss. I think I saw him earlier. He didn't want any dinner. I gather he ate in town earlier."

"Oh, I see. Thank you."

I picked at the food. My stomach rebelled slightly. That wasn't normal surely? Kate would no doubt say it was. Migraine was known to cause stomach upsets. Forcing myself to eat the smoked salmon and grilled vegetables, I pondered over Cameron's absence. For the past few weeks not a day had gone by when he hadn't sought my company. But today, he was noticeably absent; anyone would think he was purposely avoiding me.

The grey dusk of evening turned into a black velvet night as I sat and watched the moon, large and full, shining down on the water of the cove. The *Cobblestones* swirled in foam topped currents, as they had on the day the boat capsized and we'd felt their full power, but now they twinkled in the moonlight as innocent and inviting as a lover's kiss.

The long-case clock in the hall chimed eleven as I climbed the stairs to my bedroom. My legs felt weak and my body still ached but my mind was working overtime. I wondered what had kept Cameron from at least showing a scrap of concern about me.

I awoke to the sound of voices coming from above. The walkway separating the turret room and Cameron's bedroom lay directly above my bedroom. Finbar often worked late into the night, if an idea occurred to him. Still drowsy from sleep, I couldn't make out who was speaking but I heard the words. *If I find you're at the bottom of this, you're going to wish you'd never met me.* The anger with which the words were said, robbed the speaker of an identity. *You won't do anything. You can't.* This time I thought it was Finbar's voice but I couldn't be sure. A door slammed above, and then there was nothing more.

The next day when I was reading in the garden, Alice appeared through the door at the bottom of the stairs leading to the turret room. "I thought I'd bring my 'elevenses' out here to join you," she said, sitting on the garden bench. "Mr Alexander said you weren't to come back to work for a week. Is that right?"

I put my book face down on the grass. "Yes. He insisted. I'm feeling OK now though; I don't really know what all the fuss is about. By the way, have you seen Cameron anywhere, Alice?"

"I have." Her eyes narrowed into slits as she avoided the glare of the sun. "He's gone up to London for a few days. I saw him as I arrived earlier. He was in a hurry. He's up to no good I could tell."

"What makes you say that?"

"You'll see." Alice opened the plastic box containing a slab of fruitcake, "Want a piece?" she asked.

"No, thank you. I don't seem to have any appetite."

"I'd be careful if I were you. Too many bad

things have been happening to you lately. They can't all be accidents."

"You're mistaken. I'm sure of it."

"Mmm, you'd be wise to take care. Mark my words," she mumbled, her mouth full of cake.

After Alice had gone back to work, I began to think over what she'd said, analysing the events of the last week or two. Firstly, no one could have known I would be unwise enough to go swimming and get into difficulties. Similarly Cameron's life had also been in danger on the *Cobblestones*, so he would hardly have been instrumental in having us both drown, besides which, he'd saved me on both occasions. I was sure it was Alice's imagination running away with her. But somewhere in the back of my mind, I felt Cameron *was* up to something and that it had something to do with the tablets I'd borrowed from Kate.

CHAPTER 30

Steve was furious. He could hardly contain his anger during the train journey. Kate said little but she had her suspicions. Frankie's unfounded jealousy had left its mark. This was too much. Confrontation was the only way. The sabotage of her drawings was too much to tolerate; all that work down the drain.

"I'll sort this out if it's the last thing I do." Steve cut into Kate's thoughts as the train pulled into the station.

"I'm afraid it might not be enough. I am thinking of having a word with Guy."

"Hang on a minute, Kate. Don't do anything yet. Give me a chance to talk to Frankie."

"Very well, but if I'm not satisfied as to the explanation I'll have to take things further. I'm sorry, Steve but this is serious."

Finn's car was parked outside the station. He was standing in front of it drinking from a bottle of water. He raised his hand.

"About time too," he said. "Train late again?

Hello darling; I've missed you. What's the matter?"

"Don't ask," murmured Steve lifting a large brown leather folder, followed by their overnight cases, into the boot.

Conversation between them was stilted until they arrived at Ransome's Point and Finn and Kate were alone in their bedroom.

"Right now, let's have it," he said, opening the door of the small fridge situated in the corner of the bedroom. Removing a bottle of white wine, he filled two glasses, one of which he handed to his wife. "Drink this. It's sweltering out there. I'm sure it's getting hotter."

Kate sipped her wine, feeling the chill crackle through her like frost fingering a windowpane. She knew it wasn't just the wine. Her anger was subsiding leaving behind a frigidity of spirit that would be difficult to melt. She had put her heart and soul into those drawings only to have them rendered useless by a few digital snapshots.

"My designs are useless. Someone photographed them and sent them to a rival fashion house, who lost no time in sending them to Harley; all that work for nothing. The thought of having to start over is just too much to contemplate."

"Do you have any idea who did it?" Finn asked

looking at her over the rim of his glass.

"I've a pretty good idea. Frankie." Kate replied.

"Really?" Finn walked to the window. " Not surprised. Ah well, old thing. You'll bounce back. You always do. I expect you'll send the culprit packing and we can get back to normal."

"No. I don't think you realise what's happened here, Finn. This is sabotage of the worst sort. It's an offence and I want the person responsible to be arrested. I spoke to Guy before I left London. He was coming down at the end of the week, anyway. This is too important to brush under the carpet."

Finn turned to face her. "What about Steve? Surely he can handle it. He won't want Frankie dragged through the courts. Think about it. It's not as if you don't know who did it. There'll be no problem if Frankie's sent home; your new designs will be safe."

He held her hands, coaxing her to forget about prosecution.

"You surprise me. I thought you didn't care for Frankie," she said.

"I don't. But can you imagine the stink should the newspapers get hold of it? I've known enough hacks in my time. I can see the headlines, now - **Famous author's wife's designs sabotaged by**

houseguest. With the additional interest in Frankie and Steve's relationship being put on show for all to read."

Finn was stroking her cheek now. She hesitated. "I don't know. I'll speak to Guy about it all on Friday - see what he thinks." She was still angry and not about to give in to Finn's request.

Steve found Frankie taking photos at the Point, a pair of herring gulls was perched on a rock and Frankie was leaning over the cliff with the camera pointed in their direction.

"Thought I'd find you here," said Steve, the fury evident in his voice.

"Ssh, you'll disturb them. Just wait a minute." Frankie edged further over the cliff.

"A minute is just what you don't have," Steve said.

"Hang on, what's the hurry? Look you've ruined my shot now."

"Like you ruined Kate's collection?" Steve was hopping mad.

"What on earth are you talking about?"

"I suppose you're going to tell me that you had nothing to do with photographing Kate's designs, the ones we've spent months working on, and sending them to New York to a rival house?"

"Of course. Do you honestly think I'd stoop to such a thing?" Frankie scanned Steve's face. "You do. Don't you? What would I gain by doing such a thing?"

"You've never liked the closeness between Kate and me. This way it might cause trouble between us. I don't know. Maybe you thought I'd give up, come home and leave Kate to produce the new designs on her own. I don't know what to think. But I do know that your jealously might lead you to do all sorts of things."

Frankie handed the camera to Steve. "Go on take it. And if you can prove those shots were taken with this, you'll have a right to accuse me, but not until then."

Frankie marched back to the house leaving Steve sitting on a bench staring out to sea. Steve held the camera in his hand and frowned. He knew Frankie; knew when a lie was in the air and recognised the truth when he heard it. If it wasn't Frankie, then who was it? Walking back to the house later, he began to turn over in his mind the possibility that he and Kate had jumped to the wrong conclusion.

CHAPTER 31

Kate was waiting for him at the station. She was thinner than ever and Guy could see she had started smoking again. She paced back and forth at the side of the car, agitation in every step. When she saw him she stubbed out her cigarette and walked towards him.

"Guy, you don't know how good it is to see you. It seems like forever." She kissed him lightly on the cheek and slid her arms around him.

"Hello, you. Cut the weed. It'll do you no good, take it from one who knows," he said, returning her hug.

"I will, I will. Put your bag in the boot. I'll drive us to a pub I know on the edge of town. I need to speak to you before we go home."

"Sounds intriguing. Where's that rogue of a husband of yours?"

"Finn?" She looked surprised. "Oh he's about somewhere. Writing probably."

"He knows I'm coming?"

"Of course. C'mon Guy, stop hanging about.

Get in will you."

Guy decided to ignore her agitation. There would be time to get at what was bothering her later. During the short drive to the Farmer's Arms, silence hung between them, like a cobweb neither wished to break,.

The Beer Garden was busy. Couples relaxing in the sunshine sat alongside a family enjoying a cooling drink in the shade of a large oak tree, under which wooden picnic tables had been erected.

"Inside?" asked Guy, judging that she would prefer to get away from the noise coming from the kids' play area. Kate nodded and followed him into the lounge bar.

It took a while for their eyes to adjust to the interior, then Guy indicated a table near a window overlooking a field of yellow corn swaying in the breeze. As he'd anticipated, the bar area was relatively empty. Two old men sat in a corner playing cards and a young woman wearing a short skirt and white high heels sat at a bar stool talking to the young barman.

"White wine and soda and a pint please," Guy said. He glanced at his sister who was looking out of the window; remembering the scrapes they got up to as children, he felt a sudden tenderness towards her that surprised him. They'd always cared for each other but since her marriage to Finn, the time they'd spent together had been sporadic. It wasn't just because Guy disliked his brother-in-law; he recognised that his absorption in his career had played its part. Not only had it destroyed his marriage, it had taken him away from the sister he loved.

They were on their second drink by the time she'd explained in full about the sabotage of her designs. Guy said, "When you phoned you said you were pretty sure who was at the bottom of all this."

"Steve's sure it's Frankie. I think he's right but somehow I have this niggling feeling that there's more to it than jealousy." Kate lifted her glass to her lips.

"How so?"

"We've worked together before, often, and Frankie has never stooped as low as this. OK, I understand the very nature of our work means that Steve and I spend hours working closely together for weeks on end and it must get frustrating for partners, nevertheless Frankie's no fool and would realise we would soon put two and two together."

Guy thought for a moment.

"Anyone else in the frame, so to speak?"

"I don't want to even speculate. What do you

suggest we do? I'm so angry, Guy."

"I know, I do understand. I think the first thing is to take those prints to a specialist photographer in town and see if he can ascertain the make and model of the camera that was likely to have produced them. Then we'll work from there. To go through the legal system with this, you must have more than just suspicion. There must be proof of some kind and under the circumstances it might be difficult to prove. You said Frankie is denying any involvement?"

"Vehemently," Kate replied.

They drove in silence back to the house and as they arrived Finn was standing at the gate.

"Hello, hello, welcome brother-in-law. Good to see you again. Champagne is on ice. God it's hotter than hell in the house. When you've settled in, come to the garden; the drinks will be waiting."

Finn was playing the genial host.

"Champagne? The books must be doing well," Guy said, following Kate into the house.

"It's like I said, once the US market is involved, the money rolls in, so Finn is obviously making the most of it, in more ways than one," Kate said.

Guy noticed the irony in her tone and wondered what was going on now. It would wait. Kate had enough on her plate at the moment, he thought, climbing the stairs to the first floor.

Finn wasn't underestimating the truth; it *was* hotter than hell in the house. Even with the bedroom windows open, the room felt oppressive. The view across the bay was spectacular, the sky as blue as the sea, the sun burning down from a cloudless sky.

When Kate left him alone to unpack, Guy began to wonder what exactly was going on at Ransome's Point. He recognised Finn's false bonhomie, for what it was and didn't want to speculate as to what was causing it. Kate and Steve were in trouble and then there were the houseguests – what part, if any, did they play in the scenario.

Dinner was laid on trestle tables in the garden. It was just the three of them. The secretary, Rachel, had been ill and was dining in her room. Cameron Blackstone was in London, a fact that seemed to both please and unsettle Kate. He could tell by her demeanour when she spoke of him that something wasn't right. The whole place seemed to have an aura of disquiet seeping though its walls, as if waiting for some event to occur.

Guy felt light-headed after the champagne and the wine he'd drunk at dinner. When coffee was served, Finn produced a large bottle of Remy and poured a generous measure into his glass thus adding to his general feeling of inebriation.

"I'm glad it's just us three because I want to celebrate with my immediate family. In fact, my only family, for that's who you are." Finn stood up, unsteadily, and raising his glass gave a toast, "To the continued success of *'Deadlier than the Dawn'* in the U.S. of A. I've had the notification this morning, it has reached number one in the best seller lists in New York." He waited for the approbation he knew would come and then sat on the lawn in a heap at Kate's feet.

Guy watched Kate running her fingers through her husband's hair and the self-satisfied smile creeping over Finn's face and thought that he disliked the man, now more than ever. The earring he'd found in his bedroom after Finn's last visit was in his pocket. He waited until Kate went inside to refill the ice bucket then slipped it out of his pocket and handed it to Finn.

"This belongs to a friend of yours, I gather," he said.

Finn looked confused but only for a fraction of a second. Guy watched realisation dawn quickly in his brother-in-law's eyes. His gaze shifted from the earring to the French doors. No doubt deciding that it would be pointless to enter into an argument about the offending article in case Kate returned and wanted to know what the furore was about, he saw Finn shrug. "Something and nothing, old boy."

"It better be or I'll..,,"

"What had better be? Whatever it is, you do look serious, Guy?" Kate said putting the ice bucket on the table.

"Nothing, Finn just asked if I'd like another drink and I said I'd better make it my last or I'll be useless in the morning," Guy replied, holding out his glass for a refill.

"Better make it a large one then. If it's to be your last," said Finn ironically.

Guy was fuming. He wanted to take Finn by the scruff of his neck and beat the living daylights out of him. What Kate saw in him he couldn't fathom. Once you got beyond the good looks and charm there was nothing left but a good for nothing liar, who took his pleasure where and whenever he could.

"If you'll excuse me, I think I could do with a walk. The heat of the day, the brandy, you know how it is, I need to blow away the cobwebs."

"I'll come with you if you like," Kate offered.

"No, I wouldn't dream of it. You're enjoying yourself. Just relax; I won't be late, don't wait up.

I'll see you in the morning." He bent down and kissed the top of Kate's head.

The moon was full, illuminating the cliff path and touching the sea with silvered fingers. Guy took a deep breath and inhaled the scents of the night. Salt, bracken, and baked earth mixed with the heady scent of the roses forming a hedge bordering the garden. As he walked with no particular aim in view other than to put as much distance as possible between him and the loathsome Finn, he began to unwind.

Ransome's Point, after which his sister's house was named, was bathed in moonlight. The cliffs fell away from the point in silvered folds like a roll of satin. He saw a figure sitting on the seat at the highest part of the point, which was a marvellous place to view the surrounding seascape, even at night. As he drew closer he could hear the sound of sobbing.

"You OK?" Guy asked, and immediately knew the identity of the figure. "You must be, Frankie? I'm Guy, Kate's brother."

Frankie sniffed. "Hi. I expect you've heard what they all think of me?"

Guy sat down. "Well now, I understand you are number one suspect at the moment. But I have advised Kate to keep an open mind on the subject."

"Open mind? That's a laugh! I don't think anyone, including the man I love, knows the meaning of the words. They've been Judge and Jury and have condemned me in their hearts already." Frankie sniffed again.

"Are you telling me it wasn't you?"

"Of course, I am. What do you take me for? Won't anyone listen? I didn't do it. I couldn't do it. I admit to being mad with jealousy but to do such a thing would make Steve suffer and I could never willingly do that. He means too much to me."

Frankie's sincerity struck a chord with Guy. "For what it's worth, I believe you." he said.

"Well you'd be the first." Frankie looked at him in astonishment.

"In that case, we'll have to do something about it, won't we? I suggest I make some enquiries about the type of camera used for a start and we'll work from there. Kate is just fuming at the moment, she'll soon see reason, when the bare facts are presented to her, don't you worry."

They sat in silence for a moment watching the moonlight dancing on the waves. "You've given me some hope, at least. I can't thank you enough," Frankie said standing up. "I think I'll make another attempt at getting Steve to see my point of view, especially now Kate's illustrious brother believes me."

"Glad to be of some help." Guy smiled.

He watched Frankie walking back along the path and frowned. Someone had copied those designs and if not Frankie, then who?

CHAPTER 32

Two days after Guy's arrival, Finn contacted Laura and arranged for her to come down to stay at the cottage the following day. She sounded eager. "I'll be down on the nine thirty, darling. Will you meet me at the station?"

"Er no, my love. That might pose a bit of a problem. The less we are seen together the better. So I'll make my own way to the cottage. You know the address and you've got the key I sent you. Just get a taxi from a taxi from the station. Then, as far as anyone knows, you are the newcomer to the area who is taking up residence for the summer. You wouldn't believe the people around here; they want to know the ins and outs of a pig's backside."

Laura's laughter tinkled down the phone like champagne falling into a crystal glass. It was one of the reasons Finn was attracted to her. She laughed at all his jokes. But it was only one of the reasons. He felt the sweat trickling between his thighs as he thought of her. "See you tomorrow then, my love. I can't wait, you know that don't you?"

"Me too." Her voice was thick with longing.

Finn slipped his mobile into the pocket of his shorts and walked along the sand until he reached the steps leading up from the cove. By phoning Laura in such a place he was making sure there was no possibility of him being overheard. If wind of his latest escapade reached Kate's ears then that would be the end of it and goodness knew what the consequences would be. But then that was part of the thrill.

As he climbed up the stone steps he began to wonder what had happened to Cameron. At first he'd not noticed his absence, thinking that he'd reappear as quickly as he'd left but as the days had gone by, he started to become uneasy. Their relationship had been founded on need. He needed Cameron. He was the only person in the world who knew about Melody; it was as it had always been, they needed each other. And Melody's death had drawn the ties even tighter.

Where was he, Finn wondered again, as he climbed the steps? A feeling of unease made him shiver. He never liked it when Cameron wasn't where he should be; it unnerved him, especially as Laura was due to arrive tomorrow.

It had been like this ever since Falklands, ever since the accident. He felt sweat trickling down from his armpits and clinging his shirt. Whatever had happened to Hal Stewart since was a mystery. The last Finn had heard he was covering a story in the Arctic. Perhaps he'd never returned; the thought was appealing but highly unlikely. It suited Finn to believe he'd disappeared for good because there was always the chance he'd pop up somewhere unexpectedly. He began to fear that it might be the reason Cameron had gone off without a word. Maybe Hal had contacted him. Finn pulled a handkerchief out of the pocket of his shorts and wiped his damp forehead.

Stopping to catch his breath, he recognised that he was not as fit as he'd once been. His breath rasped in his chest as he breathed in. Once more he broke out in a sweat when he thought of Melody.

Then his anxiety lifted as Laura's face swam before him. The past was just that, dead and buried but she was his future and no memories or ghosts from his earlier life were going to keep him from her.

At the top of the steps, Finn looked back to the cove and across the bay. The view was magnificent. The cottage he'd rented lay out of sight of the cove but near enough for him to visit without arousing suspicion as to his whereabouts.

He could easily explain it away as a need to get a breath of air for an hour or two. However, Cameron's continued absence bothered him and past memories, tumbled back into his mind like snowballs on a slope, gathering layer upon layer until, what had once seemed insignificant now assumed a much greater degree of importance. His earlier feeling of euphoria had been transient. He needed to see Laura, to feel the elation the sight of her brought him. Tomorrow would come, whether Cameron Blackstone returned or not.

CHAPTER 33

Carrying Frankie's camera in one hand and a brown envelope containing the photographs in the other, Guy left his car in the car park at Witcombe town centre and walked to *Jespers*, the specialist photographic shop in the High Street. He'd spoken to Carl Jesper the previous day and had been assured that he would be able to give him the information he required.

A bell tinkled above the door as Guy stepped through into another world. It was like slipping back in time. The interior of the shop, although well lit, appeared like something transported from a sepia tinted print. The floor was made up of oak strips, which could have been laminated but looked authentic. A wooden counter ran the length of the shop below which were glass display cabinets showing the latest in digital equipment. At the back of the shop stood a shelving unit lined with cameras of a bygone age, each with a replica print of what they were able to produce standing alongside. Advertisement posters lined the cream painted walls interspersed with framed photographic prints, which added to the overall picture the owner had, no doubt, been trying to re-create.

Carl Jesper emerged from behind a curtained alcove at the back of the shop.

"Mr Jesper? I'm Guy Ripton, we spoke yesterday," Guy explained.

"Of course. Pleased to meet you, sir." Guy smiled at the old world charm of the young man who peered over the top of a pair of gold-rimmed spectacles at him.

"Now if you would give me a moment to inspect the camera together with the prints, I'll let you have an answer." Carl Jesper took a cursory look at the camera and walked towards the alcove. "While I make my assessment perhaps you'd like to look at our latest catalogue?" He indicated a chair near the counter on which stood a glossy magazine and the store's catalogue.

Guy sat down, inhaling the scents of the place. A mixture of leather, wood, oil and developing fluids filled his nostrils. It was an evocative mixture which Guy found quite pleasing. He picked up the catalogue and was leafing though it when, sometime later, the curtain slid back and Carl Jesper walked towards him. Guy raised his eyebrows enquiringly.

"Yes, well, I can give you the answer to your first question immediately, Mr Ripton. This camera did not produce these prints, most definitely. The second however is a little more difficult to ascertain. I can tell you, a camera usually used by a professional was responsible, of that I am certain. It could be one of a number of top quality makes. I have complied a list of the most probable. I'm sorry I am unable to pinpoint it exactly for you but I gathered from your phone call, the most important fact was to rule out this camera?" He held up Frankie's camera.

"That's right. Thank you for your help, Mr Jesper. I'll take the list if I may."

Guy slipped the sheet of A4 paper inside the envelope containing the prints and left the shop.

Walking back to his car, he wondered where he should go from here? He had to talk this over with Kate and make her realise it had nothing to do with Frankie. Then he would set about trying to discover who was really to blame. He walked faster, a spring in his step, he was beginning to enjoy himself. It was something to take his interest that had nothing to do with the city. Work had become routine, his family life was non-existent and there was always the possibility that concentrating on the task at hand would make him forget. He'd planned a summer break and was determined to stick to it. It was years since he'd been able to do so, ironically it had come too late to save his marriage.

He was whistling softly to himself when he saw Cameron Blackstone. He was walking down the High Street on the opposite side of the road. He hadn't seen Guy and was making his way towards the chemist's shop on the corner. There was something about him that rang alarm bells; Guy shook his head, he was imagining things, too long working in a profession which encouraged distrust, he thought.

Kate was bent over the drawing board when her brother opened the studio door. She was alone. "Got a moment to spare?" he asked.

She stood up and pressed her palm to her lower back.

"Occupational hazard?"

"You could say that. If I hadn't had to deal with all this," she spread her arms in a semi circle, indicating the mounds of drawings piling up on the large cutting table in the centre of the room, "then maybe my back wouldn't be in two."

Guy walked towards her and slipped his arm

around her shoulders. "Poor you. Come and sit in the conservatory for a while; or somewhere where we are unlikely to be overheard."

Kate studied his face wondering what was on his mind. She nodded and opened the double doors leading to the conservatory making sure to close them firmly behind her. From their seats near the garden they could observe anyone entering the room via the doors leading into the hall.

"This do?" Kate asked pouring chilled lemonade from the dispenser into two large glasses and handing one to her brother.

"Fine. I want you to listen to what I have to say, Kate and understand there is no way Frankie could have taken those photographs."

She was about to protest but saw that Guy was adamant. She waited until he'd recounted his visit to the photographic store and then frowned. "I don't understand. If not Frankie, then who? And more importantly why? It doesn't make any sense. Why would anyone wish to cause me so much work and inconvenience, if they didn't have a hidden agenda of some kind?"

"Well in view of what I've just told you, the answer to whom might be seems pretty clear cut. The photographs were taken by the sort of camera used by a professional photographer and you just happen to have one staying here at the moment."

"You mean Cameron Blackstone?"

"Who else?"

"You know I can't stand the man but even so, I can't see why he would do such a thing. Or what he would gain."

"Well, yes, I know how you feel about him, but I'm not exactly sure why you dislike him so much." Guy refilled his glass.

"We have a history. I'd like to leave it at that but all I will say is this. I believe he has been responsible for Finn going off the rails on countless occasions." Kate looked out of the window and caught sight of her husband climbing the last of the steps leading up from the cove.

"You do know we are all the architects of our own destruction, dear sister," Guy replied.

Before she could answer, the door to the garden opened and, Finn entered. "Has anyone seen Cameron?" he asked.

Guy thought for a moment and then said, "Why, isn't he about?"

"No. In fact I haven't seen him for ages. I thought he was popping up to London overnight but he hasn't come back and that was three days ago."

Guy thought Finn looked agitated and decided not to mention his earlier sighting of the man in question. He didn't hold Kate's black and white views where her husband was concerned so, for the moment, decided to hold his cards close to his chest and see which way they fell.

CHAPTER 34

My mobile rang whilst I was sitting at my desk. I had just started on the dictation Finbar had left in my in-tray. Alice Phillips had hardly spoken to me since my return, which didn't bother me unduly as I had the peace in which to work uninterrupted by her chatter.

The clatter of my phone on the desktop drew a mutter from Alice and a frown, as I turned to pick it up. I didn't recognise the number so stood up and took the phone on to the landing in order not to disturb the uncommunicative Alice still further.

"Rachel, are you alone?"

It was Cameron. I greeted the unexpected phone call with a mixture of pleasure and annoyance. Pleasure, because I'd begun to like the man and annoyance at his unexplained absence, so soon after I'd become so unwell.

"I am. Alice is in the turret room and I'm on the landing," I replied.

"Be careful how you answer me. Pretend it's a phone call from a friend."

I stared at the phone nonplussed for a

moment. He sounded so mysterious. "I want you to promise me you won't eat or drink anything that you suspect hasn't been prepared by Mrs Goodrich or yourself and please don't go for walks along the cliff path alone, especially not after dark. Take great care. Do you hear me, Rachel?"

"I don't understand. I..."

"Don't try to make sense of this, just be very careful. I'll explain when I return but I'm not sure when exactly. Remember….."

His voice petered out amongst static and then the line went dead. I walked down the staircase to the stained glass window situated on the landing where the stairs curved back on themselves then held the phone up to the light but the connection was broken and it didn't ring again. The patterns of coloured glass distorted the view from the window but I could just make out the curve of the bay and the sun shining on the sea. The phone call was disconcerting; what was it all about? And where was he?

As I walked towards the turret room, I became aware Alice had stopped typing. When I opened the door it was to find her standing behind it.

"I thought I'd pop downstairs and bring us up some lemonade, it's so hot in here," she said, looking flustered.

"Not for me thanks. I'll get something later." I put my phone back on the desk.

"Everything all right is it? No bad news?" Alice had recovered herself enough to give way to her curiosity.

"Yes thanks, just a friend from London, wanting to catch up."

"Oh, right. You're sure I can't get you a drink?"

"No thanks," I replied, picking up Chapter 23.

CHAPTER 35

The sun was low in the sky when I finally shut down my computer. Alice had gone home over an hour ago but I'd decided to finish the rest of the work. I knew Finbar wouldn't care whether I left it until tomorrow, as we were well ahead of his publisher's deadline, but I couldn't get the strange phone call I'd had from Cameron out of my mind. I'd tried ringing him back but the call register on my mobile refused to give me his number just a screen reading saying no number available.

Stacking the manuscript on the shelf, I caught sight of Steve and Frankie waking arm in arm along the cliff path towards Alice Phillips's cottage. My long sight is good, besides I would have noticed Frankie's flamboyant shirt-top anywhere. It looked as if they had made up after their fight. I wasn't sure what it had all been about but knew it was something to do with the theft of Kate's designs. No one confided in me and I was mostly left in the dark, apart from the odd snippets of gossip that flowed like lava from Alice's lips and I knew it would be a mistake to take too much notice of her.

My living quarters were staggeringly hot. I'd thought the windows were open when I left the room that morning but now they were firmly closed. The air smelt stale. Leaving my handbag on the table, I moved to open the windows and was surprised to see Alice near the garden gate in deep conversation with Finbar. I was surprised because I'd assumed Alice had left for home much earlier, as was her intention. There was something about the way they stood which seemed to indicate their conversation was not superficial but of a more serious and secretive nature. Cameron's warning had unnerved me and I felt as though I was suddenly suspicious and wary of everybody and everything.

Moving away from the window, I decided to seek out Mrs Goodrich in the kitchen. Perhaps I would fill a plate with a light salad and maybe some fresh fruit for dessert. Unaware that by doing so, I was subconsciously heeding Cameron's warning, I made for the kitchen.

Kate could see Finn was restless. He'd hardly eaten anything at dinner and afterwards complained that the heat was getting to him.

"I'm going to take a walk into the village and

then across the cliffs. I need some air," he said, standing in the conservatory.

"Good idea. Perhaps I'll come with you," Kate suggested.

"Um, wouldn't hear of it. I'm bad company at the moment. I've a few ideas for plots in my head but I need to be alone to think them out. Besides, it will give you some time to talk to your brother without me interrupting you. You don't get much chance to be alone with him, as it is." He bent his head and kissed her cheek. "Don't wait up. You know how it is when I need to think about a story."

It was then Kate remembered the letter. In all the trauma of the last few days she had forgotten her chance meeting with the estate agent. The letter had been addressed to Finn but she hadn't given it to him. She'd meant to open it but had placed it on her desk in the studio as Steve had distracted her with some final adjustments to the drawings before their following day's visit to London. She knew exactly where she'd left it and decided that now might be the time to find out what was in it.

She felt no tugs of guilt at the prospect of opening a letter addressed to her husband. The circumstances were suspicious to say the least and she'd been caught out by Finn's little games once too often. Although she loved him with a longing she'd never thought possible, she didn't trust him. He'd lost her trust many years ago and it had never been fully regained. It was a pity, because lately she'd begun to feel that perhaps they were travelling down a new path which would eventually make things better between them.

Lengthening shadows fell across the drawing board and cast elongated shapes on to the floor. Kate walked towards her desk; an old-fashioned roll top affair she'd picked up in market in San Francisco over a decade ago. She'd loved it as soon as she'd laid eyes on it with its numerous compartments, leather writing pad and pen tray. She'd put the envelope down on the writing pad, meaning to get back to it.

It wasn't there. The letter was gone. She knew she wasn't mistaken and hadn't put in anywhere else. She remembered putting it there quite clearly. Steve was concentrating on the drawing board whilst talking to her and she had placed it on the pad feeling the soft leather beneath her fingers, meaning to get back to it at a more appropriate moment. Someone had removed it and she had a pretty good idea who. She couldn't confront him directly. He would deny it of course. She would have to be subtler than that. Experience had taught her a valuable lesson in how to deal with her husband, without him being aware of the fact, and she would use the experience to find out exactly what he was up to now.

Later, lying in bed unable to sleep, Kate watched the moonbeams dancing across their bedroom ceiling. The green illuminated numerals on the clock on her bedside table read 2.30. Finn's side of the bed was empty. It was a quarter past three when she heard him climbing the stairs. She closed her eyes feigning sleep, heard him clean his teeth and then click on the shower. He would say it was to wash off the heat of the day and maybe it was the case but Kate was already beginning to wonder if it was for a different reason altogether and she felt the familiar gnawing ache in the pit of her stomach at the thought.

Closing her eyes she lay still as her husband slipped into bed alongside her. She felt his hand caressing her thigh and travelling up her body to her breasts. She wanted him, but something made her keep her eyes tightly shut until he turned on his back and after a while she heard the familiar sounds of his breathing as he drifted into sleep. Then she turned on to her side and watched him. His face outlined by moonlight looked surreal; what was it about him that she found irresistible? If only she knew the answer.

She lay awake until the sky turned colour heralding the dawn, greys fading into primrose yellow and deepening into gold. Another hot sunny day lay on the horizon waiting to pounce like a sleeping tiger. Kate slipped out of bed and stood at the window.

Cameron Blackstone was sitting near the low garden wall, his back was to the house and he was looking out to sea. He held his camera in front of him then with a few swift clicks captured the scene. She shivered. He still turned up like the clichéd bad penny. Whenever she saw him she was reminded of how foolish she'd been, a memory that refused to stay buried, however hard she tried.

CHAPTER 36

The early morning sunlight awakened Guy and like his sister he too stood at his bedroom window admiring the view. But unlike Kate the sight of Cameron Blackstone sitting on the garden wall gave him satisfaction. There were many unanswered questions that he needed to discuss with him before the day was out and as far as he was concerned, the sooner the better. Splashing water over his face, he slipped on a pair of shorts and Tee shirt and went downstairs. There was a slight breeze blowing in from the coast bringing with it the smell of salt and seaweed.

"Great view," said Guy. "Get a good shot?"

"Yes, I think so." Cameron slung his camera strap over his shoulder.

"I don't think we've met properly. Guy Ripton, Kate's brother." Guy held out his hand and noticed the hand that met his was as cold as ice.

"Oh I see. Then I expect you know who I am?"

"Indeed. Fine camera you have there."

"It is."

"I should think you need the best in your line of work."

"It does help." He stood up as if to go through the gate. "If you'll excuse me, there's someone I need to see."

Guy stretched his legs out in front of him and stroked his chin, a photographer with a state of the art camera, staying the summer at the house. If he was one of Finn's detectives, he would have concluded that everything pointed to it being an open and shut case but Guy was never fooled by the obvious - he always took the extra step. His instinct told him it was a mistake to take things at face value and in his line of work it had been a distinct advantage. He was relatively sure Cameron hadn't copied Kate's designs just as he was sure Frankie had nothing to do with it. The problem was, if not them, then who? Alice, Rachel or maybe Steve with a grudge of some kind? The latter suggestion seemed as preposterous as the rest, more so in fact for why would he cause himself so much trouble and hard work? It didn't make any sense.

Finn was in the turret room. He was alone when

Cameron opened the door.

"We need to talk," Cameron said.

"Where have you been?"

"Doing some research."

"Well you might have let me know." Finn sat down on the window seat.

"Worried?" Cameron sat on the edge of Rachel's desk.

"Well, yes. I suppose you could say I was worried. No one seemed to know where you were and there's been a bit of trouble here one way and another," he replied

"What kind of trouble?"

"Kate's in a state because her designs were photographed and sent to a New York fashion house before she could get hers registered. She's sure Frankie did it out of spite. That brother of hers is sniffing around like a dog chasing a rabbit. He has discovered that the photos were taken using a state of the art camera not a bog standard digital like Frankie's. I should look out, he might start looking at your equipment and I don't mean your wedding tackle."

Cameron laughed, a dry humourless sound. "He's welcome. I'm not interested in Kate's designs. Wouldn't know where to start anyway."

Finn stood up. "Mmm, I wonder how long it

will take my brother-in-law to reach the same conclusion.

Cameron raised his eyebrows. The expression on Finn's face always preceded trouble.

"Anyway, old man, don't go running off without telling me will you? I need an ally in a house full of Kate's cronies."

"Seen Rachel about?" asked Cameron.

"No. I told her to take a few days off. I've finished my dictation and the two of them are going to find the next few weeks a chore, as they have to proof read the copy before sending it to the publishers. They edit my chapters as I go along but even so, it will be littered with inconsistencies, I've no doubt. If I see Rachel I'll say you're looking for her, shall I?"

Cameron hesitated. " No. Don't bother, it's nothing important, I'll catch up with her later I expect. I'll leave you to get on."

Taking the staircase leading to the garden Finn's voice echoed down the stairwell from the walkway. He was talking on the telephone.

"Tonight, yes. No problem. I can't wait either."

He felt a twinge of alarm. Finn was a loose cannon where women were concerned. Frowning and deep in thought, he reached the garden to find

Rachel standing in front of him.

"I know. I've got some explaining to do," he said taking her arm and guiding her to the cliff path. " Walk with me and I'll try to put your mind at rest."

"That might take some doing. You do know your phone call unnerved me to say the least." She slid her arm out of his grasp but continued to follow him through the gate.

The air was heavy, not a breath of wind stirred the bracken as we walked towards the point. Silence hung between us and I felt the hairs on the back of my neck stand up. I wondered why this feeling of unease had descended on me so suddenly but was unable to shake it off. I'd wanted to see him for days but now he was here I didn't know what to say to him. Anxiety robbed me of the prepared conversations I'd imagined in his absence. Conversations where he would make me feel at ease and where we would share the sort of companionship we'd enjoyed prior to him leaving Ransome's Point.

The bench was occupied by a young couple, who sprang apart when they heard our approach. Cameron smiled and guided me toward the cliff path leading to Brandy Bay. Uneven though it was in places, we managed to reach a spot on the cliff top overlooking the beach that was hidden from the path by an overgrowth of bracken. Someone had beaten an opening through the brambles beyond which lay a grassy knoll. The ground was dry, the grass springy under our feet.

"Let's sit for a moment," Cameron said, taking my hand and helping me over the brambles.

When we were seated, I removed my hand from his and immediately felt uncomfortable. I recognised that the touch of his hand had made me relax.

"I can see why they're attracted to this place. What a view!" he said, taking a deep breath and looking out to sea.

I said nothing, waiting for his explanation.

"I'm sorry. You realise I'm avoiding this." He turned to face me. "The thing is, I can't really explain without it all sounding so ridiculous. You see when I made that phone call to you, I was frantic, so sure someone in the house was trying to poison you.

"I don't understand," I said.

"No, I'm not surprised. Don't misunderstand me. I still feel you should be careful, as long as you are staying at Ransome's Point because things are not as they might seem. I'm sorry to sound so mysterious but I just want you to stay safe. In order to clear up a few things, I'm going to have to leave here for a while. I haven't told anyone yet but I'm booked on a flight to New York tomorrow afternoon. I don't want anyone to know where I am. I'll make some excuse about having to go to London for a week or two. But I wanted you to know the truth. In particular don't mention our conversation to Finn."

I touched his arm. "You're not in any sort of trouble are you?"

"No. But while I'm away you may hear things that will make you distrust me. Please be guided by your instinct and know that I will never do anything to hurt you." Cameron took my hand in his. "No matter what you hear, trust me. Will you do that, Rachel?"

The warmth of his hand seeped into my body. I desperately wanted to believe in him.

"Yes, of course," I replied.

He sighed. "That's what I hoped you'd say." He reached for my hand. "Will you keep in touch? Let me know how you are?"

"I'll try, but I can't promise. Don't worry if you don't hear from me. I'll be back as soon as I can." He stood up, reached down for my hand and said, "Come on, let's enjoy the rest of today."

I followed him to the steps leading down to the beach. 'For tomorrow we die' I thought, the words frozen like icicles on my lips.

CHAPTER 37

"There, that's another book finished, until financial constraints encourage the creative juices to flow again in the not too distant future." Finn rested his elbows on his knees and gave them his 'special' look.

Alice giggled.

"However, I haven't lost sight of the fact that you two have a mountain of work in front of you and I want you to know I'm eternally grateful for your help. How else would this little beauty reach the shelves?" He tapped the manuscript draft on Rachel's desk as he passed it. " Oh by the way, Rachel, have you seen Cameron today?"

"Mr Blackstone? No I don't think I have."

"I wonder." he said.

"Er, I think I did hear him mention he had a few weeks' work lined up in London," said Rachel, picking up the first two chapters in order to proof-read.

"Oh? I see, right, ...thanks."

Finn left the room and hurried down the stairs leading into the hall. He'd covered his back with the 'turret room two', as he liked to call them, all that was required of him now was to let Kate know he would be away for a day or two.

Steve and Kate had their backs to him as he opened the door. They were looking at fabric samples and were in deep discussion. "Hi, darling. Won't disturb you, just wanted to say, I'll be away for a couple of days." Kate looked up and turned to face him.

"Away?"

"Research for my new novel. Don't worry I'll be back before you miss me." Finn crossed the room, kissed her cheek then hurried out through the doors leading into the garden. "Thought I'd walk to the station, get in some exercise. See you."

The only person he met whilst walking across the cliffs was a stranger with a large white dog. He nodded and walked on. At the bottom of the cliff path Laura was waiting, as they'd arranged. Her small blue car was innocuous enough not to arouse attention. Finn folded his long legs into the passenger seat and said, "Like the tinted windows," as he leaned towards her and kissed her lips.

"Mm, I think of everything, sweetie. I'd

planned on taking the train but when you said you wanted me here for a while, I thought, I couldn't be stranded without a car. I must say I was surprised to hear from you so soon."

"Couldn't wait."

Laura put the car into gear and pressed her foot on the accelerator. The car shot forward at speed out of the small car park and into the road.

"Engine adapted too, I see." Finn laughed.

"My car and I have a lot in common. There's more to both of us than meets the eye," Laura said, pulling down the sun visor as she turned into the narrow road leading towards the cottage.

The front of the building faced the lane. There was a small garden filled with summer flowers and a hardstand for off-road parking. The cottage itself was a stone-built two-storey structure with four diamond paned windows and a centrally situated front door. It was the sort of building a child might draw. On the other side of the lane were fields of corn rippling in the breeze, and bordered by a dry stone wall.

"Let's get inside," said Finn, as Laura stopped to smell a bright red rose blossoming near the gate.

"There's plenty of time," she replied bending towards the flower.

"Not for me. I'll be a lot happier when I'm out

of the way of prying eyes."

She laughed. "What eyes. There's not a soul in sight."

"That's as maybe but I'm taking no chances." Finn held the door open and when she was inside he turned her towards him, wrapping his arms so tightly around her body that she gasped. "We are in a hurry aren't we?" she said as he half carried her towards the chintz-covered settee and undressed her with the speed of an accomplished lover.

Afterwards, Laura took Finn's small overnight case up to their bedroom. It faced the back of the cottage and overlooked the cliffs. There was no cliff path, as there was at Ransome's Point, the back garden stopped at the cliff top. It was one of the reasons Finn liked the place. There was no chance that anyone taking a walk would reach the cottage, as the cliff fell away on both sides towards the coast. *'Majestic in its splendid isolation'* were the words Finn had used. Laura dragged her fingers through her hair and looked in the mirror. Her cheeks were flushed. Fluffing her hair up into wayward curls, she smiled at her reflection. Her luck was in the day she met Alex Finn. He would never know how low she had sunk, meeting him had been her salvation and she wasn't about to let anything spoil it. It was why she had travelled to Ransome's Point the previous week without his knowledge. It always paid to be one step ahead of the game, she'd found.

The sound of a champagne cork popping downstairs broke into her thoughts. Finn was waiting for her in the small conservatory, a glass of bubbly in one hand, her camera in the other.

"This yours?"

"Yes."

"Looks expensive. You into photography?"

She hesitated. "No, not really. It belonged to my brother. He was a photographer; did weddings, that kind of thing."

"Was?" Finn asked

"Yes, He died in a car accident three years ago." She sighed, took the camera from Finn, and placed it on the table as he handed her a glass of champagne.

"To us," he said raising his glass and bending forward to kiss her.

"To us," she echoed, tasting the champagne on his tongue.

"This view is even better than at Ransome's Point," Finn said walking to the window. "No stray walkers to spoil the view." He opened the door and walked to the cliff edge. "Just smell the sea."

"Mm. All I can smell is champagne," laughed Laura, filling his glass. "Oh no, look, it's empty.

"Lucky I popped another in the fridge then isn't it?" Finn said turning on his heel. "And I suggest we drink this one in bed. What d'you say?"

"I'm right behind you, sweetheart." Laura followed him up the narrow staircase, thinking. "If this is all I have to do to keep him sweet, then I'm laughing."

CHAPTER 38

Guy shut his bedroom door and picked up his mobile. Lance Rodway had worked in New York on the same newspaper as Cameron Blackstone. Lance and Guy went back a long way, to their student days. Looking at his watch Guy calculated the time difference and decided that it was acceptable to ring Lance's number. After the preliminaries were over, he got to the point of his phone call.

"Cameron Blackstone, that's a name from the past," Lance said. "What d'you want to know, although I don't think I can tell you much?"

"I understand you knew him when he was covering the Falklands War?" Guy asked.

"That's right. Look, if you're not in too much of hurry for the info, I'm travelling to your neck of the woods in two days' time. What if I dig around, see what I can find out about the man in question and then perhaps we could meet up. I'll be in London on the ninth and tenth."

"Great. It will be good to see you again, Lance.

Shall we say the Savoy Grill at two thirty on the ninth?" Guy asked.

"Sure. See you then. By the way how is that gorgeous sister of yours keeping?"

Guy traded news for a few minutes then put his mobile on the bedside table. Lance had known Finn too, before he and Kate got married. He'd always had a soft spot for Kate and was gutted when Finn and she hooked up. Guy also had his hopes dashed because he'd nursed the idea that his much loved little sister would one day marry a man he could respect and Finbar Alexander fell far short of the ideal. He had fallen from grace too many times. In his opinion Blackstone and Finn were two sides of the same coin, a fact, which had failed to endear the photographer to him, in spite of himself. Any long-term friend of Finn's was bound to be a dodgy character in Guy's eyes. It would give him immense satisfaction to be the instigator of the train of events that would lead to his downfall and it was looking increasingly like he'd taken the photographs which had caused Kate so much pain and additional work.

Picking up his diary from the bed, he wrote up his appointment with Lance and then phoned Mrs Dawson, the lady who looked after his flat, to let her know he would be staying overnight on the ninth. He had no reason to inform her of this fact, other than courtesy, but since Stella had left he'd found it reaped dividends. Mrs Dawson was a treasure he was anxious to keep.

When he informed Kate that he would be in London for a day or two, she said, "I don't know what's wrong with everyone lately, no one seems to want to stay put. Finn's gone walkabout, Cameron Blackstone has disappeared again and now you."

"I'll be back before you miss me," Guy said, raising his hand in farewell.

"That's what Finn said," she muttered in a desultory tone to his retreating back.

The foyer of the Savoy Hotel was crowded. There was a charity lunch going on in the restaurant, which was being attended by the rich and famous. Guy spotted a young surgically enhanced actress chatting to a famous football star. The girl was scantily dressed in an evening gown and wearing heavy stage make up, both of which being unsuitable for the time of day.

Making his way through the throng to the bar, Guy was waylaid by a barrister acquaintance who'd taken the phrase ' liquid lunch' rather too literally.

"'Lo old man, what you up to these days?"

"This and that, Gerald. I'm only in town for a day or two. I'm on holiday actually; spending a few weeks with my sister and her husband," Guy replied trying to move away from the man, who at the best of times was obnoxious.

"Saw your brother-in-law at his book launch a while back."

"Oh really?" Guy picked up his drink from the bar and looked around hoping to see Lance.

"Nice little bird he picked up afterwards."

Guy felt his stomach lurch. The man was drunk. There was probably nothing in it. "I must go, Gerald, people to meet, you know."

Gerald put his hand on Guy's arm to detain him and leaned forward. He could smell his whiskey-laden breath drifting towards him like a bitter wave. "Young actress by the name of Laura Crighton. I acted for her in a case against an agent who'd tried to take a larger than normal cut of her income." He belched loudly. "Nice bit of skirt. Bit young for him but then fame has its own attractions and he is doing rather well I hear."

"Guy?" Lance made his way through the throng gathered at the bar.

"Excuse me, Gerald," Guy said, taking Lance by the elbow and steering him in the direction of the restaurant.

Lance had aged since Guy had last seen him. His thick fair hair was now almost non-existent and he'd put on weight. Throughout the meal their conversation focused on catching up on news of their families and friends. Lance told Guy he'd decided at last to abandon his bachelor status after finding a young woman who seemed to fit his ideal. "It took years for me to get over your sister, you know that don't you." Lance said.

"I did wonder."

"If Finbar Alexander hadn't come on the scene, who knows? We might have been related to each other by now." He laughed and shrugged. "Emma looks a bit like her actually."

"Lance!" Guy looked momentarily shocked.

"Don't worry. That's where the resemblance ends. Have no fear, I'm not a hopeless case trying to replace my lost love with a replica."

"I'm glad to hear it. It would never work."

"I discovered that a long time ago. No, Emma is the one for me. You must come to the wedding."

"I'd be delighted." Guy reached across the table and shook Lance firmly by the hand. "Congratulations, when's the big day?"

"Haven't asked her yet. Thought I might, when I get back from this trip."

After lunch and over coffee and drinks in the

lounge, Lance opened the small black leather case he'd brought with him.

"This is all I could get on Blackstone. It's not a great deal but I've included some articles he wrote on the Falklands war, which I thought you might find interesting. Also, there's a newspaper report about an incident which occurred some time later."

Guy glanced at the report. It concerned the death of a young woman called Melody Cassidy during a party in the Hollywood Hills. He read the report and frowned. "What has this got to do with Cameron Blackstone?" he asked.

Lance frowned. "None of what I'm going to tell you has been reported to the police. Most of it is circumstantial, second hand stories doing the rounds at the time. But I knew someone who was at the party on the night in question. He was a young actor called Mickey Coburn. He admitted he was stoned on pot at the time but he did remember seeing Melody and Finn disappearing into a bedroom on the second floor, and not long afterwards he saw Cameron Blackstone enter the same bedroom."

"And?" Guy was sitting forward in his seat.

"You can see from the newspaper cutting that Melody Cassidy met with a tragic accident that night. No one else seemed to be involved. She was deeply under the influence of drink and drugs and it appears she fell over the balcony and hit her head on the slabs surrounding the swimming pool. No one saw her fall and it appeared she was alone at the time.

"What about this friend of yours? Didn't he report what he'd seen at the time?"

"No. Firstly because he was stoned and couldn't be sure what he'd seen. Secondly he didn't know who the men were and he never saw them again, not that night anyway. The other reason he was reluctant to be noticed at the party was that he was seeing a young starlet who was fiercely jealous and would not have been too happy to know he'd been to the party without her."

Guy took a deep breath. "How did you find out about it?"

"It all sounds so complicated but in actual fact it was by a series of coincidences. Some years after the event, Mickey was hired to work on a film which had been adapted from a book called *Through the Glass Darkly.*"

"By Alex Finn," finished Guy.

"Exactly. At the end of filming party, he was introduced to Finn and a friend of his."

"Cameron Blackstone?"

"I can see you're one step ahead of me," Lance said. "It was then the memory of that night came flooding back. There was nothing he could do about it but it left a nasty taste in his mouth. So much so that, when he met me at a film festival bash I was covering for a week-end supplement, he took me aside and told me the story."

"Why you and not someone else? The police, another journalist, it doesn't make sense."

"He knew I was acquainted with Finn, also that I was an investigative journalist and had worked on similar stories in the past. I promised to look into it for him."

"And did you?"

"Yes. It was about the time Kate and Finn were touring the States on the bandwagon that was promoting them as the latest glittering celebrity couple. I dug as deep as I could but there was nothing to link Finn or Cameron Blackstone to that night. Nothing except the reminiscences of a young man who was admittedly stoned out of his head at the time." Lance picked up his coffee cup.

"I see." Guy said. "I can't thank you enough for this."

"Is it significant then?"

Guy paused before answering then said, "Yes, I think it might well be. Now let's change the subject, all this must be very boring for you. Tell me more about Emma and this new job your working on."

The flat smelled of polish as Guy opened the door. Mrs Dawson had left some fresh flowers on the kitchen table with a note giving him instructions on how to heat up the food she'd left for him in the fridge.

It was nearly midnight when he finally went to bed. He pulled back the sheets and inhaled a newly-washed smell, thanking heaven for Mrs Dawson who'd rescued him from a life of dirty sheets and cold baked beans. Then he put out his hand to switch off his bedside lamp and as he did so, he remembered the earring he'd given to Finn. If Gerald was to be believed, he now knew who the owner was likely to be. Guy's lips drew into a straight line, fury was boiling up inside like an inferno. Cursing the day Kate had ever laid eyes on Finbar Alexander and his duplicitous friend, he stretched out an arm and turned out the light.

CHAPTER 39

The house was unusually quiet. Finbar's booming voice was not in evidence as he'd left to seek inspiration for his new book. In addition to which Cameron was mysteriously absent with still no comforting word to me as to his whereabouts. Apparently Kate's brother had also left Ransome's Point as he had been called to London on urgent business or so Alice, the fount of all knowledge, had informed me.

"Mrs Alexander looked quite ill when I saw her this morning. Looked as if she'd been up all night, dark circles under her eyes, clutching a cup of coffee as if her life depended on it." Alice picked up Chapter's five and six and put them down on her desktop with a thud.

I was in the middle of reading through the first four chapters, editing mistakes as I went along. It was a tedious enough task requiring concentration, without having to cope with Alice's constant interruptions.

"I feel sorry for her. Who could be so cruel?

She's had to work all hours to catch up, just to get those designs in on time, I understand." She sighed. "Can't think why she would bother though. It isn't as if they don't have enough money. Mr Alexander makes enough to keep them both in the lap of luxury I should think." Alice looked over the top of her glasses at me waiting for a response.

I ignored her and concentrated on the task in front of me.

"She doesn't have to work for a living, like some of us. That's for sure." Alice persisted.

"Maybe not. But perhaps she needs to feel she's doing something worthwhile. And she is very successful." I turned back to the page I was working on.

"Designing clothes aren't my idea of something worthwhile. It's not like helping to feed the hungry in Africa now is it?" Alice replied.

I stopped myself from pointing out that writing books could be placed in the same category. Ignoring her remark, I began to retype the page, which was littered with mistakes, thereby blocking out Alice and her catty asides. However, when I heard Cameron's name dripping like acid from her lips I stopped typing and listened.

"I don't care what Mr Alexander says, I'm sure he had something to do with all this fuss about his wife's designs. Mr Alexander won't hear a word against him but then the man is a saint. I've never heard him say a bad word about anyone."

"What makes you think Cameron Blackstone is the culprit?" I asked.

"Well for a start, I heard Mr Ripton telling his sister the camera that was used to take the photographs was a specialist make - the type a photographer would use." Alice looked smug.

"That's ridiculous; why would he?"

"Yes, well, that is the question, isn't it? If we knew that we'd know the answer," Alice countered, no doubt believing she had uttered a remark as philosophical as any uttered by Descartes. Although I was certain Alice didn't have the first idea who Descartes was unless she'd heard Finbar talking about the French philosopher and had soaked it up like a sponge. A smile played at the corner of my mouth at the thought.

"I can't see Cameron bothering to do such a thing. He's not interested in fashion or in spoiling Kate's career," I said.

"Cameron, now is it? You would stick up for him. I told you before that man is not all he seems. I'd be careful if I were you." Alice bent her head towards me as if to emphasise her words.

"That sounds remarkably like a threat, Alice." I

raised my head from my work.

"Be that as it may. All I'm saying is you want to watch him. That's all." Alice picked up a typed sheet from the stack in front of her signifying their conversation was at an end. Trying to seem unconcerned, I continued editing the manuscript in front of me, whilst my mind went around in circles as I tried to understand my feelings towards Cameron Blackstone.

At six o'clock, we locked the turret room door and went our separate ways; Alice leaving by the staircase leading to the garden and me to my room. The day had been the hottest yet and the weathermen were forecasting more to come. I slumped down on my bed and closed my eyes. The heat was exhausting. I heard the gate to the cliff path close and imagined Alice walking back to her cottage. Her animosity towards Cameron was verging on the vindictive. It seemed she had built up an image of the man that was at such a variance with his true nature as to be unrecognisable. I felt certain I could trust him. But then I'd been sure about Kenneth Boysey.

Thinking about Kenneth stirred me into wakefulness. I showered, dressed in a cool blue and white striped cotton dress and left the house via the same route Alice had taken half an hour earlier. At the stained glass window on the stairs, I stopped to look out. The sun was lowering in the sky and a shaft of evening sunlight hit the yellow glass panel temporarily blinding me. Blinking away the dark patches of the sun's glare, I descended the rest of the staircase holding on to the handrail for support, my sight returning with each step I took.

Out on the cliff path I made for the steps leading down to the cove. It was deserted. The boathouse was hardly used now, its usefulness relying on the small wooden punt that leaked and a modest-sized yacht in need of repair standing tied to its moorings like an errant offspring abandoned by its parents.

As I started to climb down, I noticed that a few steps from the top lay a small flat rock, a perfect viewpoint for the coast. I sat down feeling the cool stone beneath my legs. Not a breath of wind ruffled the surface of the water in the cove. Two seagulls floated on the current towards the harbour, the lights of which had begun to twinkle in the dusk of early evening. I raised my eyes to the cliff top as it curved away from the harbour and saw a light go on in an upstairs window of Alice's cottage. It occurred to me that she would have the most remarkable view of Ransome's Point. With binoculars it would be possible to clearly see the occupants as they moved about in the lower rooms and garden. I shuddered at the thought; it would be just like her to make the most of such an opportunity.

Involuntarily I looked back over my shoulder towards the house. It was like a drug to its inhabitants who seemed only able to leave it for short periods of time before feeling the urge to return. I'd begun to feel its magnetism myself as the weeks had passed and wondered what would happen when Finbar no longer needed me. I was no fool and knew the day was certain to come.

These days I never went far without my mobile phone, hoping for the call from Cameron which, as yet, hadn't come. I turned it over in my hands as if willing it to ring but it wasn't until I'd walked to the soft sand at the foot of the steps that I felt the phone vibrate followed by the ringtone.

"Hello, Rachel?"

"Cameron? Where are you?"

"New York. Listen I haven't much time. I've met two old friends who've given me some information that is very disturbing."

His voice drifted for a moment and I twisted my phone in order to amplify the signal.

"Rachel? Are you still there?"

"Yes, yes. When will you be coming home?"

"I'm not sure, it depends. Look I must go. Please take care, remember what I said. It's most important, even more so now."

He cut the connection and I was left looking at the phone as if merely wanting him to ring back would make it happen. But it was no use. I tried ringing the previous number but there was no answer. Feeling uneasy after the phone call, I was in no hurry to return to the house.

The sun was sinking below the horizon casting dark shadows over the yellow sand, my own assuming gargantuan proportions my head bending at the neck and travelling up the side of the boathouse. I turned towards Alice's cottage and noticed that it was now in darkness. Cameron's warning had unnerved me to such an extent that the sound of the small boat knocking against the tiny pier made me jump. I turned to walk towards the steps and heard another sound, this time from within the boathouse. It sounded as if someone was walking over the planks inside. Gentle footfalls, as light as snowflakes patted towards the door.

I wanted to run. What was I afraid of? I neither knew nor cared, but began walking away as quickly as the soft sand beneath my feet would allow. I'd removed my sandals when I left the steps and was relieved they weren't impeding my progress still further. Afraid to look around, I heard the shifting sand behind me as my pursuer shortened the distance separating us.

My breath rasped in my chest and beads of sweat trickled down my arms. It was with a certain amount of relief that I finally reached the steps and firmer ground. I began to run upwards as fast as my legs wound allow, feeling the rough surface scratch my bare feet as I ran. The footsteps following me had reached the steps; I could hear the pat-pat sound of rubber shoes as they slapped on the stone surface.

"Hang on. What's the hurry?"

I stopped in my tracks, relief flooding over me like a gigantic wave.

"Frankie?"

"God, you were off as if the hounds of hell were on your tail," Frankie said, catching up with me.

"I hadn't realised the time. I didn't want to be late for dinner."

"That's a very weak excuse, Rachel."

"OK, OK. I admit it. You startled me and for some reason I didn't want to wait to see who was following me. Evening shadows and all that."

"More plausible."

"Right. By the way, what were you doing in the boathouse?" I asked

We'd reached the top of the steps and could hear Steve and Kate's voices. The smell of barbequed chicken filled the air.

"Cosy, don't you think?" I couldn't avoid the bitterness in Frankie's voice. "And to answer your question. I'd hoped Steve and I would be able to take a walk before dinner but he was too busy. I see he found time to light the barbeque though. Anyway, I walked down to the cove alone and was curious about what the inside of the boathouse looked like. I was nosing around when I heard your mobile ring. I waited until you'd finished to give you some privacy."

I gave a nervous laugh. "Sorry."

"No problem."

"You shouldn't be jealous of Kate and Steve, you know. There's nothing going on between them."

"What makes you so sure?"

"I've know Finbar for a long time and I know Kate only has eyes for him." I slipped my arm through Frankie's.

"That's excluding Cameron Blackstone I suppose?" Frankie looked out to sea.

"Cameron? What's he got to do with Kate?"

"Nothing, forget I spoke."

"You can't just leave it," I said firmly.

"All I know is, Cameron Blackstone and Kate Alexander have history between them and that it involves Finn. It happened around about the time Finn and Kate got together. Steve is very tight lipped about it all. I can't mention Kate's name in anything other than revered tones because he goes ape."

"What d'you mean?"

"I know you won't believe it but Steve is so loyal to her that he imagines slights when none are intended. Even the faintest criticism of the saintly Kate and he is up on his white charger protecting her honour at every turn. That's why I get so jealous."

Frankie's word struck me as truthful and for the first time I began to see what was going on - to understand exactly how Frankie felt. "You poor thing. Look, let's forget dinner tonight. They are having a barbecue anyway, there'd be lots of burnt sausages and undercooked meat. I suggest we walk along the cliffs into the harbour and get something to eat at the Drunken Sailor, what d'you say?"

"I say, yes please. I can't face another evening of standing in the shadows of the saintly Kate."

The sun had dropped below the horizon by the time we reached the steps leading to the harbour and the sea lapped against the harbour wall like a thirsty dog. Outside the pub, the landlord had arranged plastic tables and chairs. In the centre of each table burned a thick creamy candle of the type usually seen in churches. Most of the tables were occupied but as we walked towards them a couple stood up leaving two seats free nearest to the harbour wall.

"This do?" Frankie asked pulling out a chair.

"Fine."

The menu was written on a board outside the pub. We chose the fish of the day with chips and Frankie disappeared into the depths of the *Drunken Sailor* to order the drinks.

Later, after we'd eaten and drunk a quantity of red wine, I steered the conversation back to Cameron.

"Tell me, what do you think of Cameron Blackstone, discounting his possible previous relationships? What is your impression of him, now?"

Frankie ordered another bottle of wine and filled both our glasses before answering.

"He's a bit of an unknown quantity. If you listen to Steve and Finn I get conflicting reports. I'm a firm believer in speaking as you find and he's never done anything to me, in fact I've found him to be very understanding where my relationship with Steve is concerned which is more than I can say for Finbar Alexander." Frankie's mouth turned down. "But as they say, one man's meat is another man's poison."

I grinned and Frankie suddenly saw the funny side of it and laughed. "Anyway, you seem very interested in Mr Blackstone, Rachel dear, so spill the beans."

Much to my dismay my cheeks began to burn. "Just wondered, that's all," I replied and Frankie, filling our glasses, just smiled.

"But to be serious for a moment. On the face of it Cameron Blackstone seems a decent sort of person. The trouble is he changes when he's with Finn."

"Changes? In what way."

Frankie thought for a moment. "I know it's difficult for you to believe but I think most men are macho egotists at heart. And however hard they try not to be, it usually resurfaces. When those two are together I think they bring out the worst in each other. Finn becomes a lout and Cameron his first lieutenant."

The sun was sinking beneath the horizon

leaving pink clouds and an amber tinted sea in its wake. I felt my stomach tighten and a wave of panic swept over me. I trusted Cameron and was disturbed to hear another less than positive opinion of him.

Unaware of my concern, Frankie ordered more wine and, as the evening gave way to the navy darkness of night, thankfully my senses became anaesthetised. Thoughts of Cameron slipped away as if taken by the tide, drifting slowly over pebbles, sliding over the wet sand and out to sea as if pulled by the innocent face of the moon.

Walking back along the cliff path, our unsteady steps outlined by moonlight, Frankie suddenly drew to a halt. "You haven't fallen for him have you, Rachel?"

"Who?"

"Cameron Blackstone of course. You have, haven't you?"

In the darkness I replied, "You're drunk, Frankie Gordino."

"Drunk or not you'll still feel the same, but tomorrow I'll be sober."

My laugh sounded forced as we weaved our way along the path towards the house. We reached Ransome's Point and were opening the garden gate when we heard the sound of raised voices coming from the conservatory.

"Siblings' quarrel by the sound of it," muttered Frankie making for the main entrance. "I don't want to be involved in all that tonight. Best make our way to bed. What d'you say?"

I stopped for a moment, in spite of myself, and listened.

"I've met him now, that last time you kept him under wraps, ask yourself why did you? You were a fool about him once, that's all there was to it. I thought you'd decided to give him a wide berth. The truth may hurt but it needs to be faced, Cameron Blackstone is trouble with a Capital T. You said yourself you think he's a bad influence on Finn."

Guy was speaking the words I dreaded to hear. Confirmation yet again, as to the true nature of the man I'd begun to trust?

I climbed the stairs unsteadily then opened my bedroom door and lay on the bed. My head was spinning from the wine but also from the remarks I'd overheard. Did I have the strength to believe my instinct when logic pointed to me being deceived yet again?

When I eventually fell asleep, one nightmare followed another until the sound of my mobile ringing on the bedside table woke me. Outside, there was a faint glow in the sky heralding the early dawn of yet another hot and sunny day. I looked at the clock as I picked up my phone. It was three thirty-five and the call was from Cameron.

CHAPTER 40

Lying in bed, watching Laura brushing her hair in the dressing table mirror, Finn felt happier than he had been for months and he couldn't find a rational explanation for his euphoria. He'd had love affairs before and recognised the first flush of passion; the being 'in love' phase. It soon passed, they all managed to bore him in the end. This was different. He loved Kate, or at least he'd always thought he did. He'd never found any of his previous mistresses able to tempt him away from his beautiful wife. To him they were playthings; a welcome diversion from the routine pattern of life, inspiration for his writing, a man thing, any number of excuses slipped into his mind.

"Penny for them?" Laura asked.

"Just wondering how I was going to tell you I have to get back to Ransome's Point later to-day."

She turned to face him, her bathrobe falling open to reveal the swell of her breasts. "Can't you stay a bit longer?"

Finn groaned. "'Fraid not. There'll be questions

asked as it is. If I stay any longer it will be difficult to make an excuse to come again."

"You're sure?" Laura slipped the bathrobe to the floor and walked towards him.

It was evening by the time Finn dragged himself away from the cottage. He walked along the path towards Totbury station and waited at the taxi rank until a cab arrived. As the cab approached Ransome's Point, he could see a plume of smoke rising in the air from the direction of his garden, and searching in his pocket for the means to pay the cab driver, the aroma of food cooking drifted towards him.

Kate and Guy were standing under the awning attached to the conservatory; Frankie and Steve were drinking cocktails on the patio. Neither Cameron nor Rachel appeared to be in the garden and their absences made the hairs on the back of Finn's neck prickle with unease.

"Here's the absent husband," said Guy as Finn approached.

"And hello to you favourite brother-in-law. Kate, my darling, miss me?" He slid an arm around his wife's waist unable to stop comparing her slight frame to his lover's voluptuous curves.

"Don't I always? A productive escape I hope?" Kate seemed to be unaffected by his absence but he noticed a tightening in the muscles of her arms as he embraced her. Always a bad sign, he thought, drawing her towards him and kissing her firmly on the lips.

"You could say so. I'm starving."

"Saw an old acquaintance of Blackstone's the other day." Guy speared a piece of chicken on the end of his fork

"Oh?" Finn tried to appear disinterested but failed. "Who was that?"

Guy walked towards the perimeter hedge, out of earshot of the others. Finn followed. "I was in London for a few days and I met up with Lance Rodway."

"Rodway?"

"Yes. He worked on the same paper as Blackstone in New York." Guy watched for Finn's reaction.

"Don't know him." Finn turned away.

"He seemed to know you."

"Yeah, well lots of people know me. It's the downside of being successful," Finn replied.

"What I meant to say was, he remembered you and Cameron at the time of the Falklands' war."

Guy heard Finn's sharp intake of breath. It whispered towards him like secret spoken in the dark.

"Long time ago. Can't remember much of it myself. Rodway is a name I can't recall."

"He said that you and Cameron were inseparable; thick as thieves was the phrase he used."

Guy waited for Finn's reply but his brother-in-law changed the subject.

"How long are you staying this time?" Finn asked.

"Fed up of me already, are you? Kate seems to want me to stay for the rest of the summer and I'm owed a long break. The Truman case was enough to drain anyone."

"It was a success for you personally though. Your picture was plastered over the papers for weeks. We only had to turn on the T.V. news to see your ugly mug on a daily basis. Anyway, you're welcome for as long as like. Problem is I'm busy at the moment, new book on the horizon, another in my head. I won't be around much over the next few weeks."

"I see."

The words hung in the air, the conversation having run its course. Finn drifted back to his wife's side and Guy towards the barbecue. Finn tried to make small talk with Kate whilst his mind picked over what Lance Rodway might have said to Guy. He cursed Cameron for doing a disappearing act, as he absentmindedly fingered the buttons on his mobile in the pocket of his shorts. He'd tried to ring him on numerous occasions over the past few days but there'd been no reply. His anxiety was beginning to border on paranoia.

At the barbecue, Guy, chewing on a piece of chicken, wondered what could be the cause of Finn's proposed future absences. He didn't swallow the bait, which was as tough as the overcooked chicken. He knew he was up to something. If the inebriated Gerald was to be believed then Laura Crighton might be a strong contender. He'd stood opposite enough liars, in his time at the bar, to recognise the truth when he saw it and his brother-in-law was a stranger to the concept.

CHAPTER 41

Throughout July the temperature steadily rose. Hosepipe bans were in operation up and down the U.K. The grass in the garden at Ransome's Point had long since lost its lush green appearance and lay withered and dried into yellowed strips. Along the cliff path the brambles drooped, wild flowers wilted, their heads brushing the dust of the trodden earth. A feeling of expectancy hung in the air as if waiting for the first clouds signalling the approach of rain to appear, whilst I waited for the sound of the taxi that would bring Cameron back to me.

His earlier phone call had roused me from a fitful sleep where dreams of Kenneth Boysey, Finbar and Cameron intermingled with each other in a stream of nonsense, which in sleep had seemed perfectly reasonable. I'd awoken with a start, bathed in sweat and my head pounding like an African drumbeat. The bedroom was filled with an amber glow, the precursor to yet another blisteringly hot day. But that had been three days ago.

When he'd rung, Cameron's voice sounded muffled and indistinct; music was playing in the background. He'd told me he'd spoken to a woman called Ginny Monroe and that he'd learned something about Finbar - something that had changed his mind. He'd said he couldn't go into detail and he was coming home to put things right at last. His voice sounded slurred and I'd wondered if it was the connection or whether he was drunk. I'd heard nothing from him since. He'd told me not to mention his whereabouts to anyone and although I desperately wanted to confide in Finbar, I'd managed to resist the temptation

Alice was proof reading another chapter when I heard footsteps on the walkway joining Cameron's bedroom to the turret room. My heart skipped a beat. Someone must have left Cameron's room and be making their way towards us. It must be him. He must have come home in the night and was now coming to see me. I felt a flutter in my chest as the footsteps came nearer. Then it seemed, whoever was out there had thought better of it and was retracing their steps. Alice seemed not to have heard. She was concentrating on the manuscript on the desk and didn't look up even when I stood up and made a pretext of opening the door leading to the walkway in order to get some air,

I slowly drew the door back on its hinges. I could see someone closing Cameron's bedroom door. I recognised the broad shoulders, and the twist of hair curling at the nape of his neck. What was he doing in Cameron's room?

I turned around and saw that Alice was still engrossed in her work. Edging forward on to the walkway I followed Finbar, opening the door as quietly as I could. He was looking through the items in the top drawer of a chest. But I hadn't been as quiet as I'd thought. Hearing a sound from the doorway he turned.

"Rachel?"

"I heard someone on the walkway. I thought perhaps Cameron had returned." I waited for him to explain why he was looking through his friend's things.

"I see. Look, I know this may look a bit sus,." He gave a nervous cough. "The thing is, I've lost a cufflink and wondered if Cameron had picked it up by mistake."

The excuse was a thin one and he realised it as soon as he'd said it. He tried to make amends.

"Silly really. It's just that it was a wedding present from Kate. Sentimental nonsense, I know." He moved away from the drawer, towards me.

"Why would you think Cameron had it?" I was getting annoyed. Did he think I was a complete fool?

"Oh I don't know; last place to look, that sort of thing. I meant to ask him about it before but as he's not around, I thought I'd see for myself. You any idea where the old devil is?" He was looking at me expectantly. I shook my head. "No? Just a thought. I expect he'll turn up soon. A bit unlike him not to let me know where is though." He stroked his chin and frowned. "Anyway it's as hot as hell in here, let's get back to the turret room and you and Alice can fill me in on how all that mundane editing is going."

He held the door open for me and followed me back along the walkway. I was sure he was up to something and wished I could tell Cameron about it.

Alice's face was wreathed in smiles as she explained how far we had progressed since the completed manuscript had been left with us. She played up her own part in the process whilst subtly failing to comment on my involvement. Finbar listened attentively, nodding and smiling in all the right places but I could see he was rattled.

Before long, he made his excuses and left. The sound of his footsteps descending the staircase echoed up to us. I walked to the window and saw him in the garden. He was biting his fingernails and pacing back and forth over the sun-bleached lawn. Warching him, I heard the sound of his mobile ringing and saw him answer the call.

He was too far away from me to hear the conversation but his shoulders stiffened then relaxed. He walked towards the cliff path, the phone still clasped to his ear. It was obvious that the conversation was one he didn't wish to be overheard. He walked towards the steps leading down to the cove. Then I caught sight of a flash of white cotton. Kate was standing in the garden beneath the turret room window. I couldn't see her face but recognised the white cotton sundress she'd worn that morning. The skirt billowed out in front of her and it was clear she was watching her husband intently.

"What's so interesting out there?" Alice asked.

I turned away from the window. "Nothing much. I was just wondering how long this heat wave is going to keep up."

"Not a cloud in the sky again. You should see

my garden, the grass is as yellow as mustard." Alice stood up. "Time for a brew?" she asked.

CHAPTER 42

Moving out of the shadow of the back porch, Kate followed the route she'd seen her husband take five minutes before. Her suspicions had resurfaced when he'd arrived yesterday. There was something about his demeanour that she'd recognised. He was furtive, excited and high as a kite. She was sure a woman was the cause of his euphoria. Her brief conversation with the estate agent in Witcombe had lain dormant in her brain, buried under a mountain of worry concerning the sabotage of her collection. The fact that the envelope had disappeared hadn't really registered at the time. She'd thought it had probably lain hidden underneath a pile of drawings and post that had littered her desk for weeks but deep down she knew it wasn't the case. She was certain Finn had removed it.

At least she had managed to finally produce the designs in time for the new season's collection. Steve had driven to the station that morning in order to fly to New York to hand over the collection in person. He would only be gone for a few days but Frankie was already complaining about his absence.

Kate tasted salt on her tongue as she descended the steps leading to the cove. She could see Finn making for the boathouse. His head was bent and he was talking on his mobile. She felt her stomach turn over and swallowed the bile rising in her throat. The sand was warm beneath her feet. She felt the rough grains rubbing between her toes as she lifted her feet from one sand hole to another, treading in Finn's footsteps. She heard his voice as she approached.

"I know it's only been a few hours, darling, but it seems like a lifetime."

His words held a longing that she'd almost forgotten. It seemed years since he had used that tone with her. She bit her bottom lip, placed her hand on the door and watched it slide open a fraction.

"I'll do my best. Give it a day or two and then I'll convince everyone I need to have some space." He was eager now, his tone light and amusing.

Removing her hand from the door, she turned away - this time she would play it differently. She was wiser and more determined to find out who this woman was before confronting Finn. It would only drive him to meet her in secret or make him plead with her that it would never happen again. But now, she wouldn't give him the chance to do either.

Returning the way she'd come, careful to tread only in the marks made by Finn's footsteps she reached the steps. Not a trace of her was left on the sand. She ran up the steps and was sitting on the top step when Finn emerged from the boathouse. He saw her immediately and raised his hand. She noticed that with the other he was slipping his mobile back into the pocket of his shorts. He was breathless when he reached her.

"Hello, my sweet. Having a breath of air?"

He sat beside her and it was all Kate could do not to shrink away from the arm he placed casually around her shoulders. "Something like that," she replied. "What have you been up to?"

He hesitated, turned towards her, but deciding there was no irony in her tone, replied in an offhand manner. "Nothing much. I thought perhaps I'd have a look at the boat, see if it was seaworthy."

"And was it?"

"What?"

"Seaworthy?"

"No. Turner and his boys would have to look

at it first I think. It's been neglected for too long." Finn stood up and offered her his hand. "Come on old thing, let's join the others, not to early for a drink I think."

Kate slipped her hand into his, marvelling at her self-control. She believed she could do it this time. This time he would pay.

Rachel and Frankie were drinking Pimms in the shade of the canopy erected outside the conservatory. Guy was inside. Finn and Kate could see that he was on the telephone. His expression was grim. When he saw them approaching he took the phone into the hall.

Finn filled a glass from the jug on the table near Rachel and smiled at her, pointedly ignoring Frankie. "You look as if you're enjoying yourself. Here, Kate, have some of this." Kate took a sip and then set it down on the table.

"How long d'you think Steve will be away?" Frankie asked Kate for the second time that day.

"He'll be back as soon as he can, Frankie," Kate replied, moving inside in search of her brother.

The phone in Finn's pocket began to vibrate. He removed it whilst walking away from Rachel and Frankie towards the perimeter hedge. It was a text message. It was from Cameron.

Contacted Ginny Monroe, remember her? Will speak when I get back.

Finn frowned and wiped the sweat away from his forehead with the back of his hand. He needed a drink and a big one at that. Walking into the house he went in search of a brandy bottle.

At first he didn't see them. They were standing outside Kate's studio. They hadn't seen him slip into the library to find a bottle he kept in the drawer of the desk. Their voices were indistinct, muffled by the closed door leading into the hall. Finn poured a large measure of brandy into a glass and opened the door a fraction.

"Apparently it was something to do with a young starlet called Melody something or other." Guy's voice was lowered.

"You're sure?"

"Certain. I warned you about him years ago, Kate."

"I know, I know. Things are different now."

"Forgive me if I say, I've heard that before," Guy replied

"No. This time it *is* different. Trust me. I can't tell you any more at the present but I will make sure I handle it to my advantage."

Kate sounded more positive than Finn had ever heard her. The tone of her voice made him uneasy. It would be just his luck for her to put a spanner in the works now, when he 'd found Laura, the love of his life. He tipped the contents of his glass down his throat and gulped as the fiery liquid slid into his stomach. She wouldn't stop him. No one could. Not even Cameron.

CHAPTER 43

Kate woke up at four a.m., the sun had risen and tinted the horizon a burnt orange. Flames of morning light tipped the ripples on the sea sparkling like diamonds thrown on a sheet of blue velvet. Finn had been home for two days.

She watched her husband sleeping. He was on his side breathing heavily, his breath smelling of brandy. Sleep had robbed his face of the fine lines creasing his eyes and fanning out from the corners of his mouth, so that he looked almost ageless. Kate felt the usual tug somewhere in the region of her heart but refused to accept it. She clamped her lips together, turned away from him and slid her feet soundlessly over the edge of the bed to the floor. The carpet felt warm beneath her toes as she padded over to the window seat then sat down curling her legs underneath her. She loved this house; nothing would make her leave it, whatever Finn was up to.

He'd come to bed at three. He was drunk. She heard him stumble as he undressed and kept her eyes tightly shut feigning sleep. He'd been drinking heavily since he'd returned from his supposed inspirational break, another sign a woman was involved. He was a fool. She recognised that now; she wasn't naïve, he hadn't the sense to be less obvious. Anger was welling up inside her, hot and hard. She couldn't bear to look at him lying there sleeping the sleep of the innocent.

As quietly as she could, Kate left the seat and went into the bathroom, closing the door with care. She knew the sound of the shower wouldn't wake him. They'd had the room soundproofed before they'd moved in. Finn had argued that a writer's muse would not be tethered to a nine to five existence. He often rose in the middle of the night and made his way to the turret room to begin his day. Admittedly it hadn't been his practice for some time but when they'd first moved to Ransome's Point and his novel was at the initial draft stage, he'd been filled with enthusiasm which of late seemed to be lacking.

The jets of water played over her body, spilling brisk streams of warm water over her head, between her breasts, over her flat stomach to flow gently between her legs and rest for a moment at her feet before disappearing in a gurgle beneath her. The repetitious process calmed her anger, freeing her of its constraints so that she could think more clearly.

He was still asleep when she left the bedroom half an hour later, wearing a green and white cotton dress. It was nearly six o'clock.

The house was silent. Kate left via the conservatory and took the cliff path in the direction of the harbour. It was cooler than she'd expected. A welcome offshore breeze ruffled the hem of her dress as she walked along the path. The tide was out. Mud flats lay baking in the early morning sun and a smell of engine oil hit her nostrils as below her she saw a collection of sailing boats resting on top of the sand, mud, and shingle, waiting for the sea to lift them up and carry them on the current for the short distance their moorings would allow.

It felt good to be doing something to escape from Finn's deceitful presence for a while. The sun was still low in the sky. Kate looked at her watch - half past six, still too early. She walked to the edge of the cliff and sat on an outcrop of rock. She had hours to wait yet. The estate agents' office opened at nine. Breathing in the early morning air, she felt a wave of tranquillity sweep over her. It felt good to be taking hold of her life with both hands again. For far too long she'd been like a puppet dancing to the tunes of others. Once, Cameron Blackstone had been responsible for her every thought. Now Steve and Guy played their parts, and Finn? Finn, in his own way, controlled her far more than the others put together. Watching the sea sweeping in over the rocks and creeping into the harbour, she felt as though a burden had lifted from her shoulders. Whatever happened now, she knew she was the architect of her own destiny.

The sleepy village of Totbury sprang to life later than the nearby town of Witcombe. Percy, Darcy and Thoms had branches in both locations but it had been at the Totbury branch where Kate had seen Richard Darcy.

To kill some time she breakfasted in the coffee shop overlooking the harbour. Earlier, she'd watched the first of the fishing boats come in on the tide as it unloaded its catch. Although she'd seen this happen on many previous occasions, it seemed to her as though she was seeing it for the first time. Every fish sliding into the waiting containers gleamed and sparkled in the morning sunlight. Even the odours rising from the harbour, as she left the coffee shop, smelled new and exotic.

It was half past nine when Kate opened the door and walked towards the reception desk in the office of Percy, Darcy and Thoms. A young girl dressed in a green and navy striped dress with the firm's name badge pinned to her lapel, smiled at her as she approached. "Hello, my name is Debbie, how may I help you."

It was the voice of an automaton. A stock phrase repeated ad nauseam throughout her working day. Kate smiled back. "Is Mr Darcy available? Perhaps you could tell him Mrs Alexander would like a word with him?"

The girl picked up the phone, relayed the message and then indicated that she should follow her through a door situated at the back of the office. Richard Darcy was sitting behind a desk. He rose and held out his hand in greeting. "Thank you, Debbie. Mrs Alexander, good to see you again. Please sit down. Now how can I help you?"

Kate had rehearsed the words whilst sitting on the cliff top as dawn spread across the bay. She decided to appear casual. Her manner would be relaxed. Taking a deep breath to calm herself she replied, "I'm not sure whether you can help at all really but I thought, as I was passing, it would do no harm to enquire."

Sitting opposite her, Richard Darcy nodded then rested his chin on his steepled fingertips as Kate continued. "Some time ago you acquired a property for my husband to rent. Well, we loved the property and enthused so much about it that two of our dearest friends wondered if there was anything else for sale in the vicinity." Kate beamed. "You see, Mr Darcy, my husband needs a bolthole, away from everyone once in a while, a place for him to exercise his creative powers. I'm sure you understand."

"Quite, quite, Mrs Alexander. I thought it might be the case, when your husband requested that the property should be isolated from its neighbours. And Willow Cottage is certainly that."

"Indeed. That is why I'm afraid you might not be able to help. Where would the nearest available property be, do you think?" Kate asked.

"Mmm.. a tricky one." He stood up and consulted a large wall map behind him. "Let me see. Ah yes, now Willow Cottage is here."

Kate watched him trace his finger along the coastline on the map and made careful note of the exact location of Finn's love-nest, for she was sure that's what it was, then feigned interest in a development further along the coast.

"Our Witcombe office may have some details about properties in this area. Would you like me to give them a ring?"

"No, thank you, Mr Darcy. You have been very helpful. I'll pass on the details to our friends. I'm sure they will pay your Witcombe office a visit before too long." Kate stood and moved to the door. "I really mustn't take up any more of your time."

"Not at all, Mrs Alexander; always a pleasure to see you. Give my regards to your husband and tell him if there is anything else we can assist him with...."

The muscles in Kate's jaw tightened. "I will, thank you."

Outside, in the street, a group of holidaymakers were strolling down the high street, having stepped out of a coach with a large painted Welsh dragon painted on the side. They ambled into shops, ate ice cream and filled carrier bags full of souvenirs. Kate envied them, wishing her life was as uncomplicated as theirs appeared to be, then walked in the direction of Willow Cottage.

CHAPTER 44

"No, it's not possible, my sweet. I know. I feel the same. Be patient, I'll come as soon as I can, believe me."

Finn put the mobile in his pocket. He was frustrated. Kate was suspicious, Cameron was digging the dirt God knew where, and Guy Ripton was sniffing around like a bloodhound. He scratched the back of his neck. He'd been bitten, he was sure of it. This heat was hatching out all manner of creatures, half of which had decided to feast on his body.

He sat in the boat and stretched his legs out in front of him. No one would keep him from Laura. He was determined to see her come what may. The water in the boathouse smelled of oil and salt. Finn could hear it slapping against the side of the boat. Flicking open his phone, he rang Cameron's number and for the umpteenth time heard the metallic tones of his voice mail asked him to leave a message.

"Ring me ASAP," he said, knowing somehow

that he wouldn't. The familiar metallic taste was back in his mouth. It tasted of fear.

The pavilion had been a wreck when Kate and Finn bought the house but Kate had insisted it be renovated. She believed that it would be useful during the long damp days of a normal British summer, when the air was warm and drizzle moistened everything it touched.

The renovations had been completed and what remained was a sturdy wooden structure with a green tiled roof. Casement windows faced the gardens on one side and on the other, the cliff walk. Inside, the furnishings consisted of bare wooden floors and walls and a large framed aerial photo of Ransome's Point hung on one wall opposite a water colour Kate had painted - it was of Finn.

Guy pushed open the half-timbered door with one hand, easing his laptop through the opening, and sighed. This was just the place. Two bamboo armchairs and a twin-seater settee littered with brightly coloured cushions were situated around a square table. He opened the windows as wide as possible and a rush of air from the seaward side brought with it a smell, so pungent, that Guy could almost taste the salt on his tongue. The whole place reminded him of a small summerhouse they had at the bottom of the garden, where he and Kate used to play as children. The warm smell seeping out of the wooden walls brought back memories of card games played on a small green baize-covered card table. He could almost hear the rain sliding over the tiles and tapping at the windowpanes. The summerhouse had been their sanctuary on wet days, a place away from their parents where they could do, as they liked.

Opening his laptop, Guy accessed the file named DES.SAB. A meticulous child, Guy had systematically worked his way through school, University and later during his Bar exams. Stella said that his meticulous manner, although admirable in some repsects, was difficult to live with. Guy had shrugged and argued that she'd known what he was like before she'd married him.

Sabotage was an ugly word. It smacked of wanton destruction and malicious damage. Thankfully he'd come across such cases rarely in his professional life but it was with a certain amount of satisfaction that Guy watched the folders open in front of him. He'd cross-referenced every bit of trivial information he'd amassed since Kate had told him of the problem and he was surprised at the result. The obvious saboteur was Cameron

Blackstone and, although it was not in Guy's nature to accept the obvious, he didn't altogether rule him out of the equation, preferring to paste his name at the bottom of the list of suspects, which to his amazement had grown since his investigations had begun.

"Good Lord, so this is where you're hiding?" Finn was standing in the doorway a drink in his hand. "What are you up to? Too hot to sit in here I'd have thought.

Guy closed the lid of his laptop. "Just catching up with work. It doesn't do to let everything slide, even on holiday, I find."

He slid the laptop into the leather case at his feet and spun the dials on the combination lock. Finn seemed not to notice.

"Seen Kate?" Finn asked. "Everyone seems to have their own agenda these days. Can't find a soul when you want one. I could do with a week or two away from here. The heat's intolerable. I told Kate we should have added air con when the builders were here but she just said, 'What! In our summer temperatures? We'd be lucky to get above twenty C.' Well, who's having the last laugh now?"

Finn sounded petulant and, not for the first time, Guy wondered what sort of brainstorm had resulted in Kate falling for such a man.

"Sorry, haven't seen her. I expect she's off shopping somewhere. She's due to have a bit of R and R after the way she's been working. If I could get my hands on the rat who'd copied her work, I'd throttle him with my bare hands."

"Yes, well it looks very much as if that trail has grown cold. Doubt if we'll every find out who did it." Finn closed the door of the pavilion behind Guy."

"I wouldn't be too sure," Guy said, walking back towards the house.

CHAPTER 45

The tar in the lane was tacky; the sun had melted its surface so that it clung to the soles of Kate's espadrilles as she walked near the hedge. Flakes of hay drifting in the air floated above her head like a yellow mist settling on her hair and clothing. Opposite the cottage, a man with a young child was sitting on a stile watching the farmer. The young child sat on the man's lap mesmerised by the gigantic harvester as it ploughed its way through the field transforming the dried hay into bales of white plastic littering the ground like enormous snowballs

Kate heard a car behind her and flattened her body against the hedge. A small blue car with tinted windows drove past her and parked on the hardstand in front of the cottage. A young woman stepped out. She was wearing a red dress and her hair hung in curls to her shoulders. Kate knew immediately that this was her rival. The woman turned towards her, so addressing to the man in an attempt to persuade an onlooker they were together, Kate said, "Amazing sight isn't it?"

The man was pleasant and happy to talk at length about haymaking, his child, the holiday he was having and the state of the weather in general. Kate heard the front door of the cottage close and a shiver ran down her spine. Her brain was spinning; how could she tackle this? Part of her wanted to confront the woman now, tell her to leave Finn alone. But the still small voice of reason advised caution.

The child, becoming bored, began to cry. The man raised the youngster to his shoulders. "Time to go back to your mother," he said.

"Mind if I walk with you?" Kate asked.

During the walk the man explained he was giving his wife some free time. She was pregnant and the heat was unsettling her. Kate let him talk, grateful that he required little input from her just the occasional nod of agreement. Inside, she was seething at Finn's behaviour and planning what she would do next.

Reaching the harbour, she left them and walked back along the cliff path. Alice was in her garden.

"Mr Alexander was looking for you," she said, and the statement sounded like a reprimand. What was it about Finn that produced such loyalty,

Kate wondered?

"Thank you, Alice." Kate didn't look up. She walked with her eyes cast downwards, Finn's latest conquest's face swimming in front of her. Was this the life she had chosen? It seemed she was destined to tread this path whether she wanted to or not. He'd promised faithfully, the last one would be just that. So much for his empty promises; Kate was determined he wouldn't rob her of some last shreds of dignity. There was no way she would let this go on. She risked leaving it too late and continuing to watch a succession of younger women fall in and out of her husband's life like butterflies landing on a flower. A look of determination spread across her face. If she had anything to do with it, this butterfly was about to have her wings clipped. And as for the flower - it had bloomed once too often.

As she approached the house, Kate saw Rachel and Frankie walking towards the point. She watched them sit on the seat and felt a pang of sympathy for Frankie who was missing Steve. Love makes fools of us all, she thought, biting her lip. Walking towards the steps leading to the cove, she saw Finn sitting on the sand, his mobile glued to his ear as if were a permanent fixture. No prizes for guessing who he was talking to.

In the garden, she passed the pavilion and took a step back. She saw Guy bending towards his laptop and moved quickly into the conservatory without being seen. It was Mrs Goodrich's day off; Kate was alone in the house. Picking up the telephone she rang the number of the estate agents' office in Totbury.

"Hello, I'd like to speak to Mr Darcy please. Tell him it's Kate Alexander."

The sound of Handel's Water Music tinkled in Kate's ear, then after a while, "Mrs Alexander, good to hear from you so soon after your visit. How may I help you?"

Listening to Tom Darcy's business-like patter Kate almost lost her nerve. Then an image of a young woman with curly dark hair removed her hesitation.

"I've been discussing Willow Cottage with my husband and I'm sorry to say, we've decided it's not for us. We'd like to terminate our agreement as soon as possible."

"Really? I see, forgive me but I thought you said your husband was thrilled with the place?" The agent sounded confused.

"He was, but you know how temperamental artists are, Mr Darcy." She gave an embarrassed laugh, hoping he would realise that she was in a difficult situation. It worked.

"I understand completely. Leave all the details to me, Mrs Alexander. We're going to put it on the market straight away. I'm sure the property will sell very quickly. Perhaps those friends, you were telling me about, might be interested?"

"Friends? Oh, er, yes, those friends. Unfortunately they've bought somewhere further around the coast," she explained.

"No problem. As I said, I'll sort things out without delay."

"Thank you, Mr Darcy. Perhaps you could address all correspondence regarding the cottage to me. I don't want my husband to bother about it. He's very busy at the moment."

Kate put down the phone and felt as though a weight had been lifted off her shoulders. And that is just the beginning, she said, as she picked up a magazine with a photograph of Finn on the cover. It was out of date but he liked to keep it resting on the wicker-topped table just the same.

CHAPTER 46

The atmosphere at dinner was tense. It was lightened somewhat by the unexpected arrival of Steve, who breezed in as Mrs Goodrich was serving the main course. He kissed Frankie, thanked Mrs Goodrich for hastily arranging a place for him at the table, and sat down.

Kate could hardly wait to hear his news and when they'd finished eating, she said, "I hope Frankie will forgive me if I whisk you away for a moment or two. Perhaps we could drink our coffee in the pavilion." She stood up. " That's if you're not too tired after your journey?"

Steve glanced at Frankie who seemed to be in deep conversation with Rachel. "No of course not. Jet lag will kick in tomorrow I'm sure but I'll be glad to get you up to speed with things in New York. My apologies everyone."

Finn grunted, Guy raised his hand but Rachel and Frankie appeared not to notice their departure.

Kate opened the back door of the pavilion allowing the night air in. The moon large and clear hung in the sky like a silver hot air balloon. "Was it my imagination or was there an atmosphere?" Steve asked.

"Not your imagination," Kate said and he heard the bitterness in her voice. "Anyway forget it. Tell me all."

According to Steve, this time the visit was a success. He told Kate that the new designs were well received and totally original, which was a relief under the circumstances. "I was almost waiting for them to tell me they'd seen them all before," Steve said.

"Believe me whoever was responsible is not going to get away with it."

"Any movement in that direction?"

"Guy's working on it. I believe Cameron is at the top of his list. Proving his involvement is however, a different matter."

"Where *is* Cameron, by the way?" Steve asked.

"That, my dear, is the question. Up to no good I expect and planning to lead my husband into even more trouble I've no doubt."

"Finn in the dog house then?"

Kate hesitated before replying. "No more than

usual but let's just say, *he* might not have changed, but *I* definitely have."

"Intriguing though the concept is, my dear Kate, I think it's time I looked for Frankie. I don't want to join Finn in the dog house just at the moment."

Kate laughed. "I'm so glad you're back, Steve. I've really missed you."

Steve leaned towards her and kissed her lightly on the cheek. As he stood up he saw Frankie standing in the doorway carrying two brandy balloons. "I came over with a drink for you both to have with your coffee. I wish I hadn't bothered now." Frankie thrust the glasses at Steve and walked away.

"Hope that dog house is big enough for two," mumbled Steve handing the glasses to Kate and following Frankie into the night.

I saw Frankie leave the pavilion and rush into the house. It had been impossible not to feel the tension in the air over dinner. Ignoring Cameron's warning, I decided to walk along the cliffs. My temple was beginning to throb and I hoped a walk would clear my head. I set off in the direction of Alice's cottage and was surprised to see her talking to Finn in the garden as I approached. Something about the way they stood made me think of co-conspirators. Alice was looking up at Finn and he had his hands placed firmly on her shoulders his head bent towards her. It was impossible not to miss their reaction when they heard me approach. They sprung apart like frightened lovers.

"Rachel," Finn said. "Walking into Totbury?"

"No, just taking a stroll."

"Well perhaps I'll join you. We've finished chatting haven't we, Alice?"

She hesitated, "Of course, Mr Alexander." Becoming the deferential secretary once more, she turned away and walked back inside the cottage.

His steps matching mine on the cliff path, Finn said, "Still no word from Cameron?"

"I shouldn't think he'd keep me informed as to his whereabouts Finbar. He's much more likely to contact you, don't you think?" I was aware of him looking at me as if, there might be a hidden meaning behind my words, then shrugged.

"Yes, perhaps you're right. Anyway tell me, how do you like staying at Ransome's Point?"

For the next hour it seemed as if the years had been stripped away. Finn was his old self, making me laugh, talking about mutual friends and about lunchtimes spent in the *Bunch of Grapes*. I began to relax in his company, something I knew I hadn't been able to do since my arrival. Then he mentioned Kenneth Boysey. He slipped his name into the conversation as innocently as his smile.

"It was all a bit messy, so I heard." he said.

I didn't answer.

"Mmm, you were very close and there was all that talk at the time."

I felt beads of sweat break out under my fringe. He knew about the trouble my relationship with Kenneth Boysey had caused and I was amazed he would resurrect the topic, in view of what happened.

"What did Cameron think, when you told him?" It sounded like a threat.

Although the moon was bright, beyond the edge of the path the cliff fell away into darkness. I could hear the sea lapping against the rocks at the base of the cliffs and the rustle of the breeze through the gorse bushes. But the idyllic scene had been transformed into something menacing by Finn's words. The implication, that if I stepped out of line in any way he would tell Cameron about Kenneth Boysey, hung between us.

Was I imagining it, becoming paranoid? I didn't think so. " I think I'll walk back now. I have a headache," I said.

"Ask Kate for some tablets," he said, concern

for my welfare back in his voice.

As I walked away, I was certain I heard him chuckle.

CHAPTER 47

The turret room was pleasantly cool in the early morning. The two women were seated at their desks. Finn poked his head around the door at ten to ask if they had any questions then, satisfied that he had the rest of the day to himself, left the house via the staircase leading to the garden.

Kate and Guy were sitting in the conservatory so he avoided them by walking towards the back of the house and letting himself out of the garden via the gate leading to the cliff path. His mobile began to throb in his pocket as he closed the gate. It was Laura.

"Finn, what's going on?" She sounded agitated.

"What d'you mean?"

"There's a FOR SALE sign in the front garden. I woke up and there it was."

Finn's brows knitted together in a straight line. "It's got to be a mistake. I'll contact the agents and get them to remove it. Don't worry. I'll see you later this morning."

Walking back towards the house Finn felt fear mixed with anger. He was fearful that Kate had found out about Laura and what the consequences might be and angry that it would mean he would have to ditch her. He wasn't ready.

Retracing his steps, through the garden, he hurried up the staircase and opened the door to the turret room. "There's a telephone directory on the window ledge, Alice. Pass it to me, please."

He leafed through the pages, wrote the number on a yellow 'Post It' note and left the room via the walkway leading to Cameron's room. Once inside and sure that he wouldn't be overheard, he dialled the offices of Percy, Darcy and Toms.

Tom Darcy was his usual sycophantic self. Finn waited until he'd run the gamut of complimentary phrases then said, "Why have you arranged for a FOR SALE sign to be erected at Willow Cottage?"

There was a moment's silence from the other end then, "Er, I'm sorry. You didn't want a sign put up? I thought Mrs Alexander made a point of expressing that she wished it. I must be mistaken. Of course, I'll have it removed today."

Finn's legs buckled and he sat on the end of the bed. "Mrs Alexander?"

"Yes, she called in here the day before yesterday. I spoke to her myself."

"Look, I think my wife has made a mistake. We did talk about leaving the place but I decided against it. Maybe she misunderstood. In any case, the property is most definitely NOT up for sale and I would be obliged if any further discussions regarding Willow Cottage are kept purely between ourselves."

Tom Darcy began to stutter. "Yes, sssir, I, er, I understand, Mr Alexander. The property will be taken off the market immediately."

Finn put down the phone. This was the last straw. He wouldn't give up Laura, not for Kate, Cameron, nor anyone else for that matter. Leaving the house, he decided it was time to teach Kate a lesson. If she thought she could meddle in his affairs she was very much mistaken.

Arriving at the cottage, Finn saw the sign being loaded into a van. Laura opened the door to him.

"What's going on?" she asked.

"Nothing. It's sorted; there was a mix up at the estate agents. Now come here and let's make up for lost time."

Later, lying alongside Laura and watching her as she drifted into sleep, Finn realised his feelings for her had intensified. He wanted to be with her every minute of every day. His love for Kate suddenly seemed like a feather blowing in the wind, however hard he tried to capture it, it drifted out of his grasp.

Laura sighed, her hand settled on his arm and he felt the longing returning. He began to stroke her breasts, heard her moan as she turned to him and lost himself in her. He was travelling a road from which he was aware there was no return.

After her talk with Guy, Kate went in search of her husband. Unable to find him, she knew at once where he would be. Backing the car out of the drive and into the lane she wondered what she would do when she reached the cottage. There would be no surreptitious surveillance this time. The car would be instantly recognisable and besides, confrontation appeared to be the only course of action left to her.

She began to bite the corner of her thumbnail at the traffic lights, not a good sign. She was nervous. She was at a metaphorical crossroads in her life. The road she decided to travel was up to her. She could turn around, forget the woman, who Finn had installed in Willow cottage, or she could seek them out and face the consequences.

It seemed she had made up her mind. The car edged forward into Leaping Lane.

CHAPTER 48

Walking back to her cottage, Alice dabbed at her forehead with a white cotton handkerchief. The heat was almost unbearable. Yellowed grass crunched under her sandals and scraped at her ankles. The water in the cove looked inviting. She wished she could shed her sensible cotton frock and plunge naked into the sea. That would raise a few eyebrows, she thought.

However, heat or no heat she was happier than she had thought possible. He'd made her position clear at last. There was to be no enforced retirement. She could work with him as long as she liked. She knew her own mind now. Loyalty was a commodity she knew how to cope with; she'd made it plain. She'd been loyal to Robert and look where that had landed her. This time she knew how to handle it. She'd told him he didn't need to worry but she'd made it perfectly clear that it came at a price. She was smiling to herself when she saw someone standing at her garden gate. What was the problem now? She could feel trouble drifting towards her like a bad smell.

I'd been sitting at my desk for over an hour. I walked over to the window, threw open the casement then glanced at my watch; it was a quarter past ten. Craning my neck, I looked back along the cliff path. There was no sign of Alice. It wasn't like her to be late.

At half eleven I switched her computer into stand-by mode and left the turret room. In the garden I found Frankie and Steve. "Have you seen Finbar?" I asked.

Steve raised his eyes from the book he'd been reading. "No. I think he's spending a few days away, working on his latest plot I gather."

"And Kate?"

Steve looked guarded as he replied, "I'm not sure. I think she left the house early this morning."

"I don't suppose either of you have seen Alice? I'm worried about her. She hasn't turned up for work and she's never late."

"Perhaps she's overslept," mumbled Frankie, whose hangover looked as if it was assuming monumental proportions.

"I think I'll take a walk over to her cottage. She might be ill."

Frankie suddenly groaned. "I'm off to get my head down for an hour or two, or perhaps a day or two."

"Hair of the dog is what you need," Steve suggested to Frankie's retreating back.

I was at the garden gate when I felt a hand on my arm. "Hang on a minute. I'll come with you," Steve said.

"There's no need, really."

"I know, but I feel like stretching my legs." He linked his arm through mine.

"How are you and Frankie getting on?" I asked, as we walked towards Alice's cottage.

"Better, I think. We had a bit of a set to last night about Kate, but it cleared the air. That's why Frankie's suffering this morning. We drank too much and talked way into the night." He turned to face me. "And it's why I'm blowing the cobwebs off by joining you on your mission of mercy."

We walked past the cove to where the path divided and met the road. In the distance I noticed a lone figure walking from the direction of Totbury station. He was carrying a small leather case and his shoulders sagged under the weight of a backpack. I would have recognised him anywhere. I gasped. "It's Cameron. He's back."

"Certainly looks like it," agreed Steve.

The figure raised his head without acknowledging us then turned into an adjacent field and walked in the direction of the house. "Couldn't have seen us," said Steve taking my arm once more.

I didn't reply. I knew Cameron had seen us but couldn't understand why he was acting so mysteriously. Part of me wanted to run back and demand an explanation for his recent behaviour but instead I listened to Steve's chatter and tried to concentrate on the reason for our walk.

When we reached the cottage we saw that all the windows were closed.

"She must be out," I said "No one could stay inside with the windows closed in weather like this. Especially post-menopausal Alice."

"Meeeow. Perhaps we should just ring the bell and see." Steve opened the gate and marched down the path. The front garden was a mass of colour. Begonias filled the borders to either side of the path and an overgrown lavender bush scented the air. To one side of the white painted door, a large pink rose tree climbed up and over an ornamental porch.

"High Hopes," I said pointing to the rose. "Alice told me it was called High Hopes."

Steve smiled, "There's optimism for you," he said as he rang the bell.

We waited for a while and then Steve turned

towards me. "There, I told you. I expect she's gone off for the day. She's taken a sicky."

"Without ringing in? Never, that's not like Alice." I moved towards the door. "I don't suppose it would hurt if we called her through the letter box. Perhaps she's fallen, or something." I lifted up the brass letter flap and peered into the hallway then took a step back and pressed my hand over my mouth.

"Rachel? What is it?" Steve lifted the brass flap. "Oh no!" He put his shoulder against the door but it opened without any effort. It wasn't locked, just on the latch.

In the hallway, Alice lay on her back with her head and upper body in the small hallway and her legs stretching into the kitchen. Her face bore the rictus of death, her skin the colour of parchment. Two livid marks stood out each side of her neck and there was an unpleasant smell filling the overheated air. I noticed she'd lost a shoe and felt tears streaking down my cheeks.

"She's stone cold," Steve said. "She's been dead for a while."

I gasped.

"Oh, poor Alice." I felt helpless as I gazed on her lifeless body.

Steve stood up and taking my arm led me back

into the front garden. He made me sit on a garden bench situated in a shady part of the lawn near the cottage wall.

"Stay here whilst I ring the police." He moved to go back inside. "You're shaking like a leaf. I'll fetch you some water."

I nodded, too shocked to speak and wrapped my arms tightly around my body. The sun had climbed in the sky and was now overhead. I checked the time on my watch and as I did so noticed something shining near the path. I bent forward and picked up a small half sovereign attached to a thin gold chain. I recognised it immediately. Hearing Steve walking towards me, I slipped it into the pocket of my skirt.

"Forget the water, I've found the brandy. I figured we both need it," he said, handing me a china mug. "The police will be here soon. They said not to touch anything but I don't suppose they meant the brandy."

The warmth of the spirit did little to stop me from shaking. Steve said it was shock and in a way it was, for although I had been shocked by the discovery of Alice's body, it was my later discovery that put me in fear for my life.

CHAPTER 49

"It's probably the post. All right I'm coming." Laura drew the belt of her cotton dressing gown tightly around her waist. It did little to cover the contours of her figure but she was at ease with her body and saw no reason to hide it.

Finn watched her as she walked towards the bedroom door and smiled. He lay back and sighed with contentment. The bell rang again; a sharp insistent sound that spoiled the moment. "Bloody post girl," he fumed leaping out of bed and throwing open the bedroom window. Looking down he saw Kate, who raised her head at the sound of the window opening. Finn drew back, hoping that there was an explanation for his wife's visit other than the obvious one. He heard Laura open the door and Kate's voice rising up the stairwell.

"Please inform my husband that I would like to speak to him."

Finn threw on the jeans he'd hastily tossed on the chair last evening and rushed to the top of the stairs. "Kate. I can explain," he began.

His wife had pushed Laura aside and was standing in the hallway. "Can you? I do wish you would," she said. "Even by your standards this will be some story. But then you are used to creating fiction so I'm sure you'll have no trouble now."

Laura was standing behind Kate. "Yes, do explain, darling. I'm dying to hear what you have to say."

Finn could see a smile playing at the corner of her lovely mouth. 'She's enjoying this', he thought, and felt a tingle of excitement running through his veins. This should be a disastrous moment for him but for some reason he felt alive for the first time in years. He'd been about to try and lie his way of it but changed his mind. If only he'd realised before that it didn't matter.

"Well actually I can't," he heard himself say.

"What?" they said together as Kate stepped away from Laura.

"Explain," said Finn walking into the living room. "I can't explain. I've fallen in love with Laura. That's the top and bottom of it."

Kate raised her eyebrows. This wasn't what she'd expected at all. She'd expected to have to rant and rave at him, while he begged her forgiveness. Chilled to the bone by his words she followed him into the room.

"I see. In that case, you know I have no option but to sue for divorce."

He was calm. He didn't even raise his voice. "Do what you must. I suppose it's no use saying I'm sorry."

"None at all. But you will be sorry, Finbar Alexander, very, very sorry." She turned on her heel, pushed past Laura who was standing in the doorway and left the cottage.

Her hands shook as she drove down Leaping Lane towards Totbury. Her breath coming in short gasps. She'd often imagined what it would feel like to be in this situation but nothing had prepared her for the anger which was throbbing through her like an infected wound. She would make him suffer for the humiliation she'd been made to endure through years of his countless infidelities. As for this final indignity - she would hit him where it hurt, in his wallet. Then let him see how long his young lover would stick around.

It was well past midday when Kate drew up outside *The Feathers* in the centre of Witcombe. A large sign outside boasted that two people could eat as cheaply as one. She sighed, wondering why the innocuous sign was causing her so much pain.

Ignoring the feeling which she knew would not go away, she walked into the bar, sat at a table overlooking the street and ordered a fillet steak and salad, stating clearly to the young waitress that the meal was for one.

On the opposite side of the street Kate saw the offices of Percy, Darcy and Toms. This time she would make sure the cottage was sold once and for all. He'd always been useless with money. He lost track of his royalty cheques, forgot to cash his advances and ran up huge bills with the wine merchants. He'd been happy to let Kate arrange their finances, pay bills, supervise his accounts, give him money to spend whenever he asked for it. It removed an unwanted burden from his shoulders.

As she forced herself to eat the steak she decided on a course of action from which there would be no turning back. She took her mobile from her bag and rang their bank manager. Whilst waiting to be put through, Kate took measured breaths to calm down, so that when William Grainger spoke to her he would never have guessed his client was anything other than her usual charming self. He was totally unaware of the turmoil seething through her as she calmly discussed how she would be closing both of Finn's working accounts. She explained that her husband was too busy to see to the transactions himself.

"No problem, Mrs Alexander. I see that the authority controlling the account is on an either to sign basis. I hope you aren't closing these accounts because of any dissatisfaction with our services," the Manager sounded anxious.

"Not at all, Mr Grainger. In fact I'm sure my husband will be coming in to see you about increasing his investment portfolio in the near future. By the way, if you could arrange for me to have the closing cheques on both accounts I will pick them up this afternoon, as I'm in town."

She was amazed at how easily the lies tripped off her tongue, she thought, as she slipped the mobile back into her bag and leaving *The Feathers* walked in the direction of the estate agents' office.

CHAPTER 50

Inspector Arthur Lawrence of the Witcombe C.I.D and a uniformed woman P.C. stepped out of the police car and walked through the narrow lane leading to the cottage. When they arrived at the front gate they saw a couple sitting on the bench outside.

"Mr Fiori? We spoke on the telephone." The Inspector held out his hand. "This is WPC Byways. Jenny, perhaps you could look after the young lady."

The Inspector followed Steve into the cottage.

"She was like this when you found her?"

Steve nodded.

"And you didn't touch anything?"

"That's right, Inspector, apart from the brandy. Rachel, well we both…." He hesitated, "It was such a shock."

"I understand. So those mugs on the sink?"

"Yes, they're the ones we used." Steve tried not to look at Alice.

"I've arranged for a forensic team to come over and then we'll get the body down to pathology. The quicker the autopsy is completed, in this weather, the better."

Steve grimaced.

"I'd like a word with you and Miss Weston; perhaps outside in the fresh air?"

Steve nodded and followed the inspector into the garden. The colour was beginning to return to Rachel's cheeks but her hand was still thrust into her skirt pocket. The WPC was sitting on the bench alongside her but stood up when she saw the inspector and Steve.

"I appreciate that you and Mr Fiori have had a shock, Miss Weston, but I need to ask you a few preliminary questions, while the events of this morning are still fresh in your mind. However, if you don't feel up to it, I'll arrange for you to come to the station sometime tomorrow." The inspector sat in the recently vacated space alongside Rachel.

Biting her bottom lip, she replied, "I don't mind, if it will help."

"Good, good." Inspector Lawrence motioned to the constable. "I've spoken to Mr Fiori, Constable Byways. Perhaps you could take some details. You know the drill, telephone, contact numbers etc., I noticed some deck chairs and a table at the side of the house."

I couldn't stop shivering, even though the mid-day temperature had escalated. I knew the inspector wanted to speak to me alone to see if our recollections were similar. I'd typed enough of Finbar's work to know this was procedural, under the circumstances. My fist tightened around the sovereign in my pocket.

"Now then, Miss Weston, Mr Fiori has recounted his version of this morning's events and I want you to tell me what you remember. Take your time. Try not to miss anything out. In cases like this the smallest scrap of information is often the vital piece that leads us to the perpetrator."

"I don't suppose there is any mistake? Alice *was* murdered, it wasn't an accident?" I searched his face willing him to reply that Alice had died of natural causes.

"No mistake, I'm afraid. It looks very much as though Miss Phillips was strangled but we'll need a further investigation by our forensics team to establish the exact cause and time of death."

I took a deep breath and began to recount how we'd found Alice, telling him what I remembered, with the exception of finding the coin. That piece of information I needed to share with Cameron, or Finbar; for the moment I wasn't sure which. Alice had distrusted Cameron and now she was dead. I tried to hold back the tears but they fell anyway.

"I've nearly finished." Inspector Lawrence handed me a white cotton handkerchief smelling of fabric conditioner. "Just one more question. When you arrived, are you sure the door was on the latch?"

"Certain, it opened as soon as Steve pressed against it."

"That's odd. You see, I can't find a door key. It's a mortise lock and I would have expected it to be either in the back of the lock or somewhere in the kitchen. It appears that Miss Phillips was murdered soon after arriving home from work yesterday evening. Her bed hadn't been slept in and from the state of the body, I should think there was no possibility of her being attacked this morning."

He stood up as two men in white coveralls appeared at the gate. "Here are the people who will confirm the actual course of events with a degree of certainty. Thank you, Miss Weston. We will be in touch when we require you and Mr Fiori to sign witness statements."

He walked down the path. "Constable Byways,

when you're ready."

Afterwards, as we walked back to the house, Steve slipped his hand through my arm. I wondered if he'd noticed that my other hand was still firmly thrust into my pocket. Neither of us spoke until we were in sight of Ransome's Point

"I suppose it's fortunate Finn's away, I'm sure he'll be devastated," Steve said.

"It's such a shock. I still can't believe it," I replied. "I don't know how we're going to tell them."

It looked as if the inhabitants of Ransome's Point were already gathered in a group in the front garden. As we approached, Steve said, "I don't think we'll have to. If I'm not mistaken it looks as though the police have already notified them."

As we opened the garden gate, I heard Guy say, "Finn must be told immediately."

Kate, Frankie, Guy and Cameron turned to face us, expressions of concern etched on each face, to varying degrees. Kate took my arm as Steve drifted towards Frankie.

"Rachel, sit here, it must have been quite awful," she said, handing me a cool drink. "The police said Alice has been murdered? It's so hard to take in. Who would want to murder an old woman? They said it didn't look like a burglary that had gone awry."

Guy raised his voice. "Why is no one listening? Finn must be told. He employed the woman for God's sake."

"I don't want his name mentioned in this house." Kate stood up. With a steely edge to her voice she repeated, "He is no longer welcome here."

Steve looked at Frankie, who whispered, "He's been at it again, apparently."

I couldn't look at Cameron. He tried to attract my attention but I refused to meet his eyes.

"I hope you don't mind but I think I'd like to lie down," I said.

As I stood up, murmurs of sympathy filled the over-heated air. I could hear them discussing Alice as I climbed the stairs. At the entrance to the first floor where my bedroom was situated, I stopped and looked up the stairs to the turret room. No more Alice. I fought with feelings ranging from the utmost sadness to gratitude that I would no longer have to suffer her poisonous tongue.

I didn't remove my hand from my pocket until the bedroom door was firmly closed behind me. The coin had cut into my palm so that a livid mark in the shape of a crescent had imprinted itself between my thumb and forefinger. I stood at the window and craned my neck. Unable to see Cameron but managing to catch a glimpse of Guy as he paced back and forth, I felt my stomach heave and rushed towards the basin.

Wiping my lips and rinsing the acidic bile from my mouth, I went to sit on my bed. The coin lay on my bedside table. I picked it up and turned it over. What was it doing near Alice's front door? I couldn't avoid the obvious answer. The one I'd been sliding to the back of my mind ever since its discovery.

The question remained. Why had I hidden it from the police and what did I intend to do about it? I stood up, opened my wardrobe door and removed the red jacket which had a hole in the lining. Slipping the coin inside, I felt it drop into the hem. I didn't want to think about it now. I needed to sleep, needed to forget that I'd ever decided to go in search of Alice.

CHAPTER 51

"What is it darling? Not regretting leaving home?" Finn missed the slight note of sarcasm in Laura's voice. He was agitated. The discovery of Alice's body so soon after his confrontation with Kate had unnerved him. When the telephone rang, he jumped.

"Why so edgy?" Laura asked, slowly stretching out a hand to pick up the phone.

Finn watched her expression change. Her eyes flew open and her face lit up like a supernova. "Yes, yes, that's fantastic. No, no problem at all. In fact I'll leave here within the hour. I can't believe this is happening. Yes, sure, I'll ring you when I arrive." She slammed the phone down, took hold of both Finn's hands and pulled him to his feet. Then dancing around him in circles, her face flushed with excitement, she managed to say, "That was Fiona. I've got the part."

Finn looked blank. "What part, and who's Fiona?" he asked

"My agent Fiona, that's who. Before we met, I

auditioned for one of the lead roles in a new adaptation of the Emlyn Williams play *Night Must Fall*. I never thought I'd get it. In fact they'd already cast the part of Olivia but as luck would have it Grace Beranger has broken her arm. I was the next choice it seems." She spun around. "Oh God, I can't believe it - me starring in the West End."

Finn looked petulant. "I don't know what all the fuss is about," he said.

Laura drew him to her and kissed his mouth. "Finn, it's a real step up for any actress, let alone an unknown like me. It's just lucky the director and producer agreed that an unknown should play the part. After all, Susan Hampshire was relatively unknown when she starred in the film alongside Albert Finney."

She broke free of him and ran towards the stairs. "I've got to pack. I'm already behind; the others have been rehearsing for weeks."

"You're leaving me?" Finn hung his head.

"Only for a month or two, darling. Anyway you can come up to town, can't you?"

"I suppose so. It's no use, me trying to persuade you not to go?"

Ignoring his hangdog expression, she said, "None at all," then ran up the stairs.

The phone started ringing as soon as Laura's car disappeared into the distance. Finn felt the hairs on the back of his neck stand up.

It was Kate. "I thought I'd better inform you that I am the new owner of Willow Cottage and you and your mistress are now my tenants."

"Don't be so ridiculous." Finn laughed.

"I think you'll find that you'll be laughing on the other side of your face when you contact the agent and our bank."

Kate recounted her recent effort to clear their joint bank account in order to buy the cottage. He began to shake with anger when she told him she'd taken legal advice as to her position regarding their joint investments. It seemed there was no way Finn could attempt to remove any money without her authority, until the divorce settlement was agreed upon. She was making absolutely certain every avenue was closed to him.

"Brother Guy been giving you legal advice, has he?" Finn spat at her.

"Let's just say, having a Q.C. in the family is a distinct advantage and leave it at that, shall we? Oh and by the way, any further discussions between us will be held via my solicitor. It's not Jeremy in case you're wondering. I've left you in his tender care."

Finn felt trapped and tried to gain some lost ground. "Look, Kate; it doesn't have to come to this, does it?"

His pleading tone floated down the phone line like feathers on a breeze. This time it was Kate who laughed. "You'll be suggesting that we remain friends next."

Finn put down the phone; he'd lost the battle. He caught sight of his reflection in the mirror above the fireplace. A deep line was furrowing his brow and his mouth was turning down at the corners. He was beginning to look his age. "Lost the battle, but let's see who wins the war," he told his reflection.

The quayside was busy. Outside *The Drunken Sailor,* the tables were set for dinner. It was a quarter past six and already most of the seats were taken. Families with young children were making the most of the warm evening air by eating outside. Fishing boats ready to go out on the tide lined up one behind the other at the mouth of the harbour and teenagers sat on the sea wall drinking beer. Their laughter floated towards Finn like an irritating spot which needed to be scratched, a reminder of a time when freedom meant being free to do as you pleased. Although he was approaching being free of Kate, he realised that he would never be totally free of her. The money - his money - was tied up so tightly it would take years to unravel. In the meantime, he would have to survive on a restricted income and how long would Laura hang around then?

"What have you been up to now?"

Finn spun around. "Cameron?"

"I see your powers of deduction are as sharp as ever. What's this I hear about you and Kate?" His words were robbed of their frivolity by the tone of his voice. He was angry. A shiver ran down Finn's spine, which was intensified when they were sitting at a table overlooking the harbour.

Cameron said, "I've spoken to Ginny Monroe."

Even his attempt to appear otherwise couldn't hide the fact that he was shaken. Finn raised his pint to his lips and felt the cool beer sliding down his parched throat.

Cameron leaned across the table. "Alice Phillips's death came at a rather convenient time, all things considered, don't you think?

CHAPTER 52

The turret room looked the same but of course it could never really be the same again. Alice's desk was where it always had been but there was already an air of abandonment hanging over it. Finbar's mini-recorder sat on the shelf waiting for him to compose his next novel but it looked forlorn, as if it knew. In view of what was happening between him and Kate, I began to wonder if it would ever be used again and if so, certainly not here at Ransome's Point.

I'd spoken to him briefly and he'd instructed me to carry on with the work, until the proof read and edited copies were ready to be submitted. I'd felt it was only right to speak to Kate about it but she dismissed it by saying, "Whatever; I've other things to think about. Stay, by all means."

It was all very unsettling. Then there was Cameron. I'd been avoiding him. The sovereign was an issue I knew I'd have to deal with but for the moment I let it rest in its hiding place. It was too much. I hadn't come to terms with the fact that a murderer had been in the vicinity and if I began to think about it too deeply, I'd have to face the fact, he might be even closer than that.

Picking up the manuscript that lay on Alice's desk, I stacked it on top of the pile near my laptop. The police had been to the house and searched the room for anything which might be significant in the hunt for her killer, but now it was left to me to tidy things up and transfer Alice's files to my in-tray. It felt like an invasion of her privacy to be opening drawers and rummaging through her things, almost as if I were a thief.

The top drawer contained the usual office equipment, pencils, pens, a couple of rubbers and a stapler. Roget's Thesaurus lay alongside the Oxford Concise Dictionary and I felt a lump rise in my throat when I remembered how covetous Alice had been regarding it. If ever I needed to borrow it, she removed it from the drawer, asked me what word I wished to look up and then read the alternative options to me before sliding it back into its resting place. After a week of this, I'd resorted to an online thesaurus and left her to it.

I picked it up. The inscription on the flyleaf read; *To Alice, my faithful other right hand, with kindest regards, Alex Finn.* I turned it over. The cover was made from the usual sort of glossy thick paper that slotted neatly inside the front and pack pages. There was nothing unusual about it in the least. Removing it from the drawer I placed it on the desktop alongside the Dictionary. It seemed pointless not to use them and they were of no use to Alice now.

The contents of the second drawer was again unremarkable, a box of tissues, a stack of A4 paper and some white envelopes, all of which I piled on top of the desk before attacking the contents of the third drawer. After tipping half-used containers of correction fluid and sweet paper wrappings into the bin, I picked up the duster and began to clean the inside of the drawers. As I leaned in towards the top drawer my elbow caught the edge of the Thesaurus and it fell to the floor splaying its paper cover flat underneath it. I bent down to pick it up and saw something was pasted to the inside of the cover.

Taking it to the window seat in order to see more clearly; I saw it was a small newspaper cutting from the New York Review. The printing had faded but I managed to make out that the piece was a report into the death of a young starlet called Melody Cassidy. It was obvious the police had missed it when they'd searched Alice's desk.

However, it must have meant something important, otherwise why would Alice have hidden it?

Kate spent most of the day on the telephone organising her new life - a life devoid of Finbar Alexander and his mistress. Her face was set in a look of determination that Guy hadn't seen since they'd been children. He recognised her resolute expression for what it was and almost felt sorry for his, soon-to-be ex, brother-in-law. He began to feel, the longer he stayed at Ransome's Point, the less motivated he became. His work and life in London seemed to drift away like a puff of smoke rising from a steam train hurtling into a tunnel. He stretched out his long legs on the lounger in the pavilion and inhaled. A mixture of salt, sand and sea mixed with an almost tangible taste of anticipation filled his nostrils. He could feel a storm brewing.

The cottage smelt neglected even though it was barely twenty-four hours since Laura had left. Finn paced the back garden, his head thumping with an ache that seemed to be permanently present. He ignored the fact that his drinking might have something to do with it. Cameron was a problem.

Was he trying his hand at blackmail? The shrill ringtone of the telephone interrupted his thoughts. At first he ignored it then rushed to answer it in case it was Laura.

"Mr Alexander? It's Tom Darcy. This is a bit awkward but I thought, in order for there to be no misunderstanding this time I, er."

"Get on with it man," Finn snapped

"Right. Well, I have been instructed by the owner of Willow Cottage that she wishes to sell it."

"Rubbish. I'm still renting the place," Finn spat out the words.

Tom Darcy's embarrassment was almost palpable. "I'm afraid that's not the case, sir. If you'd like to inspect the agreement."

Finn's fury erupted as he remembered he'd only managed to obtain the place at all because of duplicity on his behalf. Kate handled all the financial arrangements in the marriage and he'd managed to get her to sign for the cottage whilst she was preoccupied with the sabotage of her designs. At the time he'd prided himself on his adroitness. She hadn't suspected a thing.

Tom Darcy said, "In fact Mrs Alexander has effectively finalised all aspects of the agreement by paying the outstanding bill. I'm afraid it's out of my hands now, sir. The sale of the property will go ahead.

Slamming down the phone, he went into the small conservatory. He was a fool. He'd never been good with money, hated even talking about how to maximise his portfolio – whatever that meant – left it all to Kate and her brother – gave himself time to wine and dine women and to write – it had seemed so easy. The view of the coast was magnificent but he saw none of it except Kate's face swimming before him in a sea washed red by his anger. The day had gone from bad to worse and Cameron Blackstone had played a major role in it.

CHAPTER 53

Finn was half way through a bottle of Scotch when the phone rang for the first time. It was Kate. "I want you out by the end of the month," she said and slammed the phone down.

He could hear the venom in her voice. His heart began to race. It wasn't going to happen; no way would Kate be calling the shots, he was determined to make her see sense. He began to pace back and forth as he repeatedly drained his glass and was the worse for wear when the phone rang for a second time.

"Hello, darling; missing me?"

He could hardly hear her. She sounded as if she was in a pub. Anger and irritation fought each other for the ascendancy.

"God, Finn you sound awful. Are you drunk? It's only mid-day."

"Save me from nagging women," murmured Finn.

"That can easily be arranged," Laura replied.

Suddenly, he realized, he could lose her as well

if he wasn't careful. She was not as easily manipulated as Kate. The thought seeped into his befuddled brain, sobering him. "Forget it, darling. I'm missing you, that's all. Forgive me for being such a bear? When can you come down?" The background noise increased and he dug his fingernails into his palm.

"Beginning of next month I should think. It's mad here, rehearsals, meetings, with the script writers and directors, you know the kind of thing. I will try to get away then, I promise."

Finn heard her name being called, then laughter. "Sorry, darling, have to dash. Love you."

He held the phone in his hand unwilling to cut the connection. The beginning of next month would be too late, if Kate had her way. Their joint account wasn't the only thing which was frozen, like the icy tones of his bank manager when Finn had requested he release funds immediately. Admittedly he was shouting down the phone at the time. In the end the man agreed to advance a loan, which would be charged at some exorbitant rate. But it wasn't enough. He was swimming in a murky sea of financial ignorance that was threatening to drown him.

The scotch left a bad taste in his mouth but it wasn't all to do with the alcohol; his taste buds had been soured by his conversation with Kate and nothing would taste the same again. Carrying the glass to the sink, Finn caught sight of an envelope on the mat in the hallway.

The small white envelope bore his name on the front in computerised print. It had been hand delivered. Finn threw open the cottage door and rushed towards the gate, then looked down the lane from right to left. An elderly man using a walking stick walked towards him followed by an arthritic dog. Stepping back inside the cottage, he opened the envelope and removed a photocopy of a newspaper report. The one Alice Phillips had threatened him with all those years ago.

His heart fluttered, missed a beat, then pounded; he could hear every beat. It was mad. Why had this been sent to him, now? He thought there'd be an end to it, with Alice's death.

The air pressure had been steadily rising all day. I saw Steve and Frankie swimming in the cove then lying in the partial shade afforded by the boathouse. The humidity increased as the hours crept past midday and even with the relative relief from diving into the sea, it would be only a temporary measure, I thought, as I saw them dive beneath the waves.

The turret room was unbearably hot so I spent most of the afternoon sitting in a deckchair on the walkway separating Cameron's room from Finn's office, as I read over the last few chapters of Finn's book. Part of me was hoping to see Cameron and yet I was concerned as to how I was going to react to him and how much of the events of the past few days should I share with him.

Now that I'd done it, I felt bad. Reading between the lines of the newspaper article, I'd come to a decision which perhaps had been rash. Nevertheless I couldn't take it back now. Thank goodness I hadn't signed my name. He wouldn't have any reason to suspect me.

It was getting dark by the time I eventually decided to go back to Ransome's Point. I stayed in the village until the shops closed then had a meal outside *The Drunken Sailor*. I didn't want to see anyone from the house and dreaded bumping into Cameron.

Even with the sun sinking lower in the sky, the temperature was high. Not a breath of wind stirred the scorched leaves on the gorse bushes as I walked back along the cliff path. My hair brushed against my shoulders and I felt a trickle of sweat slide down my back. I lifted my hair with one hand and removed a covered elastic band from my pocket then twisted the strands of hair into a knot on top of my head.

"Mm, I love watching you do that. It fascinates me to see how such a thick mane can be tamed with just a twist of your hand." Cameron emerged from the grey dusk and stood in front of me barring my way. "I wondered how long it would be until you stopped avoiding me but decided I couldn't wait to find out any longer."

"You've been following me?"

His laughter did little to settle my nervousness. "Hardly. I was standing in the pavilion and saw you coming along the path. That's when I decided to come to meet you. It's getting dark and if you remember, I did tell you not to go out alone at night, especially after what's just happened to Alice." He slipped my arm through his. "There that's better, isn't it?"

I nodded. My tongue felt thick in my mouth as I searched his neck for the thin gold chain he always wore.

"Where's your sovereign?" I asked.

"What?"

"Your chain, the gold sovereign you and Finn have, is it missing?" I touched his neck.

He'd told me once that he and Finn bought them at an hotel in Las Vegas when they'd both won at the Black Jack table. They were souvenirs, lucky talismans from a time when they were young and fancy free, apparently. I'd never seen either Finn or Cameron without them.

"Oh right. Yes. Here it is." He slipped his hand into the pocket of his shorts. "I've been meaning to get the chain fixed."

"Then this one must be Finbar's?"

"You found it. I noticed he wasn't wearing the other day. He said he'd lost it. Where did you find it?" He was smiling.

"Outside Alice Phillips's cottage on the morning we found her murdered," I said.

CHAPTER 54

Rehearsals for the play were going well; in fact better than she could have hoped. At last, it seemed, Laura Crighton had arrived, or that was what the director had led her to believe.

The lunchtime crowd at the pub was thinning out when Finn arrived.

"Darling, it's so good to see you. I couldn't believe it when you rang," Laura said, and even she thought the words lacked conviction. She had one eye on James Moreton, who was playing the lead; last night, after the dress rehearsal, he had cornered her in the corridor outside her dressing room. The congratulatory kiss on the cheek had somehow developed into something else and if the rest of the cast hadn't crowded into the corridor behind, who knew where it might have led.

"When can you get away from the luvvies," Finn asked petulantly.

"Don't be like that, darling. I'm one of them too remember."

"I'm not likely to forget, am I?" He took her

arm and led her towards an empty table. "At least you can have a drink with me."

"Of course. But just one, we have to be back at the theatre by three. You do understand don't you?"

It wasn't so hard for her to look appealing, acting had its advantages. Laura smiled at James, who raised his glass in her direction. She began to wonder why she'd gone to all the trouble of photographing Kate's designs in the first place. Now that she had the promise of a new career in the theatre to think about, Finbar Alexander and his troublesome wife suddenly lost their significance in the scheme of things. She'd originally thought that if Kate were preoccupied with her work then it would leave the way clear for Finn to promote her in an adaptation of one of his Inspector Flately novels which had been bought by ITV. But Finn had signed away his rights and had no influence over casting and, as if that wasn't bad enough, all he wanted to do was to hide her away in the cottage in Leaping Lane for weeks on end.

As if echoing her thoughts, Finn asked, "When are you coming down to the cottage?"

"Soon, darling, I promise, as soon as I get a break I may be able to come down one Sunday morning for the day. It all depends on how long the play runs. You must see that."

In the event Laura arrived at Finn's hotel room at a quarter past twelve. She was full of apologies; the cast had a meeting after rehearsals, the director went on and on, she couldn't get a taxi, the list was endless. All Finn could comprehend was that the night was slipping away and tomorrow Kate wanted him out of the cottage. He'd consulted Jeremy, his solicitor, but it seemed there was nothing he could do. As Laura slid into the bed and he felt her smooth skin alongside him, he decided that tomorrow he would go to Ransome's Point to talk this out with Kate. He didn't relish the idea, in fact it would suit him if he never saw her scheming face again, but he had no alternative.

Kate was up as soon as it was light. She walked out to the point and sat on the bench overlooking the coastline. As she inhaled the smoke from her cigarette, she thought over her past life with Finn. She supposed part of her still loved him and part of her always would. When Cameron had first introduced her to him, she'd thought him brash and self-assured. It was later, when he'd called to ask her to meet him that she'd felt differently about him. He'd said he was worried about

Cameron and would she consider meeting him for lunch so that they could talk. They were in New York at the time and met in a small restaurant on the edge of Central Park.

She couldn't remember much of their conversation apart from the fact the he thought Cameron was worried about something that had happened in their past and he wondered if he'd confided in Kate. She'd told him he seemed the same as always to her, and, reassured, Finn had begun to talk about himself. She believed she could see beneath the self-confident exterior to the man beneath. There was a vulnerable quality hovering beneath the surface she'd found appealing.

After that first meeting, there had been more. Finn seemed to appear when she least expected him. He'd turn up at her flat expecting to see Cameron and instead of leaving when he realised he was elsewhere, he'd stay. They had long conversation, often lasting deep into the night. But he never touched her and always left with the words, "See you around, Kate." As the weeks turned into months Kate found she couldn't wait to see him and when Cameron had a commission from a firm in Europe, Finn and she become lovers.

She still felt bad about the way their

relationship had ended. That was the reason she didn't want Finn to keep inviting him to spend time with them both. That, and the way Cameron had taken the break up, and his influence over Finn, who was always in a party mood when his so called 'friend' was on the scene. Then there were the girls. It was as if Cameron was saying to her - look at me - I don't need you. She was sure he'd enticed Finn into straying and had encouraged him to drink more than was good for him.

Kate watched the fishing boats sailing in to the harbour on the tide. The air was still heavy; thunderclouds hovered on the horizon unable move, as there was no breeze to carry them in. It suddenly occurred to her that Finn's latest conquest had arrived on the scene at roughly the same moment as Cameron Blackstone had appeared. Was this yet another contrivance on his part? So maybe Finn wasn't wholly to blame at after all?

"Smoking again?"

He was standing in front of her, blocking her view.

"Is it any wonder?" Kate spat out the words.

"No, perhaps not." Cameron sat on the bench at her side. "What's he been up to this time?"

Kate's laugh was harsh, a humourless sound

leaving her throat in a bark of anger.

"You're expecting me to believe that you don't know?"

Seagulls swooped towards them flapping their wings in the stagnant air. It was still early and the rising temperature creating an oppressive atmosphere didn't help the situation, as Kate waited for a reply. Finally he answered her and it was as she'd expected. "You chose him Kate. I tried to warn you. Forgive me for repeating the obvious cliché about making your own bed." He stood up and walked back along the path towards the house, leaving her more alone than she'd ever thought possible.

It was no good; I couldn't sleep. The temperature had risen even further throughout yesterday and an unsettling yellowy-grey tinged light hung over the coast as dusk had fallen. My head ached, I felt sure thunder was in the air. But it wasn't just the weather that was responsible for my wakefulness. Seeing Cameron earlier had made me re-think about the sovereign, which now lay in the palm of my hand; should I talk to Finn about it, take it to the police, or simply hand it back to its owner.

I was sure Cameron was hiding something and was terrified of what it might be. When we'd reached the house last night, I'd meant to show him the newspaper cutting I'd photocopied and sent to Finbar. I couldn't explain why I'd sent it anonymously except that I'd been afraid because Alice had taken such steps to hide it away. I suppose I was hoping Finn might approach Cameron about it without me having to be involved.

I couldn't be sure I could trust Cameron either. How could I? There were so many questions about him still left unanswered and my only source of knowledge had been murdered. It didn't help that Alice had such a bad impression of him but I had to trust my own judgement. The first glow of morning light crept over the horizon but I was wide-awake, sleep as elusive as the answers to the questions responsible for my unease. Slipping the chain into my dressing table drawer alongside the cutting from the newspaper, I came to a decision. Unfortunately it was one I would come to regret.

CHAPTER 55

Finn returned from London just as a breeze sprang up and lifted the clouds nearer to Totbury harbour. He knew he should have gone straight to the cottage but he was still angry with Kate. He was sitting on the harbour wall when he saw Cameron walking up the steps leading to the cliff path. He stood up and called to him then saw him hesitate and retrace his steps.

"Fancy a drink?" asked Finn, wiping sweat from his brow. "God, I hope it's going to rain at last."

"Look, I don't think I do. In fact I've had enough of you and your little games. I've spent a lifetime pandering to you because of what happened in the Falklands and now I know the truth, it makes me want to vomit. Go to hell, Finn."

Watching him walk away, it felt as if it all made sense at last. Well, so what, he thought, let him do his worst. He'd never truly forgiven him for Kate anyway. Walking towards *the Drunken Sailor,* he decided the time to confront Kate was fast approaching, after he'd had a drink first. He'd only stay for one.

As the one turned into four, Finn began to think about the newspaper cutting and why it had been sent to him. Alice must have either given it to someone or someone had found it. But who? It didn't take him long to come to the obvious conclusion. Draining his glass he decided the time had come to pay a visit to Ransome's Point.

I could see Cameron walking towards the house. His head was lowered so all I could see were his black curls. I sighed; I seemed to have a habit of falling for complicated men. As I watched, I saw him take his phone from his pocket soon after mine began to ring.

"You said you had something I should see? Yes, I'll be on the walkway in half an hour. No, I've just seen him and as far as I'm concerned our friendship is over."

I put down the phone. He was angry. I was certain Alice had been hiding the newspaper cutting for a reason and, as there hadn't appeared to be any response from Finn, I thought Cameron might make sense of it. Although, I'd sent it anonymously to Finn, if he was implicated in Alice's death, he might know she'd kept the cutting and come looking for it. None of it made any sense and the more I thought about it the more confused I became. It was the main reason I'd decided to show it to Cameron, in order to judge his response face to face. I knew I might be playing a dangerous game but felt there was no other way.

"Anything wrong?"

Guy was sitting in the conservatory. I'd been unaware that he was there. I wondered if he'd overheard my conversation with Cameron.

"No, I'm fine," I lied.

"Why don't you come and sit with me for a while. You look hot and Mrs Goodrich has made up a refreshing batch of cocktails. There's an iced jug with your name on it waiting in the conservatory." He was smiling at me and for the first time in ages I felt the need to relax, to shift the burden on to someone else's shoulders. I glanced at my watch.

"Well, perhaps I have time for just the one before I get back to work."

"Still working on my no good brother-in-law's script? You need a medal." There was an edge to the words, although said in apparent good humour, I felt meant exactly the opposite.

Guy was a good listener and before long we discovered we had friends in common in London.

"I heard all that fuss about Kenneth Boysey.

I'm sorry." He looked at me with genuine concern and I felt unaccountably close to tears. It all seemed such a long time ago now, ridiculous to even think about it.

"Thank you. I had no idea he was married you know?"

"Kenneth was an idiot."

To my dismay his words acted like a dam breaking. Tears ran like a torrent down my cheeks and the more I tried to swallow them away, the more they fell.

"Here," said Guy handing me his handkerchief. "You've been holding on to that for far too long in my opinion. Don't mind me. Have a good bawl, it will do you good."

I gulped, tried to smile, then said, "It was awful. His wife came into the office. She made me feel like a home-wrecker. I didn't know who she was. I had no idea he had a family. You'd think that I would have known, wouldn't you?"

Guy shrugged.

"Everybody else did. They didn't talk to me for weeks. I almost got the sack. Finn was so helpful at the time. We used to meet occasionally in *the Bunch of Grapes.* He was the only one who understood."

Guy frowned and to my surprise took my hand

in his. "If you ever need someone to talk to, I'm here. Don't ever forget that, Rachel."

Wiping away the last of my tears, I stood up. "You've been very kind. I'll see that your handkerchief is laundered before I return it. I must go now."

I'd been about to confide in him. What had I been thinking? First I needed to talk to Cameron. There was the newspaper clipping, I'd have to know what he thought about it. Afterwards, I needed an explanation from Finn and tonight after dinner I was going to suggest we meet in the turret room and once I was satisfied with his explanation as to its loss, I would return his sovereign.

But I wasn't to know I would retain no memory of certain events after dinner that night. I was unaware that the clock was ticking.

CHAPTER 56

When Finn eventually left the pub, the sky was funeral-black. Thunderclouds hung over the harbour and the lights outside *The Drunken Sailor* swayed like an inebriate, in the gathering wind. Finn had drunk more than he'd anticipated; a red mist of anger sprang up in front of him as he strode up the steps leading to the cliff path. He was furious with Cameron and unsettled by his visit to London to see Laura but the real root of his bad temper lay with Kate.

Alice Phillips's cottage was shuttered; a yellow and blue strand of police tape fluttered from the garden gate. He regretted what had happened to Alice. In a strange way he missed her. He should have been able to trust her but one never knew how far trust could be stretched before it snapped. Cameron knew that.

The air was thick and humid. Finn drew in his breath and felt an ache somewhere underneath his breastbone. He stopped and looked up at the sky.

There was no trace of the sun which had shone merciless in its intensity for weeks. A fine mist was rising up from the coast like a genie escaping from a bottle. As Finn watched, the sky was suddenly lit by a sheet of lightning spreading an eerie glow over the bay, coating the cliffs with a veneer of yellow and dappling the sea with an accompanying swirling wind. Gigantic raindrops fell on his head pounding against his scalp as, turning a bend in the path, he saw the garden lights of Ransome's Point in front of him. Thunder rumbled in the distance as the shower abated. Cameron was sheltering in the pavilion as Finn approached.

"Where's Kate?" he shouted above the sound of a thunderclap overhead.

"In the turret room I think. She said she wanted to clear out some of your things actually."

"Damn cheek. Who does she think she is?" Finn spat at him.

"Your wife, unfortunately," replied Cameron, turning on his heel and walking towards the conservatory.

I'd walked to the point in an attempt to clear my head before supper. The shower had taken me by surprise and after standing in the rain and letting it wash over me for a while, I made my way back to the house.

Opening the door, I saw Cameron crossing the hall then saw him walking up the main staircase. I walked back through the conservatory and into the garden. He was making for the turret room where we'd planned to meet. I hoped I could just make it to my room first to change out of my wet things. The storm was at its height when I reached the door to the spiral staircase. Fork lightning snaked a path from the clouds to the harbour in a spectacular display of light. I jumped as a thunderclap resounded above my head. I'd never liked storms, hated the sound of thunder and no amount of reasoned argument could persuade me that lightning was rarely fatal.

As I began to climb up the stairs to my room, I heard the rain. The previous shower had fallen heavily against the walls and windowpanes but this one was indescribable. When I reached the landing leading to my room I suddenly remembered leaving my handbag at the side of my computer. Beginning to climb the second leg of the staircase leading to the turret room, I thought I heard voices coming from above followed by the sound of breaking glass and a scream. But it was impossible to hear anything clearly above the sound of the raging storm. One thunderclap followed another accompanied by a howling wind that lashed the sea against the rocks at the base of the cliff. I climbed the staircase with a gnawing feeling of trepidation and wishing that a simple thunderstorm didn't affect me so severely

When I reached the circular stained glass window, a flash of light, so bright in its intensity, blinded me and afterwards, I remembered nothing until I was standing in the turret room with Steve and Frankie. Kate was lying in a pool of blood and Cameron was standing over her, a jagged piece of blood-stained glass in his hands.

Steve rushed forward. "Kate? Kate? He turned angrily towards Cameron. "What have you done? My God man, she's dead!"

I gasped and before Frankie could reach me, I felt my legs give way. The rest of the night passed in horrific snapshots. I was living through my worst nightmare. The police and ambulance services were called. Cameron, Steve and Frankie were taken to the police station in Witcombe for questioning; a young woman police officer gently questioned me and then suggested I should take a sedative and try to get some rest. There was nothing I could tell them that would be of any help. Frankie and Steve had arrived on the scene before me; they had heard a scream when they were on the landing below and had rushed up the main staircase in time to see Cameron Blackstone standing over Kate's body.

Steve told me later, that Cameron protested he'd taken the glass from Finn's hand and it was he who had argued with Kate, smashed the window in temper and used the jagged shard to stab her as she tried to reason with him. But no one had seen Finn and had only Cameron Blackstone's word that he'd ever been there.

Guy was spending the night with some friends at a cottage further around the coast and was appalled when the police telephone him. I was sitting in the conservatory with Frankie and Steve when he arrived the next day. He stood in the doorway and leaned against the doorframe. At first no one knew what to say to him. I looked down at my hands as if the answer would suddenly appear. Frankie wept and Steve looked ashen. Eventually it was Guy who spoke.

"Has anyone seen my brother-in-law?" he asked.

"No, he's not come over to the house," Steve replied. "The police have informed him. He's living in a cottage just around the coast from here. I gather he's taking it badly. What's going to happen now?"

Guy stepped inside and sat on the couch next to me.

"The police want us all to stay put for the time being. It would appear to be an open and shut case but in my experience one never knows."

"I can't believe Cameron would do such a thing," I said. " It's all my fault."

Guy patted my hand. "Of course it isn't. You had nothing to do this."

I began to shake. "If only I hadn't asked Cameron to meet me, he may never have gone to the turret room and Kate might still be alive."

"You mustn't say that. Cameron Blackstone is answerable for his own actions. Whatever twist of fate occurred to put him there at that particular time, it is no one's fault but his own." Guy stood up and paced the floor. "I feel so helpless. Tomorrow, I'll speak to the officer in charge of the case and see what I can do. I owe it to Kate."

Frankie stopped crying. "Don't you think he did it then?"

"All I'm saying is that I believe nothing unless it can be proven without a shadow of a doubt and just now there are a few questions which need to be answered." Guy walked towards the hall. "Mrs Goodrich has graciously offered to look after everyone as usual. And I know it's a cliché, but tomorrow is another day and one in which I'll be actively working to get to the bottom of what happened in the turret room. Now if you'll all excuse me.

Steve sighed, "I don't know about you two but I'm for a stiff drink."

Frankie and I nodded and turned towards the view of the bay.

"Looks like the storm has passed," said Frankie.

I nodded, unaware that it was only just beginning.

CHAPTER 57

Laura Crighton swore to the police that Finn and she were together at the time of Kate's death. She knew her words couldn't be disproved as she'd arrived late on the night in question and had driven her car down the deserted lane to Willow Cottage. She'd found Finn in a drunken stupor talking a lot of nonsense. At least it had seemed like nonsense in the dead of night. However, in the clear light of morning and after the police had informed them of Kate's death, Finn's ramblings began to make some sort of sense. Drinking strong black coffee some time later, Finn confessed to Laura that he'd been in the house at the time but that Kate was alive when he'd left. The problem was, the police were bound to consider him a suspect, if they knew he'd been at the house. Everyone knew they'd been having problems and that Kate had threatened to turf him out of the cottage.

After Laura had agreed and given him an alibi, Finn began to relax. He would soon argue the point about inheritance. He was almost sure Kate hadn't had time to change her will but he couldn't be certain. Unfortunately there was Ripton to consider. He would be sure to make things watertight as far as Kate's wishes were concerned and that could cause a problem.

"I've got to get back to London, darling. Sorry about leaving you alone but you do see there's nothing more I can do. The police know where to find me but I'm sure you have nothing to worry about on that score. I'll ring when I arrive, shall I?"

Laura put her finger on the button and the tinted electric windows on her car slid shut. Finn stood at the gate and waved. He could no longer see her face and wondered if she'd forgotten all about him as soon as the window had closed. He'd noticed a cooling off recently and this thing with Kate and the police had done nothing to improve things.

It was raining. Not like on the night Kate died. This was a fine drizzle sweeping in from the sea and hanging over the village and harbour like a shroud. Finn paced the back garden oblivious of the rain. His thoughts had turned to the anonymous delivery of the previous week. Alice had kept it somewhere, he was sure of it. In that case someone up at the house had found it. It couldn't have been the police or they'd have questioned him about it. It was vital he found it. Apart from Cameron the only other person he could think of was Rachel. Besides Cameron would have discussed it with him, so it had to be Rachel; it was just the sort of thing she'd do. She didn't have the guts to put her name to it; little Miss Mousy Weston was playing games. As things stood, she could make things very uncomfortable for him. Running his hands through his wet hair, Finn decided he would have to visit the house again. He hadn't wanted to, but there was no alternative now.

The desk sergeant looked up from his crossword.

"I'd like to speak to Mr Cameron Blackstone. You're holding him in connection with the murder of my sister Mrs Kate Alexander." Guy slid his business card across the counter. The sergeant raised an eyebrow and straightened up.

"I'll just be a moment, sir."

Guy waited whilst the sergeant spoke to his superior officer. There was a faint smell of disinfectant wafting in the air mixed with a smell of soup coming from the station canteen. Guy looked at his watch; it was nearly mid-day.

"Mr Blackstone is being moved into an interview room now, sir. Constable Barnes will accompany you."

The room was narrow and windowless. A neon strip blinked above a laminate-topped table and two utilitarian chairs. The chairs were arranged so that they faced one another. Cameron sat in one and the constable indicated that Guy should sit in the other then took up his position to the right of the doorway.

"So, I gather you deny all charges?" Guy asked.

There was a moment's silence. Cameron raised his eyes and stopped picking at the skin around his fingernail. "I didn't do it. Why would I? You know how I felt about her. I didn't hold any resentment about what happened; it was all too long ago."

"You're telling me - you were just in the wrong place at the wrong time?" Guy expression never wavered.

"I know it doesn't look good for me." He reached across the table and put his hand on Guy's arm. The constable took a step forward. "Ask Rachel to show you the newspaper that Alice Phillips was hiding and ask her about the sovereign. Your brother-in-law is not all he seems. I beg you, Guy, don't look at the obvious. Kate was dead when I reached the turret room. Please believe me. Besides, Rachel must have seen the murderer leave. She was on the back stairs at the time. He couldn't have left by the main staircase or I'd have seen him."

Guy stroked his chin. "You said he. It could just have easily been a she."

Cameron shook his head. "I don't know. All I know is that I didn't kill her and now Rachel can't remember most of what occurred that night."

"The police psychiatrist has seen Rachel. He said she's suffering from shock and that the pieces of her memory which are missing may never return. It all depends on how deeply they are buried. So I wouldn't rely on her coming to your aid, if I were you." Guy frowned and stood up. "I'll be in touch."

"You'll help?" He saw a faint light of hope in Cameron's eyes.

"Let's say, I'm interested in is getting to the truth and leave it at that for the moment. However, I will say, if I find you are telling the truth then I'll do everything in my power to make sure you're released."

"Thank you," whispered Cameron, as Guy nodded to the constable and left the room.

CHAPTER 58

Drizzle coated the windowpanes in the turret room leaving behind rivulets that trickled into each other then fell over the sill into the garden below and although I'd opened all the vent windows a filmy layer of condensation obscured my view. Standing in the centre of the room, I closed my eyes and tried to remember what had happened after the lightning sliced through the circular window. I'd climbed those stairs again and again but my memory continued to hold its secret.

I'd avoided this room for obvious reasons and even though Mrs Goodrich had placed a vase of fresh flowers on the windowsill every day since Kate's death, I still could not remove the stench of death from my nostrils. With eyes tightly closed I went over the events of that evening up until I reached the stained glass window, willing myself to remember. For a fraction of a second the memory would hover, just out of reach and then it would disappear. I pressed my knuckles into my eyelids in frustration but the next scene my mind replayed was of me standing in the doorway watching Cameron bending over Kate.

I took a deep breath as I heard someone close the door at the bottom of the spiral staircase followed by the sound of footsteps rushing up the stairs. I backed away from the door. Fear prickled my scalp and I clutched at my throat as the door opened.

"Thought I'd find you in here." Finbar stood in the doorway. He was smiling and for the first time in my life I wondered what I had ever seen in him. His expression suddenly changed to one of forced solemnity, it was like flicking on a switch.

"Bad memories, I understand. Poor Rachel, come here let Finbar make it better."

Even the forced use of his full name sounded like a mockery. He was trading on our past friendship. It had never been anything more, perhaps not even that, however much I'd wished it to be otherwise.

"I'm OK. Really." For some reason, I wanted to put some distance between us.

"Come along now, Rachel. None of us are OK, are we? Not since this tragic mess."

When I didn't reply, he said, "I've come to pick up my things. The police said it would be fine so I thought I'd strike while the iron's hot, eh?" He came closer and started to open the desk drawers one by one.

"Where is it then?" he asked, without looking up.

"What?"

"Don't look so innocent, my dear. You know what I'm looking for. The original of the photocopy you were so careful to see that I received."

I stammered, "I don't know..."

His mouth turned down and he took a step towards me as the door to the walkway flew open and Guy stepped into the room. "You've got a cheek. What do you think you're doing here?" he asked.

"Don't you think it's I who should be asking that? This house is mine and you are not welcome," Finbar said, pulling out the drawers and sliding them across the floor.

"I think you'll find you're mistaken. Kate made a new will weeks ago. She knew what you were up to. Taking my advice she made sure her property and finances were in order. It was the very least I could do for her under the circumstances." Guy put his hand on my arm.

"You OK?"

I nodded.

Finbar sat down at the desk but I noticed his

hands were shaking. My heart was hammering away in my chest. What was I afraid of? Menace had seeped once more into the room, which had so recently been the scene of such an horrific event. Until he'd arrived, I'd thought the traces of that night had been wiped away with the disinfectant and polish so liberally applied by Mrs Goodrich. I saw his shoulders sag and recognised it as a sign of defeat. He'd hoped to intimidate me into giving him the newspaper cutting. It's true significance was still a mystery to me, only Alice was aware of that and she'd been murdered. I shivered at the thought. "You shouldn't be here," Guy said, taking my arm. "We'll get Mrs Goodrich to make you a black coffee, you look as if you've seen a ghost."

"We'll talk again, Rachel," Finbar said.

"Finish taking your things and get out," Guy demanded whilst guiding me out of the room towards the main staircase.

There was a cold wind blowing in from the sea. The conservatory blinds slapped against the windows as Guy reached up to close the vents. "Now what was all that about?" he asked.

I was about to feign ignorance but felt anger at Finbar's intimidation. "I'm not sure I know exactly, but I think it has something to do with this." I took the cutting from my pocket and handed it to him, explaining as I did so where I'd found it and about sending a copy to Finbar. Once I started to talk the words tumbled out as I covered every detail I could remember, starting with finding Alice's body and ending in the turret room a moment ago, with the exception of the one piece of information that might have linked Cameron with Alice's murder. I still wasn't sure why I didn't mention the sovereign, even though he'd shown me he still had his. Something wasn't right.

Guy turned the newspaper cutting over in his hand. It was a report of a party held in Beverly Hills at the home of a well-known film producer. It was the sort of party where 'A' list celebrities jostled with lesser mortals in an attempt to be seen by the paparazzi. One of the resulting photographs was included in the newspaper report, which stated that a young starlet named Melody Cassidy had plunged to her death from a second floor balcony. It concluded she'd died whilst under the influence of a Class A drug. However, the reporter led the reader to consider that her death was suspicious in a number of ways. Apparently two people had occupied the bedroom prior to her death but there were no witnesses able to give any further information. It was generally accepted that the film business closed ranks in circumstances where its celebrities were concerned. There was a grainy photograph attached to the article showing guests arriving. Finbar was posing for the photographer, a young blonde on his arm. Behind him stood a man whose features were indistinguishable, as were those of the two women standing to either side of him. The caption underneath the photograph read;-

Alex Finn, the novelist, shares a joke with starlet Melody Cassidy less than an hour before she met her untimely death.

"And you say, Alice kept this hidden all this time?" Guy asked.

I nodded. "I thought it was odd, partly because it was so well hidden and partly because I couldn't think why it would be significant enough for her to go to the trouble of hiding it in the first place. It even crossed my mind that it might have something to do with her feelings for Finbar. She gave the impression of being an adoring puppy, keen to carry out her master's every wish and I wondered if the photograph of him was the only one she had."

"What made you change your mind?" Guy stood up and inspected the photograph more closely.

"I don't know really," I sighed. " I think it

gradually dawned on me there could be a more sinister explanation."

"Which is?" Guy looked up from the newspaper.

"It could be that Alice had been blackmailing him. I often had the feeling he took great pains not to upset her but always thought it was because he was afraid to lose her."

"He may have been afraid of upsetting her for another reason?" Guy bit his lower lip. "I think you could be right. And if you are - you realise what it could mean?"

I shivered. "I can't bear to think of it. It doesn't really make any sense. Whilst I am able to accept the notion that he was being blackmailed, the thought that he would have stooped to murder is something I can't believe."

"Can't or won't, Rachel? Hypothetically the whole scenario could hang on the death of Melody Cassidy. Let's say, for argument sake that Finn was involved in her death and Alice found out about it. Perhaps Alice was becoming a nuisance and had to be silenced for good. Perhaps Cameron is innocent and Finn killed Kate."

"You're not serious are you?" I stood up and put my coffee cup on the table. "I think I need a stiff drink, Guy."

"Let's go into the library. There's a bottle of Remy we could polish off."

As we crossed the hall, Finbar came down the stairs carrying a large white plastic box filled with files and manuscripts.

"I take it you have no objection to my taking my belongings until I can sort out this farce, brother-in-law?"

"How good it feels to tell you that you are no longer in a position to assume such a relationship still exists between us. Hand over your door key, please and if there are any more of your things hanging around, I'll arrange to forward them to you."

Finbar placed the box on the floor then made an exaggerated gesture of removing his keys from his pocket and sliding them across the floor.

"It will give me great pleasure to have you return these keys with an apology for misappropriating my home, once I sort out this little mess," he said walking to the door, then looking back over his shoulder, once again, he said, "I'll be in touch, Rachel."

The drizzle had turned into a downpour. The view from the library window was obliterated. "He's going to get rather wet," Guy said.

"I wish I could say I was sorry but he scares

me." I felt the brandy slide down my throat and hoped Guy felt the same urge as I to get as drunk as possible in order to forget the horrific end to a summer spent at Ransome's Point.

"I've spoken to Cameron." Guy said, pouring us both another large measure each. "He mentioned the newspaper cutting and wanted me to speak to you about it. He implied Finn was implicated in Melody Cassidy's death. But I obviously can't just take his word for it. I told him, if, I thought he was innocent, I would take the case."

"How can he be innocent? I saw him; Frankie and Steve saw him. You know what we all saw." I shivered.

"Of course, I don't deny that he is up to his neck in trouble right now but in my experience things are never quite as clear as they appear to be and I owe it to Kate to find out the truth. I'm going to book a flight to the States, first thing in the morning. I have a contact there called Lance Rodway, I'm sure he'll be able to help me get to the bottom of this." Guy held up the cutting, "Now I think it's time I got my head down - a busy day tomorrow."

I sat in the library long after Guy had gone to bed. The usual sounds in the house were absent.

Mrs Goodrich was staying in Totbury with her sister. Steve and Frankie had booked into an hotel in Witcombe. They couldn't bear to stay in the house. Kate's death had affected Steve badly. Staying at Ransome's Point a moment longer than was necessary wasn't an option as far as he was concerned. He said that, once the police gave them the go ahead, they'd book the next flight back to New York.

The wind had dropped and the house stood like a pupa cocooned in a web of drizzle, waiting for the truth to set it free.

CHAPTER 59

Emerging from the arrivals gate at John F Kennedy airport, Guy searched the throng waiting to meet travellers from abroad. At last he saw Lance, who raised his hand in greeting.

"Good flight?" Lance asked, walking towards his car.

"Not bad. Thanks for meeting me. And thanks for bothering to get involved in all this."

"Nonsense. I was going to say it's my pleasure but as the reason for your visit has been instigated by Kate's death, there can be no pleasure in it."

"That's for certain."

They drove through the busy New York traffic to Lance's apartment, which was in a converted warehouse building. An ironwork lift deposited them on the fourth floor opposite which was a stout double door leading to Lance's apartment.

When Guy had unpacked his things, Lance called from the living area.

"Jack Daniels on the rocks, waiting."

"Just what I need," said Guy, sinking into an

overstuffed sofa over which a cream mohair blanket was draped. "I detect a woman's touch," murmured Guy, his eyes taking in the general décor of the room.

"That's down to Emma. She's a smart cookie. I'm a lucky man."

They discussed old times as the Jack Daniels slid comfortably down their throats. Later, when the topic could no longer be avoided, Lance said, "I've made contact with Ginny Monroe. She'll meet you at eleven in Starbucks, tomorrow morning." He handed Guy the address, which was scribbled on the back of an advertisement for Coca Cola. "She will be able to tell you first hand about the Falklands. Then at five thirty, in Costa's bar, at the end of the street, Mickey Coburn, the guy who saw Cameron and Finn on the night Melody Cassidy died, will be waiting for you. He said to tell you he'd have a copy of *Murder on the Main Line*, with him."

Guy laughed, in spite of himself. "Highly appropriate, don't you think? This is beginning to feel like a scene from a Hitchcock movie."

The next day, a cold wind was blowing down the street as Guy pushed open the door of Starbucks. Lance had given him a magazine article written by

Ginny, which had a small colour photograph of her alongside her name at the top of the piece. She was sitting on a high stool at a counter near the window cradling a large coffee mug in her hands. She looked cold and ill at ease as Guy introduced himself.

"I don't know if I have anything to tell you that will be of help." She looked uncertain. "But Lance seemed to think it might be relevant."

"It's very kind of you to meet me, " said Guy, ordering a large black coffee and drawing up a stool to sit alongside her. The view from the window was of a busy New York street, shoppers and workers hurrying by, each intent on their own business, not one person stopping to admire the trees in the park or the majestic skyline. "I'm sure whatever you can tell me about Finn and Cameron's activities during the Falklands conflict, will help me build up a picture of their past. At present there appears to be something of an unholy alliance between those two and I'm trying to understand the mechanics of it all.

Ginny shifted uncomfortably in her seat. "Where to begin? As I said, I really knew very little about them at the time, other than that Finbar Alexander was a journalist and Cameron Blackstone a photographer. I believe they met up when Blackstone was freelancing on the same newspaper which employed Alexander." Ginny shivered and drank the last of her coffee.

"Another?" Guy offered.

"Please. I think I'm starting a cold."

Guy ordered two more drinks and waited until she felt she could continue with her story.

"We were young and keen to make names for ourselves. Hal Stewart and I travelled together and met up with Finn and Cameron on the journey. I always believed Finn was the more driven of the two and in the light of experience it shows I was right. And although we all made reasonable careers for ourselves, it was Finn who made the big money."

"And spent it." Guy sounded bitter.

"I'm not surprised to hear you say that. He loved the good life and the trappings of fame even then."

"If it wasn't for my sister he'd have got through it all."

"I was so sorry to hear about Kate. I always felt she was too good for him."

Guy sighed, "Love makes fools of us all, " he said.

"True enough, I should know, I fell for it."

Guy looked puzzled

"It's a difficult time for all of us to remember. The sinking of the Argentinian cruiser the General Belgrano had taken us all by surprise." Ginny sat back on her seat and continued her story, whilst watching the unfolding drama of life on a busy New York street. "Unfortunately my memory is sketchy as to what happened when we first arrived but I do know we had our work cut out. The conflict was at its most dramatic, news reports were being sent out every few hours."

She sighed and Guy noticed that her grasp tightened around her coffee mug. Her knuckles shone like a line of white marbles underneath her skin. "It was when Cameron was photographing the troop ships arriving far below us that the accident happened. Finn and I were some distance away from Hal and Cameron. Finn had made a pass at me the night before when I'd drunk more than I should have. He believed he could press home an advantage the next day and had encouraged me to hang back behind the others."

She shivered again and Guy wasn't sure whether it was from the cold or the memory of her encounter with Finn, then she continued, "At the time, Cameron was perched on a great vantage point above a rocky outcrop. There was a drop below him of approximately seventy feet. He lay on the grass and stretched the upper part of his body over the drop trying to angle his zoom lens to get the best possible photo. It had been raining and the grass was slippery. Finn was trying to take my attention away from what was happening on the cliff but I watched anxiously as Cameron eased his way nearer to the edge. When he slipped and disappeared from sight, I remember Finn being frozen to the spot."

She sneezed, apologized, and continued. "He didn't move until Hal peered over the edge and clambered over the side I got up and ran down the incline followed by Finn. I could hear his footsteps sliding over the wet grass, so I know I didn't imagine it. He was **behind** me." She frowned. "Cameron lay on a ledge some ten feet down. Somehow Hal managed to lift him back on to firmer ground. But he was unconscious and knew nothing of his dramatic rescue until he opened his eyes and found Finn cradling his head. He naturally believed that he'd saved him. I remember thinking it was odd that Finn did nothing to correct his assumption and, as Hal had shot off on a mission of his own, there was no one but me to disprove it."

The door to the café opened and a blast of cold air hit the back of Guy's legs.

"That sounds like Finn alright," he said.

"I was in a very difficult position. Once he'd made sure Cameron was safe, Hal told me he'd seen the opportunity of a story further around the headland. He said to make sure Cameron had someone to keep an eye on him but he thought he was just suffering from cuts and bruises, nothing more. Hal had studied medicine for two years before deciding he was more cut out for journalism and changed courses mid stream, so I assumed he knew what he was talking about."

She took a sip of coffee. "The minute Hal disappeared, Finn took charge; he carried a protesting Cameron, over his shoulders, to a wildlife observation station nearby, where they radioed for help. Finn wouldn't let me go with them to the field hospital but insisted I join Hal. I remember him saying something like, 'there's a great story unfolding in the harbour, don't miss it, it could make your name.'"

"Did Cameron ever discover the truth about his rescue?"

"He didn't hear it from either of us and I don't think Finn would ever have put himself in such a bad light by confessing the truth of the matter. You see, I believe that Cameron has always felt grateful to Finn for saving his life. I gather they were extremely close after that. Whenever I saw news reports of Finn's escapades, Cameron was usually somewhere in the background."

"You never felt like telling him the truth?"

"It wasn't my truth to tell and Hal wasn't interested, so I tried to forget the whole incident."

"Until now?"

Ginny nodded. "I did mention it to Hal a while ago. It was when I came across some archive footage of a report into the death of Melody Cassidy. There was a photograph of Finn talking to her and I thought I could just make out Cameron in the background. No one would ordinarily notice him but I enlarged the copy on the computer and sure enough, there he was.

"And you think it's significant?"

"Not unless you know that trouble has a habit of following those two around." Ginny shivered and this time Guy was certain it wasn't from the cold. "He phoned me a while back, you know."

"Who?"

"Blackstone. He wanted to meet me, said he had some business in the area but I made an excuse. He was the last person I wanted to see."

"Really?"

"There was something about him that always made my skin creep. I can't explain it. Anyway, I've heard a rumour Miles Chance is looking into the death of Melody Cassidy. He seems to think there is something odd about it."

Guy had heard of Miles Chance; his reputation for investigative journalism was well known. If anyone could get to the bottom of it, he was the man for the job. He looked at his watch. "Look I'm sorry, I have to go. Thank you so much for meeting me. Perhaps we could have lunch together before I fly home."

Guy handed her his card. "Give me a ring when you have a moment"

"Thanks I'd like that but unfortunately I'm flying to the Middle East the day after tomorrow. I've to report on the Palestinian crisis for an article in Time magazine."

"Pity. Anyway thanks again."

Guy helped her into a taxi and watched her disappear into the gaping mouth of the city's traffic system. He felt uneasy. In the back of his mind something was niggling away at him. And he'd learned by past experience that to ignore it would be a mistake.

CHAPTER 60

The man conspicuously carrying a copy of *Murder on the Main Line* was tall and thin. He was standing at the bar alternatively turning the pages and drinking lager from a pint glass. From time to time he kept looking over his shoulder as if waiting for someone, it was obvious that the novel wasn't holding his attention. Guy knew he was unused to covert meetings of any kind, let alone one as potentially damaging as this one.

"Mr Coburn?" Guy asked touching him lightly on the arm.

"Mickey, please," he replied, indicating two chairs and a table situated in an alcove. "Shall we?"

When they were seated, Mickey Coburn began to relate the events of the night Melody Cassidy fell from a bedroom window in a house situated in the heart of the Beverley Hills district.

Apparently Harry King's party had been the kind of affair which had started off as an invitation only party but which had rapidly deteriorated into a melee of invited guests and favoured hangers on. Finn and Melody being a member of the former category and Cameron and Mickey relegated to the latter.

"They were standing around the pool drinking champagne when I arrived," Mickey said. " At least the two men were, Melody was smoking pot. I recognised Alex Finn, the author, but didn't know the other man. Melody kept disappearing through the double doors leading into the house and emerging higher than a kite on a windy day."

"I'd read somewhere that she was addicted to cocaine," Guy said.

"Coke, heroin, speed, anything she could get her hands on. She was as thin as a pipe cleaner but sort of sexy with it, if you know what I mean?"

Guy nodded.

"Anyway, I was looking for a story and bored with watching the three of them getting high on the stimulant of their choice, so went inside in search of new fodder."

"The three of them?"

"What?"

"You said, 'The three of them', did you mean Finn and Cameron were taking drugs as well?"

"No, they were getting high on alcohol. I never saw evidence of anything more sinister. If I had I might have had a story - *Thriller writer, high on coke* - too good to miss. But alas, I saw nothing unusual in their behaviour. Well not then at any rate. It was much later and I must admit, I was high myself at the time, so I didn't think to much of it."

"What did you see?" Guy prompted.

"I was looking for the bathroom. I was in desperate need of a piss. I saw the three of them going into a bedroom along the corridor."

"And?"

"And that's that."

Guy looked disappointed. Was he wasting his time here?

"The next day I had the hangover from hell and missed all the fuss on the news, but the day after that, I got the full story. Melody had fallen from a balcony and was dead. It appeared there were no suspicious circumstances and she was believed to have entered the bedroom in order to snort cocaine in private. It was generally accepted she'd been alone at the time. There was no mention of the other two."

"And you said nothing? Wasn't that a story which had fallen right into your lap?" Guy looked incredulous.

"Not so. I was messed up with drink and pot and to be honest all I had was an impression of three people entering the room so, although I thought it, I couldn't swear to it being Alex Finn and his friend. I couldn't even say what time it was. She may well have been on her own when it happened."

"What makes you think differently now?" Guy asked.

"Miles Chance has been looking into Melody Cassidy's death. He has a feature running - Hollywood Hushed Up - I think it's called. He looks into untimely deaths in the community and from time to time investigates any he thinks may have been suspicious."

"And it would appear, he considers Melody's death to fall into that category?" Guy signalled to a passing waiter. "Same again," he said.

Mickey Coburn fidgeted in his seat.

"I suppose I've never really believed Melody was alone that night, whatever the newspaper reports stated at the time. I can't prove they were with her but I can't prove they weren't either. I did write to Lance Rodway, we met and that's how I'm meeting you."

"I'm glad you did. My sister is dead and Cameron Blackstone is being held in custody awaiting trial for her murder. He insists he is innocent and I'm determined to get to the truth."

"And you think this may have helped in some way?" Mickey was beginning to relax.

"It's a distinct possibility. I wish it was more, but it's a start." Guy stood up "I'll keep in touch and let you know how things develop."

"You've no idea how good this feels. I've had this simmering around in my brain for years. It's good to get it off my chest at last."

"Don't be surprised if Miles Chance comes knocking on your door though. I've heard he's like a dog with a bone when he gets his teeth into something," Guy said.

"At least I'll know how to deal with it now. At last it doesn't seem so impossible. I'd begun to feel like it was a bad trip or a figment of my imagination."

Mickey stood up and shook Guy's hand. As they walked outside into a grey drizzle Guy turned up the collar of his coat. Behind them, on the table lay an unread copy of *Murder on the Main Line*.

CHAPTER 61

It was six weeks after his visit to New York that Guy realised he'd been a fool. Past prejudices and gossip had clouded his path to the truth. He had allowed emotion to rule his actions and had failed miserably in his assessment of the events leading up to Kate's death.

It was gone eleven when he received the phone call from the Cedars Psychiatric Unit in San Diego. He put down the phone, unable to believe he hadn't seen it before. He'd always prided himself on his judgement; could spot a wrong one a mile away. This time he couldn't even take comfort from the fact that it was by any skill on his part, after all, it was purely by chance he had bumped into Lance Rodway, which had led him to this breakthrough.

Stewart Grant flexed his muscles and stood in front of the open window. "Come back to bed darling," Laura said, yawning. She enjoyed watching him preening like a peacock but preferred to feel his muscles tighten around her body as they made love. He was young, beautiful and talented and she meant to keep him happy.

The morning paper thudded onto the mat in the downstairs hallway. It would hold the reviews of the play and she was sure they would put a smile on his face. Stewart left the bedroom and Laura listened to the sound of his footsteps hurrying down the stairs. She smiled at the thought of his naked body being seen through the glass fanlight above the front door. The old lady who lived across the street was in for a rare treat.

When Stewart returned, he held the paper up to face her. "Hey, isn't this the guy you were shacked up with?" he asked, handing her the newspaper.

The photo showed a grim faced Finn handcuffed to a policeman as he left the cottage in Leaping Lane. The headlines read;- *Alex Finn, the prominent author of The Inspector Flateley detective series, was to-day arrested in connection with the murder of his wife, Mrs Kate Alexander, the fashion designer. Mr Finn declined to comment to our reporter as he was being led away from his love-nest in Leaping Lane, which he is believed to have shared with his latest conquest, a young actress named as Laura Crighton.*

"My God," exclaimed Laura, sitting up. "How did they find out?"

"You knew he was involved in his wife's murder?" Stewart looked incredulous.

"No, no, of course not. I mean how did they find out about me?"

"Don't worry, darling, no publicity is bad publicity."

Laura breathed a sigh of relief. "Yes, yes, I'm sure you're right. But as for killing Kate, there's no way Finn did it. He hasn't got the bottle.

NOW

CHAPTER 62

There is no point in delaying the inevitable. I'm shocked that the house has deteriorated so much in ten years. After the trial, neither of us had any wish to see the place again. There were too many memories hiding within its walls and some were better left forgotten.

My therapist is responsible for this visit. He believes that by visiting the place, where it happened, it will nudge my memory into releasing the details of the thirty minutes or so which are still locked inside. At first, I thought, why bother? Whatever I've hidden, it couldn't have any bearing on what happened later. But with the support of my husband, who thought it might put an end to the flashes of memory that disturb my dreams, I decided, I'd nothing to lose. Everything is different now but perhaps it's the right thing to do, to close a door, which will always remain partially open unless I can remember.

I move away from the front of the house and walk towards the garden door leading to the spiral staircase. A cold wind whips around me lifting the remaining leaves from the trees and tossing them at my feet. Although the lock is rusty, the key turns and for a second I feel the heat, as I did on that fateful night. Underneath my warm coat, I am sweating. The stale air rushes down the staircase towards me and I fall back against the wall.

Taking a deep breath, I close my eyes and exhale. My heart rate slows until I feel ready to climb the stairs. With each step I take, I am slipping back through the years. I can hear the sound of voices coming from the turret room above me, the words are indistinct, but the voices are raised and angry. I reach the circular stained glass window through which I again see the storm raging around the coast. A thunder clap sounds overhead and a flash of lightning streaks through the glass illuminating the colours into a rainbow of light so bright it blinds me. I hear footsteps thundering down the stairs.

I close my eyes, afraid to open them. And then I hear his voice.

"Rachel?" he says.

My eyelids fly open. His hands are covered in blood. His shirt is torn and his eyes are wild.

"Finbar, what is it? What have you done?" I ask.

There's a gash on his forearm and his shirt clings to it. "It's not my fault, I tried to stop it. I was too late."

"What is it? Tell me."

"You haven't seen me, Rachel, remember, you haven't seen me."

He shakes his head then rushes past me into the night.

So this is the memory I refused to accept? My feelings for Finbar were always complicated. The horror, of what he might have done in the room above, must have locked into my brain. I begin to shiver, thinking what could have happened, if I'd remembered at the time.